DEVIL IN THE DETAILS

SAVANNAH BLAIZE

ACKNOWLEDGMENTS

I want to acknowledge the many readers and friends who have been supportive in my quest to deliver Domenic's story. I appreciate each and every one of you who have taken the time to connect with me with such encouraging words.

Special mentions to:
My brainstorming partner and beautiful friend, Lisa Grant Sleeman, who endured long phone conversations and many messages during this journey. Her passion to get this story out was equal to mine. My talented friend and actress, Vanessa Ellen Powell who wants to make this into a stage production and play the role of Harper. Sue Thompson my friend from the Netherlands, and also a fellow Lucifer fan, who assures me that if she was in the movie business, she would be knocking down my door to get this on the big screen. Sue, I truly appreciate your encouragement and proof-reading skills. My lovely friend Sue Brierley, who allowed me to chat about my characters every time we had a phone call catch up. My American friend Jessica Eiden Smedley, who read for "Aussie" content. My friends Heidi Catherine, Michelle Duffy, Tricia Baggs, Liza Marshall, Phoebe Grant Sleeman, Beth Prentice, Julie Westwood, Rebecca Saunders, Dorothy Shorne, and Elvina Payet who all provided feedback and encouragement. And many, many, more. Andrew Campbell my handsome Audiologist who allowed me to use his name and his likeness for my character.

The Sparkle Sisterhood:
To Maria Nicola (of 10 Way Necklace fame) and her sister Gina Marbot.
Thank you for your encouragement and allowing my Luc Nightingale stories
to be a part of the fun and laughter on your Sisterhood conversation page. I
am forever grateful. I have made many new Sparkle friends.

Ladies of the Sparkle Sisterhood, remember. "Amethysts look their best when
worn naked."

DEVIL IN THE DETAILS

PROLOGUE

DOMENIC
BORN 6TH MARCH 1992

The wonder of the human body is not lost on me. Holding a man's beating heart in your hand, knowing you have the ability to prolong or enhance his life, is something I do not take for granted. Some may say I'm privileged to be a heart surgeon, at the tender age of twenty-five, and to have my own private patients. But I know that, besides being born gifted, it has taken a lot of hard work and determination to get to this point. You see I was born with a truly remarkable and unique ability to be able to detect if someone needed medical attention, purely by laying my hands on them. I've spent my life being intimately aware of the health and wellbeing of the people around me. I've also spent my life keeping this ability a secret to all but my family.

Of course, some may say that my gift was heaven sent. But I know that the Devil had more to do with it than anyone else. My name is Domenic Ericson and my Godfather happens to be Luc Nightingale, the Devil himself. The way my mother Harper tells the story, she didn't have a choice in accepting the deal she made in Hawaii back in 1990, to divorce her husband and change her life. As a consequence, she was required to provide the Devil with her firstborn son, to train as his successor in Hell. She hadn't been convinced Luc was sane at the time, and she had no intention of having children, but she shook her hand on that deal. She was indeed able to divorce her first husband Dean. She married Richard, my father, and when I came along nine months or so later, Luc decided that he would allow my mother and father to raise me to adulthood, before he called in his marker. The untimely death of my father in a boating accident meant that my mother was left to that task. My Godfather stepped in to lend a hand and I've been living in the Devil's shadow ever since, learning all I can to be a better heart surgeon, while enjoying the benefits of being the Devil's protégé.

DOMENIC

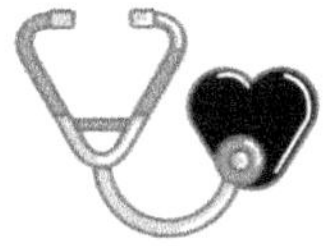

5th March 2017

The operating room at Cedars-Sinai Medical Center hummed like a well-oiled machine. The operating staff were used to my work procedures, and idiosyncrasies. The subdued lighting, the classical music playing softly in the background, the soothing hum of the medical equipment, provided a calm ambiance for the hours spent on our feet, and ultimately had an effect on the outcome and success of an operation. The scrub nurses in attendance today were very familiar with my meticulous process and anticipated my needs. My appreciation for their skill in reading my body, or expressions, while wearing a face mask, protective goggles and a head lamp, knew no bounds. My patient, Dan Adams, had come through the difficult operation well. After a few nerve-wracking hours on the operating table, and with mechanical assistance, his vital signs, blood pressure, and heart rhythm were now pleasing. I concluded the procedure and left Dan, and the OR, in the nurses' capable hands.

As I approached the family waiting patiently for news, his wife Patricia shot up out of her chair.

"How is Dan? Is he . . .?" Patricia faltered, not wanting to hear any bad news.

"Dan's fine. He came through the operation with flying colors."

"When can I see him?"

"The nurse will come and collect you in a little while. You'll have time to go and get something to eat. I know you've been in here all day, and you've probably had enough coffee. You can relax now."

"Thank you so much. I was very worried. I'll call the children and let them know." Tears trickled down Patricia's face. She brushed them off quickly with the back of her hand. "Or is it too soon to tell the children?"

"Let them know. I'm sure he'll be fine now we've repaired his heart. When he goes home, it's imperative he stays on the diet I prescribed. And he gets back into some gentle exercise in a few weeks. Walking is good. Okay?"

"Yes. I'll make sure he stays away from high calorie junk foods."

"Take care. I must get back to OR." I turned to leave.

"Thank you again." Patricia swiped at her tears once more. Two family members joined her, and the older of the two gentlemen took her arm. They walked off down the corridor, presumably to call the children.

The satisfaction in helping to give patients a longer life, never gets old.

❧

I poured a glass of red wine and sat back in my favorite chair to listen to an aria on my state-of-the-art sound system and to watch the sun going down. My newly acquired open plan apartment was sparsely furnished but I had been taking my time getting used to it before filling the space. It was one of four apartments on the top floor of a building not far from the hospital. The best thing about it, and the aspect which sold it to me, was the natural light pouring in through the floor to ceiling double glazed windows in the main rooms and the master bedroom. The hardwood floors and spacious kitchen with the long marble counter came in at a close second. I don't mind living so close to the hospital, as I can be on site at the drop of a hat. If I want a change of pace, or company, I can visit the family home, and my mother, in the Hollywood Hills. If I'm lucky, I might even see Lucia, my younger sister, if she isn't out dancing or dashing around the countryside with friends. My mother tears her hair out, but trying to control Lucia, is like trying to control a tornado.

I worry about my mother, since I moved out, although I know she isn't alone, unless she wants to be. Cameron and Aimee Crawford, a married couple who've been with the family for many years, attend to the house and live in the gatehouse on the large estate. Cameron is the chauffeur and looks after the grounds and any maintenance required on the estate. Aimee is a fabulous cook, and is primarily responsible for the household chores. My mother spends her time writing movie scripts, painting abstract artworks, and is a member on the board of the company she owns. She has written and directed some well received short films over the years, of which I am very proud. And Luc, my Godfather and also the Devil, pops in now and again to check up on everyone. My mother is at her best when Luc drops by for a visit.

A low voice behind me startled me out of my reverie. *Speak of the Devil.* I turned away from the view, toward the kitchen counter. Luc was pouring himself a glass of red wine. He was dressed in his signature style. Black pants and shirt, all beautifully presented, not a crease in sight, with his top button undone, and his black tie hanging loosely from his collar. The shoes polished to a high shine. His black suit jacket was draped over a barstool. He appeared tired, worn down, as if he'd had a tough day at the office.

"You did very well today." Luc lifted the glass to toast, then took a sip.

"Thank you. It was a particularly difficult operation." I took a sip of my wine.

"I watched from the observation platform for quite a while. You're impressive when you're focused."

"I learned that from you."

"Compliment accepted, thank you."

"Have you seen Mom today?"

"No. I came straight to you. Is there a reason I should visit tonight?"

"I presumed you would, since you're here."

"Actually, I came to give you an early Birthday gift."

"Really?" I looked around for something tangible.

"Yes. Oh, you won't see it. It's an enhancement to add to your talents."

"I'm intrigued."

"We both know about your insight into the human body. I'd like to give you an insight to more aspects of the humans you operate on. I'd like to give you the ability to gauge their worth. Their morality, their selfishness, their depravity."

"Won't that interfere with the treatment I give them?"

"Possibly."

"Ah. I see where you're going with this."

"You've always been able to see things clearly, Domenic."

"Your motives are not as altruistic as they seem. You have an ulterior motive, don't you?"

"I do. I'm searching for souls. And you can help me with this."

"You want me to see if they're worth your time and effort. You want me to make deals for you?"

"Well I don't want you to be the one to make the deal. I'm perfectly capable of doing that. I want you to steer me in their direction."

"And if I decide that these candidates are perfect for you, and corruptible, does that mean all my efforts in keeping them alive will be for nothing?"

"Let me ask you a question. If you were going to save a man's life on the operating table, and you knew he was going to rob a bank as soon as he was out of hospital, and in doing so was going to kill many bystanders . . . would you still save him?"

"You're going to make me judge and jury?"

"No. I'm going to give you the ability to help the human race. If your patient on the table is more in my league, then he isn't worth saving, and you should just send him on his way to me. He'll come to me sooner or later anyway."

"I don't know that I want this extra talent. It seems more like a burden than an asset."

"I'll tell you what. I'll give you a chance to see if you like it. If you don't find it useful, I will remove it. Deal?"

"You're making deals with me now?"

"Sorry, wrong choice of words. What do you say?"

"Okay. You've given me something to think about."

"Excellent." Luc beamed at me and held out his hand to shake mine.

"Deal." I grinned back at him. "When will this take effect?"

"It has already been done. Happy Birthday Domenic."

As Luc disappeared into thin air, I heard a faint chuckle. Theatrical exits were his specialty.

2

DOMENIC

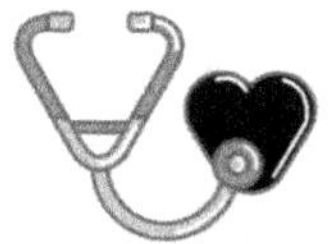

6th March 2017 – Domenic's 25th Birthday

*W*hen I awoke the next morning, the sun was still below the horizon. I stretched, checked my messages, and pulled on my exercise gear. I switched on the early TV news, set the program resistance level and climbed aboard the cross trainer. An hour later, I entered the shower to wash off the sweat and cool down. My mind wandered to the new doctor in the Emergency Department, I'd had the pleasure of meeting the day before. Dr Charlotte Benson was definitely someone I would love to get to know better. Tall and blonde and very knowledgeable, if her diagnosis of my new patient was anything to go by. I also had a glimpse of a shapely figure tucked away under the scrubs. I turned the cold water on full blast, to quell my thoughts, before I got lost down that rabbit hole.

I pulled a dark blue tie from the rack to match my navy suit and white business shirt. I had consults scheduled all day in my private rooms. No surgery scheduled for today. I knew my mother would be organizing a lovely birthday dinner, and I had planned to finish early and drive straight to the family home in the Hollywood Hills before the sun went down. I selected an expensive Italian cologne my mother gave me for Christmas, knowing she would appreciate the gesture. I found silver cufflinks, a Christmas gift from Cameron and Aimee, and slipped them into my shirt cuffs. Cameron and Aimee were like members of the family. Lucia and I spent so much time with both of them growing up, we followed them around the house and the garden and spent many hours listening to stories of their youth. They were like the grandparents we never had. They were also there for my mother when my father passed away. We all adore them.

When I arrived at my office, Amanda, my practice manager, was already sitting behind the desk.

"Amanda, don't you have a home? Isn't this a bit early for you to be here?"

"Ditto. I guessed you'd be in early. Happy Birthday, Domenic." Amanda produced a small plate containing a frosted vanilla cupcake from behind the desk. The tiny blue candle in the center was already lit.

"Perfect timing it seems."

"I heard the elevator ping, and guessed it was you. You'd better blow it out and make a wish before the smoke alarm goes off." She placed the cake on the desk.

I did what I was told, bent down and blew out the candle.

"What did you wish for?"

"Can't tell you, or it won't come true."

"I'll make some coffee and bring it to you with the cupcake."

My phone started ringing in my pocket. I knew who it would be before I looked at the screen. I gave Amanda a thumbs up sign, headed for my office and closed the door.

"Good morning, Mom."

"Good morning, Domenic. Happy Birthday."

"Thanks. You have the honor of the first phone call."

"You know I always like to be first. What time will you be coming to the house, so I can plan dinner?"

"I'm planning on finishing early, around four o'clock. I'm looking forward to sharing a glass of champagne with you before we eat. I'll call when I'm leaving the office."

"Wonderful. I'll see you later."

"Will Lucia be home?"

"I think so. She is aware it's your birthday."

"Ciao. I'll call you later." I hung up and walked to the window to look down on the streets below. Lucia's voice sounded in my head without preamble.

Happy twenty-fifth birthday, big brother.

Good morning Lucia. You didn't want to use the phone like everyone else?

Why bother with technology when we can talk like this.

I suppose you're right.

Of course, I'm right. I'm always right.

I'll see you tonight, at dinner.

Maybe. That depends on Justin. He's my new . . . boyfriend.

What happened to Paul?

Paul was last week.

And how old is Justin?

Old enough. And you can stop the questions. You're behaving like my father.

You're seventeen. I worry about you.

I may have been on this earth for seventeen years, but I'm wise beyond my years.

You are a piece of work I'll give you that. I have to go. I'm expecting a patient soon.

But I haven't told you what I got you for a birthday gift.

Get out of my head Lucia. I have to get to work.

Ciao.

My sister and I have always been able to communicate telepathically with each other, as well as with Luc, my Godfather. It's an interesting story, but due to the fact that Lucia and I both have some of the Devil's DNA, we are able to converse in this manner. It's come in handy on many occasions. We try not to do it around our mother, as she feels left out, and the last thing we want to do is upset her. Our family is a fairly tight unit. I guess we have to be, because there are so many family secrets we cannot share with the rest of the world.

My final patient for the day is late. As this is his first consultation, I presume he's changed his mind. That's unfortunate for him as he's going to receive a substantial cancellation fee in the mail. I'd begun to pack away my case files when Amanda announced that George Caruso had arrived. When I opened the door, I found an overweight but well-dressed man, who appeared to be in his fifties, and an elegant woman, sitting in the waiting room. I presumed she was his wife. Amanda handed me his patient history form.

"Please come in and take a seat." They both sat in front of my desk.

"This is my wife, Angela," George announced. Angela nervously returned my smile.

"How can I help?" I asked, addressing George.

"I've been having trouble breathing, and I've had a couple of episodes of pain in my arm and in my chest. My doctor recommended you. But you're much younger than I expected." George frowned. Concern etched into his face. "He gave me this for you." He passed over a sealed envelope.

"I can assure you my age has no bearing on my ability to treat you. I have many success stories under my belt. And as you can see from all the framed certificates on the wall behind me, I am well qualified." I opened the envelope and quickly scanned the contents.

"My doctor was pretty insistent that you were the right surgeon."

"Your doctor considers you a candidate for bypass surgery." I tapped the page in front of me with my pen.

"Yeah, he mentioned it. That's a pretty dangerous operation."

"It's dangerous to ignore the symptoms and do nothing." I said, hoping to add the correct serious tone to my voice. This man is a heart attack waiting to happen.

"I've been trying to talk him into taking this seriously for a while." Angela murmured quietly. She glanced nervously at her husband. She received a scowl in reply.

"I think it's time to examine you. If you'd like to step into the examination room over here." I opened the door and directed him to the examination table. "Remove your shirt and slip on this gown. The fastening should open at the front. I'll give you a minute." I closed the door.

I returned to my desk and addressed his wife.

"How long has he been putting off seeing someone about this?"

"A few weeks. He won't listen to me. He's worried about time away from his business."

"If he is truly interested in his business, and his health long term, he needs to have this bypass."

I returned to examine George. He was sitting on the raised table, his legs dangling off the edge. He looked very uncomfortable. I listened to his chest through the stethoscope.

"Your back has been troubling you hasn't it? Your posture is suffering from the extra weight you're carrying. If you want to be healthy after this operation, we'll have to get you on a healthy eating plan."

"I'm no good with diets."

"Think of it as a different way of eating, rather than a diet."

I asked him to swing his legs up on the examination table and lay back. As soon as I placed my hand on his shoulder to support him the room around me disappeared.

I saw a small child being helped to open a birthday gift. Then the scene changed. I saw lots of smiling happy faces sitting around a dining room table, and a family Christmas dinner spread out before my eyes. Then the venue changed again, and I saw a stack of invoices stamped overdue, waiting to be paid on the desk in a study, and a lamp turned down low. There was a handgun and a few loose bullets on the desk. I withdrew my hand and the images stopped. All these images rolled quickly through my mind, and I was viewing them from George's perspective. The last image also carried the heavy emotional burden of despair. I didn't know if this was past, present or future events. I shook my head to clear the lingering image of the gun.

"Are you alright?" George asked, concern etched into his brow.

"Yes. Let's check your blood pressure." I quickly applied my unreadable expression of experienced physician.

I continued with the examination, then returned to my desk to allow George to get dressed, and to make my notes. We agreed on a date for the operation, and I escorted George and Angela to reception, and handed them over to Amanda to finalize the bill. It wasn't until I was back sitting in my office chair that I had a chance to examine what had happened. I didn't know how to interpret the images. Did this mean he was a good guy or a bad guy? Did the despair and the gun mean he was going to take his own life? This gift that Luc bestowed upon me was going to take some getting used to.

The drive from town took a little longer than expected, due to the hour. As I approached my mother's walled estate, I called Cameron and he opened the gate from inside with the remote. He waved me through and gave me a mock salute from the front door of the Gatehouse. I pulled up in the circular drive, in front of the main building, and Aimee greeted me with a hug at the front door. She took my jacket to hang up in the hall closet.

"Happy Birthday Domenic. I've made the roast your mother requested for dinner." She lowered her voice to a whisper. "But I've also made the spicy chicken pies you like, but don't tell anyone, or they'll think you're my favorite. Your mother is in the sunroom."

"I won't say a thing. Especially if you put a couple of pies aside for me to take home."

"I've already thought about that." Aimee beamed at me and patted my arm.

My mother, Harper Ericson, looked happy to see me and opened her arms for a hug. She was dressed in a cream silk blouse and long black skirt which almost reached the floor. The afternoon light streaming through the windows caught the silver streaks in her blonde hair, which was stylishly cut to sit above her shoulders. As a child I had always thought that my mother was attractive. When I was growing up, I noticed that heads would turn whenever we were out in public, but I took it for granted because she was my mother. As an adult, I can now fully appreciate that for a woman turning fifty-seven later this year, she is and always has been, stunning.

"You're just in time to open this bottle of champagne," my mother announced.

"Sorry I'm a bit later than intended. My last patient took longer than I expected."

"No matter. You're here now. And here's Lucia."

"Happy Birthday big brother." Lucia rushed into the room like an excited puppy. She had dressed for the occasion, replacing her tight blue jeans and casual tops, with a short and flattering red party dress. It wasn't often she showed off her long, tanned legs, and at seventeen she was shaping up to be a tall woman. Not surprising as we have tall genes in the family. She had her right hand behind her back, and she grabbed my jacket lapel with her left hand to pull me down to kiss my cheek. "A birthday gift as promised." Lucia handed me a small, gift-wrapped box, secured with a silver ribbon, and tied in a bow.

"Do I open this now, or at dinner?"

"Open it now." Lucia was bouncing on the balls of her feet.

I opened the small box to reveal a black leather keyring nestled in silver tissue.

"It's a lovely keyring." I removed it from the box.

"You don't look impressed." Lucia pouted, flicking her long dark hair back over her shoulder.

"It's just that I already have a perfectly good keyring."

Luc appeared in the hall, walking from the front door. "But not for a Porsche 911. Happy Birthday Domenic." Luc tossed a car key in the air which I caught.

"I don't know what to say. That's a generous gift."

"This gift is from your mother and from me. You don't turn 25 every day." Luc said. "It's out front, do you want to take a look?"

We all walked out to the driveway. The sleek silver Porsche gleamed in the late afternoon sun. I opened the driver's door and slid in behind the wheel. Lucia jumped into the passenger seat. I love the smell of a new car, with leather seats and pristine interior. This wasn't the first car I'd owned, but it was the first Porsche. I felt ridiculously happy. Judging by the look on everyone's face, they could tell this gift meant a lot to me.

"Thank you. This is a beautiful piece of craftsmanship." I ran my hands over the leather steering wheel. I hopped out of the car, gave my mother a hug and walked forward to shake Luc's hand.

"Come on inside everyone. Let's have a glass of champagne. Aimee call Cameron. Is he going to join us for champagne before dinner?" Harper took Luc's arm and they headed inside.

"He's on his way," Aimee announced.

The table in the dining room was set for six. Three on one side and three on the other. It was a custom in our house that no one sat at the head of the table. The reason behind this was that my father always sat at the head of the table, and since his death, my mother has kept that place for him. She says he watches over us all. I have always taken it for granted that she knows what she's talking about. Cameron and Aimee always join us for special occasions. As I mentioned, they're more like family than household staff.

"I take it Justin is out of the picture tonight?" I quietly asked Lucia, who was sitting opposite me.

"I told him to come by later. I wanted to share this occasion with my family," Lucia said equally quietly.

"So, I'll get to meet him."

"Not if I can help it. It's hard enough with Cameron giving everyone the third degree, and Luc is here tonight too, so I'll be meeting him outside the gates," Lucia whispered.

"You'll invite Justin into the house so that we can all meet him." Luc announced. His sensitive hearing had obviously picked up every word. He smiled at Lucia. She wasn't going to get away with anything tonight, it seems.

"Let's have a toast. Does everyone have something in their glass? Excellent. Happy Birthday Domenic, and many happy returns. We're all very proud of you, and what you have achieved." My mother said.

"Thanks Mom."

"Now let's enjoy this feast Aimee has prepared. I see she's also made your favorite pies. She spoils you Domenic."

"Don't I know it."

Wonderful food, excellent wine, surrounded by my family. A family who obviously enjoyed each other's company. What more could I want? I looked around at the smiling faces, and wished that my father, Richard, was indeed sitting at the head of the table. I thought of him often and wondered what life would have been like if he had survived. I have no doubt it would have been less grand. Luc stepped in and has made sure that our family was taken care of, and that we wanted for nothing. He provided all the essential material things I needed and a lot of the emotional support. He is officially my Godfather, but he's been more like a father for these past seventeen years.

"Domenic it's time to make a wish," Harper said.

Aimee came back into the room carrying a white cake stand, on top of which sat a tall, frosted, chocolate layer cake, alight with candles. Everyone sang happy birthday. Aimee placed the cake stand on the table and passed me a sharp knife. I blew out the candles, made a wish, and plunged the knife into the cake.

"I hope your wish comes true," Harper said.

I wished that I had someone special in my life, someone with whom I could share happy moments like this. It had never been easy as a teenager because I never thought of myself as young. I guess I have always imagined I was an adult imprisoned in a child's body. And to a degree I was. I learned to keep to myself. The women I was attracted to were older so rather than risk rejection, I tended to keep to myself. Besides, how could I explain the fact I shied away from touch. I never let anyone inside the walls I had created. It was safer that way.

It had been a wonderful evening, but it was time to leave. Aimee pushed a package into my hands at the front door. The cold pies she had put aside for me to take home were tucked inside a cardboard box, with some birthday cake wrapped separately. I never left this house without food or a bottle of wine, or a token to show me that my family cared for me. The greatest gift I had received tonight was the genuine love passed around that dinner table, in the laughter, and the teasing and the camaraderie of family. I hope I never take that for granted.

3

DOMENIC

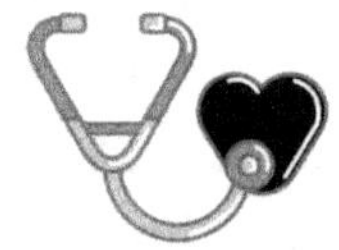

20th March 2017

The morning's surgical procedure had gone well. I had half an hour to grab some lunch before I had to be back in the OR to scrub for the afternoon session. The hubbub in the hospital cafeteria was not unusual, as staff and patients jostled for table seating, or the quick option of standing at the counter running the length of the wall near the entrance. I picked up a tray and headed down the line to the fridge containing pre-made salads, grabbing a bottle of orange juice on the way. I paid for my food and turned quickly to find a table and walked into a nurse carrying a similar tray of food. I experienced a jolt of electricity and awareness when her bare arm touched my hand.

"Sorry, my fault." I hastily corrected the tray before the contents landed on the floor.

"No. I should have been looking where I was going. Hey, you're Dr Ericson. I attended your lecture on open heart surgery last week."

"Yes, that's right." I found myself staring into the biggest, bluest eyes I had ever seen. Combined with curly, flaming red hair pulled back from her face and tucked into a bun at the nape of her neck, and lots of freckles dotted about on her pale skin, this young woman was a delightfully rare sight in this predominantly blonde and brunette world I was accustomed to sharing.

"Did you know that the blue eyes and red hair combination is very rare. Only about seventeen percent of the population have blue eyes, and combined with red hair, the percentage falls to zero point seventeenth of a percent. It's fascinating."

"Yes, I am aware of that. People point that out all the time."

"Fascinating." I registered I'm repeating myself, and I sound boring, but I can't help appraising her. Not only because of the rarity of the combination, but because this young woman was fresh faced and stunningly beautiful, radiated happiness and was completely unaware of her hidden gifts.

"Although, the zero point seventeenth of a percent is a new addition to the information shared with me."

"You are a healer."

"I'm a nurse, so I guess you could say that."

"No. I mean you have healing hands."

"Well, that is certainly the most unique pick-up line I've heard." She laughed and it was like a waterfall of happy notes tumbling over each other.

"It wasn't a pick-up line. It's fact."

She narrowed her eyes, and tilted her head, trying to work out if I was joking, I think.

"Sorry, you'll have to explain that to me another time. I have to go. My shift starts soon. See you around."

She headed for the counter near the entrance. I decided to join her.

"Hello again. My *shift* also starts soon. May I join you?"

"It's a free country." She shoveled a forkful of tuna salad into her mouth.

"I should have explained myself more clearly. Have you heard of Kinesiology and Reiki?"

"Of course."

"I believe you have the ability to not only determine through Kinesiology, but to aid in a patient's wellbeing through touch, with Reiki. You should study it. You have healing hands."

"You don't know the first thing about me. You don't even know my name, yet you tell me I am a healer. Pardon me if I'm a tiny bit suspicious of your motives. I have heard the doctors in this country are forward."

"You're Irish?"

"What gave it away? The accent? The red hair?"

"No, the last name on your name badge Sophie O'Connor. Your accent is not very noticeable."

"My family emigrated when I was young."

"Do all of your family have red hair."

"No, I'm the only one. My two brothers have auburn hair." She finished her salad and scrunched up her napkin. She grinned at me. "If you're finished with my family genetics, I'd better get moving."

"Have a great day Sophie."

"You too, doctor."

I watched her dump her trash, stack the tray, and head out of the cafeteria. She was wrong. I wasn't finished. That zap of electricity through my body when we barely touched had me curious. Was this part of Luc's gift I wondered? Suffice to say I wanted to know a lot more about Sophie O'Connor.

4

SOPHIE

I headed for my car at the far end of the multi-story staff parking lot. It was always satisfying to end a shift and know that during that day you had nursed someone through a difficult experience and made their day better. Even though my feet were sore, my back ached, and my stomach grumbled from lack of food, it had been a rewarding day.

The very serious face of tall dark and handsome Domenic Ericson kept popping into my head throughout the afternoon. I had asked around and was told he was a bit of an enigma in the nursing circles. He hadn't been an Attending Physician at the hospital for long, kept to himself, was quiet and reserved, didn't socialize within the medical circles but was a brilliant surgeon. Of course, people asked why I was showing interest, and to be honest I wasn't sure. I sensed naivety in his conversation at lunch. When I examined it later, what I took for flirting, was in fact probably genuine medical interest in my genes. It was unusual to say the least. Most guys I encountered were after one thing, and they had the impression that nurses were open minded and compliant and would provide them with all they desired. He was not the first Resident doctor that had made the assumption that I was easy prey when I first started my nursing career. I had a feeling though, that Doctor Ericson was not in the same category.

As I approached my allocated parking space, a car raced down the ramp and around the corner and slowed beside me. I glanced over at the driver's side of the Porsche. The tinted window lowered soundlessly.

"Hello Sophie. I apologize for my behavior earlier. I must have come across as rude, and that was not my intention."

"No need to apologize. I'm sorry I accused you of trying to pick me up. I must have seemed as if I had tickets on myself."

"Tickets? What kind of tickets?"

"It's an expression for being full of your own importance." My initial theory was proving to be correct. Dr Ericson was a babe in the woods.

"I see. However, I didn't make that assumption. Take care driving home."

"You too. Nice car by the way." I was impressed by the sleek silver exterior.

"Thank you. She is a beauty."

"She? Does she have a name?"

"Luna. Goddess of the moon."

"Excellent choice."

"I thought so. Have a good night." The window slid up, and the car disappeared around the corner and down the ramp.

I thought about the doctor all the way home. Not only because he was tall and good looking and intelligent. But because he was hard to work out. Someone as brilliant should be more streetwise. But then again someone so young in his field must have spent a lot of time locked away studying to be able to have achieved his level of expertise.

My house-mate Lisa, who was also a nurse, was watching a movie on Netflix, stretched out on the sofa, with a bowl of popcorn and a can of soda by her side. She waved absentmindedly in my direction as I made my way to the kitchen, helped myself to a bowl of pasta in the fridge and popped it into the microwave. When it was hot, I grated some parmesan cheese on top, carried my meal into the living room, kicked off my shoes and sat cross legged on the floor beside the sofa.

"Thanks for cooking. It tastes great."

"Not a problem. Your turn tomorrow."

"Any requests?"

"Not fish. I have a date."

"Oh. Who's the lucky guy? Do I know him?"

"A new ER nurse, I don't think so. His name is Peter Parker, like in Spiderman. But everyone calls him Pete."

"Do I have to make myself scarce or is Pete taking you out."

"I'm meeting him at a bar. A friend of his is in a band and has a gig. You should come."

"Not on your first date."

"Well technically he hasn't asked me on a date. He asked me to come listen to his friend. He just happened to ask all the other nurses on the shift. But I have high hopes it could turn into a date."

"I'm your wingman then. What if he picks me instead?"

"As if. With this embodiment of Italian womanhood under his nose." Lisa rose off the sofa and placed her hands on her hips. She turned toward the kitchen and sashayed across the room in an accentuated wiggle. She flicked her long jet-black hair out of the way, glanced back over her shoulder, and winked at me.

"You'd convince me more if you weren't wearing baggy pajama pants and a sweatshirt. But he might be extremely short sighted, so I shouldn't judge."

She picked a pillow from an armchair and threw it at me. I ducked.

"Hey, careful. Pasta sauce and pillows don't mix."

I got up and took my nearly empty bowl into the kitchen, scraping the sauce and cheese from the bottom and licking the spoon as I walked. Lisa was loading the dishwasher. She took the bowl from me and slotted it into the machine.

"Will you come? We can share a cab and have a drink or two."

"Why not. I didn't have other plans. It might be fun."

"Great. I have the early shift, so I'm about to hit the shower then bed."

"Besides, it will give me a chance to wear that dress I bought on sale."

"I don't think it is a high-class venue. I looked it up."

"If I'm going out, I may as well dress to impress. You never know when Prince Charming is waiting to sweep you off your feet."

"You read too many of those romance novels."

"I've been led to believe you should have an idea of the kind of partner you want, and you should visualize him or her. I am visualizing a Prince. I am dressing for a Prince. I am not settling for anything less. I've had some losers in the past, and I'm through with that. I want someone intelligent and strong and loving . . ."

"And rich, don't forget rich."

"Money isn't everything Lisa. I've had guys with money before. They haven't been especially kind or caring."

"When you find your Prince, see if he has a friend for me then, will you?"

"I'll make that a priority. A Prince with a Princely friend."

"Maybe I should dress up too."

"If you want this guy to notice you, to see you as something other than a work colleague, then I think it is a good idea. So, ditch the jeans, slap on some make-up and let's get glamorous for the night."

I took a bottle of water from the fridge and settled into the big armchair with the romance novel I was working my way through.

"Goodnight," Lisa said as she walked by. "You read too many of these soppy stories, and they give you high expectations. Where are you going to find a good looking, intelligent, kind and caring guy, other than in between the pages of your books? A knight in shining armor is not waiting around every corner."

I had an image pop into my head of a silver Porsche driving around the corner in the parking garage, the window sliding down, and Domenic Ericson's serious face looking over at me.

"Where indeed?"

5

HARPER

21st March 2017 - Morning

I was enjoying an early morning cup of coffee in the sunroom, when I heard Luc's distinctive voice in the distance. Walking down the hall, their heads bent together, he was in deep conversation with Aimee. Luc came over and kissed my cheek. Aimee was carrying a tray containing a coffee pot, another cup and a cream jug. She refilled my empty cup, placed the tray on the coffee table and left the room.

"Have you seen this article?" Luc asked. He produced a newspaper from under his arm and handed it to me.

"Which article?"

"The hospital is having a fundraiser. They want contributions to auction off. I was thinking that your painting of the sunset I admire so much, would be a good one to donate."

"If you admire it so much, why would I want to give it to the hospital?"

"Because I can bid for it and the hospital gets the money."

"And you get to own the painting."

"I've been trying to buy that painting from you for a while. And you always say no."

"I've told you I don't want to part with it. You can see it any time you want. On my wall."

"You might reconsider when you realize the money raised is specifically for life saving equipment in your son's cardiac wing."

Luc was right, that did make a difference. I was so proud of Domenic and the work he was doing. If I could help in any way, it was worth considering.

"The hospital might not think that my painting is worth auctioning off."

"Ah ha. You're considering it." Luc beamed. He thought the procurement of his favorite piece of my artwork was safely in his hands.

"I am considering it, yes. I'll let you know."

"I have the perfect spot for it. On *my* wall."

"Don't count your chickens, mister. If I do decide to donate it, someone else might outbid you."

"Do you honestly think that I would allow someone else to get their hands on that painting?"

Of course not. What was I thinking? If someone did outbid him, Luc would make sure that the painting ended up with him. When he wanted something, he could be very persuasive.

"Changing the subject, I'd like you to look into this new man in Lucia's life. I shouldn't call him a man, he's really just a boy. He plays the drums in a band. I'm a bit concerned he might be on drugs considering the people he's mixing with. Lucia assures me that she's not interested in drugs, but it makes me nervous nevertheless."

"I'll have a chat with her. And I will check him out. Don't worry. Lucia will not take drugs. She knows the damage they can do."

"I'll feel better when I know he's not going to lead her down the wrong path."

Luc laughed. I was worried he wasn't taking me seriously.

"It's not funny."

"Your daughter is a very independent young woman. No one. . . I mean no one . . . will make her do anything she does not want to do. Believe me, I know she doesn't need artificial substances in her system. She's wild enough . . . sorry. . . strong-willed enough, without them."

Coincidentally Lucia appeared with a backpack slung over one shoulder and munching on an apple. She showed no indication that she knew we had been discussing her.

"Good morning Mom. Uncle Luc. I'm going to study for an exam at Claire's after school. It might be a late one, and Claire's brother will drop me home tonight."

"Give Cameron the address and he'll come pick you up," I offered.

"Oh, there's no need when Claire said her brother would do it. It would be rude not to accept. Besides I don't know what time."

"I hope your results reflect the work you are putting in on this exam. What subject is it?"

"Math. I'd better go. Cameron is waiting to drive me to school. Ciao family."

I watched her ponytail bounce as she marched off down the hall. I remembered her as a little girl, walking through the school yard, full of confidence, looking neither right nor left, just heading straight for the building, eager to learn. Eager to get away from home to be the queen of her own domain.

"I'm surprised you let her get away with that." Luc arched a perfect eyebrow at me.

"She only thinks she got away with it. I was young once too. And headstrong and wanting to burst out of the constraints that my aunt and uncle put on me. I'll have her tailed."

Luc burst out laughing. Then suddenly stopped. "Oh, you're not joking!"

"When it comes to Lucia, I have learned not to stop her plans, which will make her want to be even more impossible, but I need to make sure she doesn't get hurt. I've been having her tailed for a while now, when she's out of the house in the evening. I hired an old work colleague in the stunt business. Someone to step in and take care of things if she got into trouble, or anyone unsavory approached her. So far it has been unnecessary."

"I would probably take a different approach."

"Yes, but there's very little else I can do. I could've called her out on it. But that would have meant calling her a liar in front of you, and she loves you too much to disappoint you, and she wouldn't have had a great day at school. And you're not here often enough for me to ask you to pull her back into line."

Luc's smile disappeared. An expression ghosted across his face, and sadness etched into the lines around his eyes.

"I'm here as often as I can," Luc said quietly.

"I'm sorry. That was unkind. I know you're here with us when you can be." My heart began to race as it always did when I was anxious, when Luc and I had cross words, or if I said something which hurt him or made him sad. I didn't want to hurt him. I knew it was difficult for Luc to be here on Earth for any length of time with me or my family. His place was in Hell, guarding the demons there. Luc was my best friend. The only one who really knew and appreciated what had happened in my life, and how sad I had been since my husband Richard had died in a boating accident, some months before Lucia was born. Being left with two children was draining, and I ended up having to take medication to get through that sad part of my life. I lost many months in a fog of depression. He was my rock back then and had been my support all these years.

I grasped the heart shaped twenty-four-carat gold locket I wore and rubbed the satin smooth surface between my finger and thumb. It amazed me that over the years, I had not rubbed away the delicate wings pattern etched into the design. This had become a ritual which never failed to calm me down. Richard gave me the locket after Domenic was born. It contains a picture of Richard and our son, but the catch is broken and even if I had it repaired, I couldn't bear to look inside.

I took some deep breaths, and after a few minutes my heart slowed down, and back to normal. I glanced up at Luc, who was watching me intently. When our eyes met, he smiled, and warmth returned to my heart. Good, we were back to normal footing. I relaxed.

"I'd better let you get ready for your meeting. You will think about the painting and let me know. I can have it transported to the venue. You won't have to do a thing."

"How did you know I had a meeting? Oh, silly question."

"I knew because Aimee told me when I arrived. No hocus pocus involved. She told me not to hold you up too long. You know she protects you, nearly as well as Max. By the way, where is Max?"

"I haven't seen him since last night. He hasn't been the same since Domenic moved out."

"Max! Come here," Luc called out.

Max appeared in the middle of the room, with his head cocked to one side, watching Luc and waiting for orders.

Outsiders wouldn't understand the importance of Max in our family. When Domenic was growing up Max followed and protected him as if his own life depended on it. There was nothing that dog wouldn't do for Domenic. When he grew old, and was obviously in pain, Domenic could not bear to see him suffering any more. He asked Luc to do something, anything, to help Max, even if it meant he was going to lose his best friend. Luc laid his hand on Max, and he went peacefully to sleep. Domenic wept, broken hearted, and when Luc could no longer stand to see him inconsolable, he did something amazing. He brought Max back to us.

Granted he wasn't alive. But Max still looked exactly like the Doberman we knew. As a Hellhound, he was able to take up his duties as protector, but there was far more that he could do, now that he wasn't of this world. Max had the ability to appear and disappear on command, communication was often through telepathy, he could teleport to any location to locate Domenic and Lucia. He could travel from this world to the underworld, could grow in size and shape, and his howl was deafening. Luc had managed to remove the stench that he brought with him when he came back from Hell, by adding a special collar. The bond that he had with Domenic was still as strong, and he took his job as protector of the family very seriously. Over the years, anyone human or demon attempting to break in or scale the walls of the estate had mysteriously disappeared. We surmise Max buried them somewhere, on this earth or beyond.

Luc ruffled Max's ears, and the animal leaned into the touch of affection.

"Where have you been? Do I need to check the perimeter of the yard for fresh graves?" Luc asked.

"He was probably up in Domenic's room, sitting by the bed like he used to do. Or in Lucia's room, waiting for her to come home."

"Maybe we should get Max a friend too?" Luc announced with a straight face.

"Two dogs? No Luc."

"You won't have to feed them. You don't even have to pick up after them."

"Another Hellhound you mean?"

"Why not. Lucia won't be here in a few years' time. No one to run with in the yard. No one to throw a ball."

"Thanks, now you're depressing me. I am planning on keeping my daughter here till she's at least thirty-five."

"Good luck with that." Luc laughed, and disappeared.

Max sauntered over past my chair and lay down by the window in the sun.

"You won't leave me will you Max." Max raised his head, his ears twitching at this sound of his name. He looked over at me, tilted his head to the side, and if I had been able to communicate telepathically with him like the rest of my family, I am sure we would have had a long and meaningful conversation.

I sighed and poured another cup of coffee.

6

LUC

I stayed in the shadow world for a short time, to make sure Harper had calmed down. I knew her heart was beating fast because my heart was also beating fast. I'm aware that the part of my heart beating in Harper's chest is still running in sync with mine. There are days that are harder than others to hide the truth from Harper. If she knew how difficult it was each and every time that I left her to return to Hell, if she knew I was doing this to protect her and my family, would it make a difference? Would she forgive me if she learned the truth? It's not something I'm willing to risk. The knowledge of all we shared, the close bond that we continue to share, keeps me going when I want to turn back and undo all I have done, all the sacrifices I have made for my family. I would have loved to be the one to tuck the children into bed at night. I would have loved to be the one to have the Father-Daughter dance with Lucia at school. I would have loved to slip into bed and hold Harper as she fell asleep each night. But I have to be content to always watch over them from the shadow world, and to occasionally be a part of their real world as Godfather Luc.

There was enough time to check up on Domenic at work before I had to return to Hell.

The operation was nearly complete when I arrived. The surgical team had closed the patient up and were ready to wheel him into recovery. I popped in on Domenic in the locker room.

"Tiring operation? You look exhausted."

"It was tricky. We were repairing a procedure that had been botched by another hospital earlier this year."

"Will he live?"

"Yes, he will. If he retires and takes up something less hazardous to his health. Police work is not in his best interests at the moment. Even sitting behind a desk can bring its own stress."

"How's the car?"

"I'm very happy driving her."

"Good. Have you found your other gift useful?'"

"I've had a couple of strange occurrences, which I think are connected to your gift. But I haven't worked out yet if it is a help or a hindrance. The jury is out."

"Lucia has a new boyfriend. I told your mother I would check him out. He plays drums in a band. Travels the country touring. Has she talked to you about him?"

"Lucia has a new boyfriend every other week. No, I haven't heard about this one. He sounds too old for her in my opinion. Do you want me to talk to her, ask her about him? It might be easier coming from me?"

"Find out what you can. I'll check back later. There's a plane crash I have to attend. Right now. Sorry."

I had received a telepathic message from Hell that a light plane had crashed into a mountain to the North of the state during the night. The pilot was hanging on to life by a thread when I arrived. His passenger was dead. The plane was full of illegal drugs. They had been flying low, under the radar, to avoid being detected, so no one knew of the crash. Only an experienced pilot would fly successfully through the mountains in the middle of the night. I guess this guy was not experienced. I leant into the cabin through the shattered side panel. I tapped the pilot on the shoulder, and he opened his eyes.

"Marcus. Wake up! You didn't think this scenario through, did you?" I asked. I snapped my fingers and the metal peeled away

"How did you do that? Who. . . who are you?"

"I'm your escort."

"My escort?"

"To Hell. You killed this guy beside you. And you have enough nasty white powder in this plane to kill many more. And do a lot of damage if it had indeed reached its destination. Let's be honest here, you are the scum of the earth. Coincidentally the kind of scum Hell was created for. Do you have any last words?"

"Last words?"

"Before you die, Marcus. Anything interesting you want to confess? Why are you repeating everything I say?"

"You didn't come to save me?"

"Hell no. I came to make sure you can't touch that radio and call for help. Although I see now it's shattered. I came to make sure this plane is burnt to a crisp. With the drugs and you in it of course."

He began to struggle, but his seat belt was securely locked, and part of the aircraft was wedged into his side. Blood which had trickled out before, now poured from the wound.

"You're making this easy for me. The more you struggle the quicker it will be."

"I don't want to die."

"It's a bit late to be worried about that. It's a fait au complet."

"What?"

"It's a done deal. You're dead."

He slumped back in the seat. I snapped my fingers and the plane burst into flames. I stood a fair distance away and watched it burn. The colors were spectacular. A message came through to say they had received him in Hell. Good riddance. Too many lives were ruined by scum like this, who just wanted to make money from the weakness of humans. And I knew more than anyone else how weak humans could be.

If Harper was worried about drugs, at least these drugs were going nowhere near the population of California.

7

SOPHIE

21st March 2017 - Evening

I stretched my leg out of the soapy bubbles floating in the bath and ran the safety razor down my shin. It was lovely to have time for a bit of maintenance before we make our way out for the evening.

Lisa knocked on the door and walked in.

"Are you nearly done? I have to style my hair."

"Please come right on in. You're not bothering me at all!"

"I've seen it all before a gazillion times. I need the straightener."

"I would've liked a quiet thirty minutes to myself. Today's been crazy."

"Well soak up the quiet, cos the band is loud."

"How many are in the band?"

"There's a lead singer, two guitarists and a drummer."

"Why two guitarists?"

"They usually have two guitarists to thicken up their sound and

35

maintain momentum when switching from rhythm to lead. It helps to add layers and variety to their sound."

"Did you learn that by rote? You seem to know a bit about guitarists?"

"Yeah, my brother plays guitar. He's a fount of knowledge, which he shares. Constantly."

"Did you book a cab?"

"Yes, so move your bony ass out of the bath and let me get ready."

"Okay, okay. Let me shave the other leg, and I'm out of here."

I had decided to wear a forest green bodycon dress. It was sleeveless, had a low neckline, but not too low, and came to just below my knees. The dress itself did not show too much skin, but what it did was showcase my small bust and waist and clung to my hips. I felt sexy in this dress, which did wonders for a woman's confidence when you are without a date and everyone around you seems to be paired up.

Pete had decided Lisa was worth chasing and hadn't left her side all evening. I think it had something to do with the fitted black skirt and backless top she wore on my recommendation. I noticed his hand resting on that expanse of olive colored skin many times. Lisa looked supremely pleased with herself, and I couldn't blame her, because Pete was handsome and attentive and seemed like a nice guy.

The band was indeed loud, but they managed to play covers really well, and I had enjoyed myself. Much to my surprise. The other nurses who had turned up, both male and female, from the Emergency Department of the hospital were fun to be around. I recognized a few faces, probably from the cafeteria or common areas. I had a couple of dances, but no one there caught my eye.

Suddenly, out of the blue, I began to feel uneasy. The walls of the club were closing in on me. My heart began to race, and the hairs on the back of my neck stood up. I knew the signs, and something wasn't right, I had to get out of here. I considered calling a cab, as it was obvious that Lisa wasn't ready to leave and wouldn't be leaving alone.

I turned to walk to a quiet spot to make the call and bumped into a chest of solid muscle. I looked up into the eyes of a man mountain, with shoulders and neck fighting the constraints of a polo shirt. His bicep, I calculated, was the size of my thigh. He stood his ground between the high tables

"Sorry. I need to get by." I moved to the right and his hand shot out and grasped my bare upper arm.

"No need to rush off. I just arrived."

"And I'm just leaving. Let go of my arm."

"But we're only beginning to get acquainted."

"Let me go. I won't ask nicely again."

He laughed at me. I brought my knee up to his groin, but he was too quick, and he blocked with his thigh. Now he looked annoyed.

"That wasn't a nice thing to do. Let's go get a drink and you can apologize."

He pulled me with him toward the bar, I struggled in his wake. I recognized the voice before I saw Domenic, who was blocking our way.

"Let go of this young lady now, before you get hurt."

He laughed at Domenic and pulled me to his side.

"*You* are going to hurt *me?*"

"Only if you don't let her go."

The bully laughed again. He grabbed me tighter to his side.

Domenic reached out and placed his fingers in the crease of the big man's neck. He dropped to the ground with a sickening thud. Domenic pulled me away before I toppled over too.

"How did you do that?" I asked, in awe.

"I followed Mr Spock's technique."

"But that was fictional. Wasn't it?"

"Come on, let's go before he wakes up."

He guided me through the crowd, and we hurried through the double front doors into the cool night air. Already, my heart had slowed its pace. I took deep breaths of fresh oxygen.

"Thank you for coming to my rescue. But I would've managed to get away from him."

"Really?"

"It was a public space, and I would've screamed the place down."

"I could never walk away when someone's being bullied. And from my point of view you were being bullied. He was under the impression that because of his size he could get away with whatever he wanted, and I was no match."

"In this case size does *not* matter . . . is that what you are telling me?" I laughed and Domenic joined in.

"I guess that's exactly what I'm telling you. His size will make a difference though when he comes to, as his head hit the floor quite hard. He didn't go down gracefully."

"The bigger they are, the harder they fall. He'll have a headache tomorrow." I rubbed my arms, which were cooling quickly in the chilly night air.

"Here. Take my jacket." He slipped the jacket off and hung it over my shoulders.

The lining of his jacket was warm against my skin. The intimacy of the gesture was not lost on me. His spicy cologne clung to the fabric and tickled my senses. I looked up into eyes which had turned dark charcoal in the street lighting. Warmth, and not from the jacket, skittered across my skin. He moved slightly toward me. My heart began to race. Car headlights suddenly illuminated us before driving by. The moment passed. He turned away.

We walked across the street to where Domenic's car was parked.

"I'll hail a cab. I would make sure you got safely home but have to stay a bit longer. My little sister is in there and I want to make sure she leaves soon."

"But if you go back inside, that guy might be awake."

"I'm not going back inside. I'm going to wait here where I can see the door."

A cab cruised up the street and Domenic hailed it for me. I slipped off his jacket and handed it back to him. He opened the rear passenger door and closed it when I got in. I lowered the window.

"Thanks again. I guess I'll see you around."

"No doubt you will. Have a good night. I've taken note of the cab license plate." He gave a thumb's up sign. "All good." He tapped the roof of the cab to take off.

"You think of everything." The cab drove off and I watched him pulling on the jacket, out of the back window, until we turned a corner.

He had definitely piqued my interest. I wondered why he wasn't going in to collect his sister if he was worried about her. I sent a text message to Lisa to let her know I was on the way home, and that a knight in shining armor had stepped in to save me after all, and signed off with LOL, and a smiley face.

8

DOMENIC

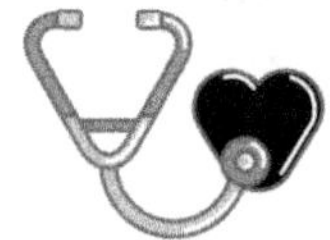

Sophie's cab turned the corner and I climbed into the driver's seat of my car to watch the patrons leave. Lucia shouldn't have been in the club as she was underage, but I guessed she would have cast a spell over the guy at the door to get past him. One of Lucia's special gifts is that she can enhance her face and body to appear older. She isn't aware that I have seen her use this to her advantage before.

Patrons spilled onto the street, and I caught sight of her and her current boyfriend, with his arm around her shoulder, making their way to his car. I tailed them until he dropped her at the gate of the estate and took off down the street.

I watched from a distance. She removed a long sweatshirt from her backpack and pulled it over her head, and down over her jeans. Heels were stuffed into her bag and exchanged for a pair of sneakers. She shook her hair loose to cover most of her face. I saw a woman change into a young girl before my eyes. She rang the buzzer, spoke into the intercom and the gate slid open, and I noticed Cameron standing at the door of the gatehouse. The gate slid closed again. She was home and she was safe.

I turned the car around and headed home. I had no idea a couple of hours ago that I would be checking up on Lucia. I had been eating dinner at a nearby restaurant when I saw her enter the club. No mistaking my little sister, no matter how she alters her appearance. She emits a certain vibration that I can sense when she's near. I hadn't thought about it much, but this vibration has become more noticeable since my birthday. Or since Luc bestowed on me the new ability to delve deeper into the very heart of what makes people tick. Although I have always known what makes Lucia tick. She sees herself as a princess, and she loves the fact that she has abilities that very few people know about. She is very intelligent and doesn't have to try hard to be top of her class in any subject. She is wise in the ways of the world and uses the weakness of others to get what she wants. Cunning? Yes, she is. Manipulative? Yes, she is. But she is also loving and sweet and kind to those around her, and generous to her few close friends.

It was fortuitous that I had been there tonight. Bumping into Sophie was a real surprise. I hardly recognized her at first. That green dress left little to the imagination, and her hair was loose covering her shoulders and framing her face with masses of bright red curls. She hadn't been wearing make-up at the hospital, but tonight she had gone all out with bright coral lipstick and something to cover up her freckles. It wasn't until I saw her big blue eyes that it clicked. She said she could've managed without my help. That may have been a fact. But I did enjoy stepping it and coming to the rescue. I have never been impressed with bulging muscles, or when the man who owns them takes advantage of his size to intimidate others. He'll have a headache tomorrow.

When we walked outside, I had the urge to take her hand. But I know from past experience that's not a good idea. I'm afraid if I touch Sophie's skin, I might get to know more than I bargained for, and I would like Sophie to remain a mystery for a little while longer.

Throughout my life, because of my unusual gift, because of my connection to Luc, and his DNA which is running through every cell in my body, I have avoided touching people. When I lay hands on a person, it is like being given a key to unlock their medical history, and to diagnose how I can help them if they are unwell. The images and the information run like a video at high speed, through my brain. It takes minutes for a diagnosis. But the images and the burden of their medical history stays with me for a long time, weighing me down. I have found It's best that I keep my hands to myself and avoid intimacy. I've been accused of lacking affection, but nothing could be further from the truth. One day I hope to be able to touch someone and not be overwhelmed by an information download.

Coupled with this new enhancement of Luc's I am almost afraid to touch my patients, the sensory overload is so strong. The bully in the bar was a classic example. My fingers were on his skin for mere seconds, and I knew that his excessive steroid use has caused problems in his liver and kidneys, and his prostate is already showing signs of cancer. The aggressive behavior was also a side effect, which would accelerate if he did not slow down using the drugs. Unfortunately, if he's being prescribed these drugs by unscrupulous doctors, they are not telling him about the terrible side effects. That, or he just doesn't care.

The drapes were drawn back in my apartment, and the moonlight shone in on the sparse furniture and solo rug I had placed in front of the black leather sofa to introduce a splash of color. The rug had come from the Middle East, and was so soft under bare feet, constructed of silken threads of a mix of deep crimson and caramel and soft greens. The pattern was intricate and exquisite. It was one of my favorite things in the apartment. I had bought it from another doctor who was returning overseas. I had visions of a man and woman making love on that carpet, on many occasions. It gave me ideas that one day it would be my turn.

An image of Sophie, laying there, her red curls spread out on the carpet, her bare arms outstretched to me, wearing that green dress she wore tonight, popped into my head. She had the look of a woman who knew her own power over a man. I think there's more to Sophie than meets the eye. I'm drawn to her on a whole other level, not just the physical.

I poured a glass of wine, turned on some classical music and took a seat on the balcony. I enjoyed this time of quiet introspection before turning in for the night.

Are you awake?

Yes Lucia. I'm awake. Why are you up so late?

I've been thinking about the future and what I want to do.

And what have you decided?

That's the problem. I don't know what I want to do. You were lucky, you always knew you wanted to be a doctor. I don't have these ideas or visions of my future.

Why are you worrying about it now?

Mom has been asking me to choose a college But all I want to do is run in the opposite direction. I want to be a free spirit. I'm over the classrooms and the teachers.

It's not a bad idea to go to college until you find your place. You're a smart girl, and you've never had to work hard to get results. You're one of the lucky ones. I'm sure you could get a scholarship to any college you set your mind on. And remember it's not all about the books and the lessons. It's about networking and connecting with people and making life-long friends.

Okay I'll think about it.

Good. Go to sleep. How about I pick you up for an early breakfast tomorrow. I don't have any patients until noon.

Great. I'd like that. Goodnight big brother.

Goodnight little sister.

I worry about Lucia. She is popping into my head to have a chat more often these days. There are drawbacks as well as benefits to being able to communicate telepathically. I just wish she would 'knock" occasionally and not just barge on in. I often wonder if I have any private thoughts, between Luc and Lucia entering at will.

I know she's struggling and wants to grow up fast. But she's too headstrong and doesn't think things through. She has made some bad choices with her friends in the past, and I know Luc has had to step in and steer her in the other direction. We have to be very careful who we allow into our homes and into our lives. Our family is not like any other.

I turned off the music, finished my wine and headed for bed. Tomorrow I will have to convince Lucia it's in her best interests to continue her education for a while longer. I know it's what Mom and Luc would want her to do. But for now, all I want is the sweet relief of slumber.

9

SOPHIE

23rd March 2017 – Afternoon

I glance around the cafeteria while waiting in line to pay for my lunch. I had hoped Domenic might be eating here or passing through, but it seems I'm out of luck today.

The hairs on the back of my arms stand up. Something's wrong, a queasy feeling in my stomach, a premonition of something bad going to happen. I glance around the room, where everything appears to be normal. But this has happened many times during my lifetime, and I've never been wrong before. Suddenly there is a high-pitched scream coming from the other side of the wall near the entrance to the hospital. My heart begins to race, because I'm all too aware of that primal sound of fear. I ditch the tray of food on the table and rush with the flow of cafeteria patrons toward the sound. A woman is kneeling on the floor in the hallway, rocking back and forth, bending over a child of about seven whose eyes are closed, and whose skin appears to have a blue tinge. The keening sound of her grief strikes at my very soul.

"Make way, I'm a nurse." I kneel down beside the child, to assess him. "What happened?"

"He just fell over. He's not breathing." The woman, presumably his mother, was weeping.

"What's his name?"

"Peter."

"Peter, can you hear me?" I asked loudly. I shook his shoulder. No response. I checked to see if his airway was clear and tilted his head back.

"Do something! Please," the woman begged.

I started CPR and was relieved when two nursing assistants appeared pushing a bed and with a doctor hurrying in its wake. I stood up to let them lift the child onto the bed and work on him. They hurried off in the direction of emergency, and the mother followed them. I heard them page Dr Ericson soon after. At least Peter was going to be in good hands.

ॐ

I had reached my car at the end of my shift, both tired and hungry, and was loading my belongings onto the back seat, when a car approached. I looked up and smiled when I recognized Domenic behind the wheel. His window lowered.

"We've got to stop meeting like this. People will talk." I laughed.

"Only if I get out of the car, or you get into mine." Domenic smiled and his eyes crinkled up at the edges.

"Is Peter alright? The boy who collapsed today. I heard you being paged."

"Yes, he's in intensive care. I think he will be fine. He is a strong young man."

"That's good news."

"I heard a nurse took care of him when he collapsed. Was that you?"

"Yes. I was nearby. Although he was in the right place for help, in a hospital."

"His mother wanted to find the lovely nurse who came to their aid, and to thank you. She said everyone around her just stood and looked. You were the only one to rush in and help."

"Sometimes people don't want to get involved, don't want to touch someone in case they do more harm than good. I'm sure there were people standing around them who just felt helpless."

"Yes, touching someone you don't know can have drawbacks."

"Why do I get the feeling we're not talking about Peter anymore."

"I'm just stating a fact."

"I'd better let you go, you look tired."

"Ditto. You look tired too."

"I hope my house-mate has cooked dinner tonight. Otherwise, it's going to be toast again."

"I'm going to have home-made lasagna if you would like to join me?"

"You cook?"

"I do. But I didn't make this. However, I can vouch for it being fabulous."

"Did your mother cook it for you?"

"No, Aimee, our family housekeeper, cooked it. She is a wonderful cook, she made extra and she dropped it off for me tonight at my apartment. It's in the oven and will be ready in . . ." he checked his watch. "Twenty minutes."

"I'm sorely tempted."

"You can eat and run. I won't be offended."

"Okay. It's a date." I ducked my head and returned to my car.

As soon as those words left my mouth, my face flushed a bright red.

"I'll follow you there," I yelled over my shoulder.

I hopped in behind the wheel and followed him out of the parking garage, cursing myself all the way for being an idiot. He was being kind. Being a friend. Why was I making more of this? The man did not say anything about a date. As traffic was light, we arrived at the apartment building within a few minutes. I wasn't aware he lived so close. I followed him through security garage doors into the bowels of the building and parked in a visitor's space. As soon as he opened the door of the apartment, the aroma of garlic and spices wafted through the air and my stomach grumbled.

Domenic invited me to sit while he washed his hands and quickly set two places at his dining room table and produced a bottle of red wine, which he opened to allow to breathe. The oven timer let out a shrill sound. He turned it off, donned thick padded oven mitts to remove the large tray of golden topped, cheese covered lasagna and set it on a wooden serving platter on the table. He opened the fridge, found a covered dish of garden salad and added it to the meal on the table, between our two places.

"I'm just going to wash my hands. The bathroom?"

"Down the hall and on the right." Domenic pointed to the hall leading off the living room.

I had the chance to look around, without being obvious. I must admit I was dying to stop and look more closely at the black and white photographs lining the hallway. The apartment was elegant and stylish, and suited my mental image of Domenic to a tee. I wandered past a room which was obviously Domenic's study, then a spare bedroom and found the bathroom on the right as he had directed. The shower in this bathroom took up one wall and would easily hold half a dozen people. Jets set into the marble tiles and two large shower heads would mean complete coverage of every inch of skin. Double white porcelain basins set into the vanity unit, a toilet along another wall, and a tall glass fronted cabinet for storage of fluffy white towels completed the space. The frosted windows set high in the wall would allow this room to be bathed in light.

I washed and dried my hands and couldn't help but peek into his bedroom through the open door at the end of the hall. Everything in the apartment was spotless and sleek and minimalist, in shades of grey and black and with splashes of pristine white. I had never seen such a large bedroom for a single person. My whole family would have lived in a house the size of this bedroom when I was a child in Ireland. The bed was huge and sat center stage on a carpeted plat-form, and the black lacquered headboard curved around to form the side tables. The large white European pillows looked inviting; the pale grey duvet was probably filled with duck down. Everything in this apartment had no doubt cost a fortune. Of that I was sure.

"Dinner is served!" Domenic called out.

I reluctantly returned to the dining room. I'd had a small insight into the doctor's private world, and I was curious to find out more.

We made a big hole in the tray of lasagna. In part because we were both hungry, and because it was delicious, as Domenic had suggested.

"I don't think I need to eat for a week. That was wonderful. Please pass on my thanks to Aimee. And thank you for sharing. If you had planned to put portions of that lasagna in the freezer, I'm sorry I've taken your Monday and Tuesday portions."

"You're welcome. I will pass on your thanks. No, I'm not going to suffer. Aimee will make more if I want it. But I imagine there will be something just as tasty in my oven for dinner in a couple of days."

"You're very lucky. I'm guessing she misses you."

"I am lucky. I'm never going to starve as long as Aimee is cooking for me. I can cook, but I know she loves to do it. So why wouldn't I enjoy the benefits."

"Yes, food is love. Especially food made by someone who loves you."

"I'm very happy that Aimee looks after my family. And her husband Cameron of course. He takes care of the grounds and the maintenance. How about you? Do you like to cook?"

"I can cook. Of course, not like this, but I'm learning. I've been buying some cookbooks. I practice on Lisa, my house-mate, but she's a better cook than me, and I feel for her."

"Maybe you could cook for me. I could be your guinea pig for a change. Lisa could have a night off."

"Oh."

"What?"

"My house is not like this. We rent a place on the other side of town. It wouldn't be safe for you to drive there in your flashy car. It might get stolen when you were eating."

"I don't think it will get stolen."

"You don't know the neighborhood. I'm telling you, it's not in your league at all."

"Tell you what. You invite me and I will make sure my car will not be stolen while we eat. I'll bring Max."

"Who's Max? Is he your bodyguard?"

"Max is my dog. Well, he's the family dog actually, and lives with my mother. Believe me when I tell you that no one will go near the car if Max is sitting in it."

"Okay. You asked for it. One fabulous meal. Cooked by me. And at least if you get sick, I can take care of you." I laughed. Domenic looked thoughtful.

"Let me know what you're cooking, and I'll bring the wine."

"We're really doing this?"

"Yes. I'm free next week. What night suits you?"

"Friday. I'm not working next weekend."

"Great. Friday it is."

I stood and picked up the dishes.

"Please don't worry. I'll do that." Domenic took them from me and put them on the counter.

"I have to go. I don't want to leave this all to you."

"I'll load the dishwasher in five minutes. Go home. It's okay."

I picked up my purse and Domenic walked me to the elevator.

"You don't have to walk me to the car. I'll be fine. Thank you again." The doors opened and I stepped in and turned around. *Do I shake his hand, or do I kiss his cheek?* I stood on my tiptoes and kissed his cheek. I got zapped by a flash of electricity. I jumped back. My lips buzzed. "Wow. Talk about static electricity. This carpet must be full of it. Goodnight." The doors closed and I looked down. I was standing on ceramic tiles.

10

DOMENIC

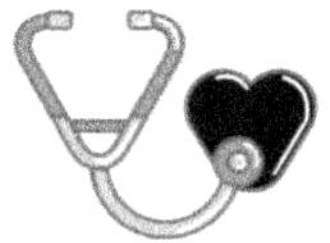

31st March 2017

I have had dreams every night that somehow involve Sophie. They are not sexual in nature, but I always wake up with a raging erection and wishing I had her in my bed. I have never had this continued reaction to anyone in my life before. Abstinence has never been easy, but it has never been as difficult before to move on from a woman I know I cannot have. My intention was to make friends with Sophie and with others at the hospital. Mom has pointed out on many occasions that I need to make friends of my own age, now that I am no longer living at home. But I have to be careful.

Last week when she kissed me on the cheek, I felt that flash of electricity Sophie mentioned as the doors were closing. Static electricity was not to blame. And with it came an awareness I had never experienced before. In that instant I recognized her kindness, and compassion, her intelligence and awareness, her selflessness and passion for nursing and helping people. She is one of the good ones and does not have a mean or nasty bone in her body. For her, family is

51

everything, and helping people is part of her DNA. I got all of this in an instant. Now I am wondering what prolonged touch would give me. Do I risk taking her hand? I guess I'll find out when I go to dinner tonight.

I bought a bottle of white wine to accompany the chicken casserole she said she was cooking. I dropped in on the family, and to let them know I was taking Max on a date.

"You're going on a date?" Lucia sounded amazed.

"Yes I am."

"She must be something special," Mom said

"She's a nurse at the hospital. She is unlike anyone I have ever met. She's not aware of the fact she's gifted."

"Gifted. How?" Lucia asked

"She is a healer. She isn't using her power, but I can sense it within her. She thinks nursing is what she is good at, but there is a whole other side to her, which I am hoping I can show her."

"I bet there is." Lucia smirked.

"Don't be crude Lucia." Mom admonished. "Your brother is lucky to have found someone he can spend time with. You will be careful Domenic, won't you."

"I'll be careful. And I'm taking Max with me to dinner. He is going to look after the car. She tells me that the neighborhood is . . . "

"Dodgy?" Lucia asked

"Precisely. Max is my secret weapon."

Max appeared on cue and nudged my hand for a pat.

"Let's go Max. You're on guard duty tonight."

"I hope he isn't required. But better to be safe than sorry. I know you love that car." Mom gave me a peck on the cheek and put her arm around my waist as we walked to the door. She has always been the only one who can touch me without the sensory overload.

"Bye Lucia," I called over my shoulder.

"Bye big brother. Enjoy your date. Make sure Max does not bring any bodies back home."

Max hopped into the back seat and lay down with his head on his front paws. He knew what he was here for. He was probably thinking it would be a long night.

I pulled up outside the suburban house. There were a few young men gathered around a car on the other side of the street. They noticed my car, stopped taking and moved in my direction.

"Nice ride." One tall guy said a couple of feet from the door. He walked up and down admiring the sleek lines.

"I've always wanted to drive one of these," another one said. A few mumbled obscenities behind him in support.

I got out, walked around the car and lifted the wine from the passenger seat along with a small bunch of flowers wrapped in brown paper, and tied with a white ribbon. I left the sidewalk and started to walk up the path to the house.

"Hey, you've left your windows open. That's not safe in this neighborhood." They all laughed.

I glanced back over my shoulder. One young hot shot decided he would reach in and open the driver's door. I stopped and turned to watch the show.

Max raised his head from the back seat. One amazing thing about a Hellhound is that he can change his shape and size at will. The angrier he gets the bigger he becomes. He feeds off fear and the young idiot who thought he would take my car for a test drive got the surprise of his life. Max's head had grown to three times its size. He stuck his head out the window, snarled, and bared his huge teeth, which shone bright in the evening light. Thick strands of saliva dripped from the viscously sharp edges of his canines. The collar he wore had large metal spikes which advertised 'don't mess with me or I'll cut you to shreds.'

The young hot shot backed away quickly, nearly tripping over in his haste. His friends backed off too. Max's head retreated into the back seat once more.

"I wouldn't go near the car. Max doesn't like strangers," I announced.

"You should close the windows. What if he gets out?" tall guy asked.

"He won't leave the car. Unless someone tries to be a hero. If you want to test that theory, I hope your medical insurance is paid up."

They returned to their side of the road, but they kept glancing back. I rang the doorbell. The door opened and Sophie simultaneously pulled an apron from her waist, which was covering a sky blue, knee length dress, the color of her eyes. She had bare feet and I noticed her toenails were painted bright red. Her hair was pulled to the top of her head, russet curls cascading down the pale column of her neck. She looked fresh, and wholesome, and utterly beautiful.

"Come on in. I see you've met the neighbors. Friendly guys, aren't they," Sophie said.

"And as long as they stay away from my car, they will remain healthy guys."

"Do you want a bowl of water for Max? Is he okay in the car?"

"He has everything he needs. I threw a cadaver in the back seat before I left home."

"You're kidding. Right?" Sophie giggled.

"Am I?"

"Stop teasing me. Come and meet Lisa, my house-mate."

"These are for you. I wasn't sure of the flowers, but Aimee said I couldn't go wrong with pink roses."

"Thank you, they are beautiful. Hey Lisa, this is Domenic." Lisa waved from the kitchen. She was stirring a pot. "Lisa took over, while I answered the door. I promise I cooked the meal."

"Lovely to meet you." I gave Lisa a wave.

"Likewise," Lisa said and turned back to the pot.

The table in the corner was set for two I noticed. Sophie took the gifts into the kitchen and poured the wine. She returned with two glasses and handed one to me.

"Cheers. Lisa is leaving soon. Shall we sit?"

I attempted to sit down on the sofa. Sophie quickly plumped up a pillow at my back.

"I'm fine. Relax."

Lisa appeared from the kitchen carrying the flowers in a glass vase. She set them down in the middle of the table.

"Everything is ready. The oven is off. The sauce is cooked, Have fun guys," Lisa said.

"Thanks for your help. Have a good night." Sophie gave her friend a hug.

"Don't go near the car on your way out. Okay. Max is very protective," I said.

"Sure thing. Although I do like dogs." Lisa smiled as she picked up her purse and looped it over her shoulder. I could tell she didn't like being told what to do by a stranger.

"Promise me you won't try to pat him or go near the open window," I said.

"If you say so," Lisa said, unconvincingly.

"He's on duty, and he takes his job very seriously. I'll bring him around another day when he's in a better mood. And you can pat him then. Okay." I could tell this was not sitting well with Lisa.

"Please don't go near Domenic's car. Max has been given instructions to challenge anyone, including a cute thirty-year-old woman, who is being asked nicely by Max's owner. Capisci?" Sophie folded her arms and raised one eyebrow to make her point.

"Sure." Lisa left the house. I sent a telepathic command to Max to raise his head off the seat and follow her with his eyes when she leaves the house. Under no circumstance to harm her, even if she ventures near the car. I could be sure Max would follow instructions. But I could not be sure that Lisa would do the same. Sophie must have had a similar suspicion because she opened the front door and watched Lisa until she had disappeared around the corner. And then waited for a couple of minutes until she was sure she wasn't coming back.

"You trust her, I see."

"She's Italian, she's headstrong, and she doesn't like being told what to do."

"I gathered that."

"Let's eat. I hope you're hungry. I made a lot."

"It smells delicious." I took my seat at the table.

"Are you okay for wine? I'm going to have another glass. I seem to have finished mine." She disappeared into the kitchen.

"One is fine for me, thanks."

"I'm a bit nervous, having you here," she called out.

"Why? I can't be the first guest you've had to dinner."

"No. But you're more . . . "

Sophie returned to the table and placed her glass of wine on the coaster.

"More what?"

"Fancy. Far classier than I am used to. Everything you own, everything you have is expensive. Your apartment is filet mignon. My house is chipped beef."

"Please don't be nervous. Your house is lovely."

"You're being kind. But thank you. I'd better serve dinner." Sophie disappeared into the kitchen.

She returned with two plates loaded up with chicken casserole and vegetables.

"I hope you like it, but I won't be offended if you can't eat it." She slid onto the chair opposite to mine.

I took a bite and found it to be tasty.

"I don't know what you're worried about, this is delicious."

Sophie ate some and her face was a picture of delight and surprise.

"Oh. It tastes good." She laughed. "Lisa must have added some extra touches. It didn't taste this good before."

The main course was followed with fresh fruit and vanilla ice cream. Sophie wouldn't let me help clear away the plates. Getting her own back, no doubt. I felt pleasantly full when we returned to sit on the sofa.

"Tell me about growing up in Ireland. It's a country I have wanted to visit. I imagine it to be magical, with little Leprechauns running around all over the place. And pots of gold at the end of the rainbows."

"I have yet to meet a Leprechaun or find a pot of gold. I don't remember much about Ireland. Other than the fact we had a large family and a small house, in a small village. I can tell you though that my great, great, great grandmother Maggie Mae was a witch. Or so I'm led to believe. I was named after her originally, but my father's family wouldn't have it. They say I take after her. She had red hair, and blue eyes too. She was the medicine woman for the village, the person the villagers went to for herbs and potions for all sorts of ailments. The person people went to when someone was giving birth, or someone was dying. Yes, she was there at the beginning of life, and at the end of life. Maggie Mae was a powerful woman. The story goes that she brought the love of her life back from the dead. She could also call upon a curse if you wronged her. Some say she worked alongside the Devil himself."

"You don't say! This is a turn of events. Sophie O'Connor is the great, great, great granddaughter of a witch. I am intrigued, especially if Maggie Mae was in cahoots with the Devil. I think that's why I'm sure you have powers you are unaware of. Remember I did tell you I believe you are a healer the first time we met."

"Yes. I do remember. Although I don't understand why you think that."

"Call it intuition on my part. I have powers of my own."

"What powers do you have? Other than being a fabulous doctor."

"I can read people"

"Like a clairvoyant?"

"No. Their character, their intentions mostly."

Sophie turned to face me. She had moved closer on the sofa than I'm usually comfortable with. She looked me in the eye. It took a great deal of willpower to sit still and not move back.

"So, read me. What's my intention?"

"You are virtue personified. You have a light glowing inside you, which spills out to those around, making their days better. Your intention is . . . "

"Yes?"

"Your intention is . . ." My heart was pumping a million miles an hour. I knew her intention. I forced myself to stay still.

Sophie leant forward and pressed her lips to mine. I was pulled into a vortex of emotions, sensations and heightened awareness, which shook my body to the core. Pleasure, pure and simple, sweet and electrifying surged through me. She pulled back slowly. Wonder reflected in her big blue eyes. She blinked slowly. She had experienced it too.

"Wow." She pressed her fingertips to her lips.

I couldn't think straight let alone speak.

"Did you feel that?" she poked me in the chest.

My lips moved but no sound escaped. I leant forward and took her face in my hands and kissed her tentatively, gently, almost afraid of what I would find. Pleasure washed over me once more. I felt more alive than I had ever felt in my life. I had thrown caution to the wind and touched her, and I was no longer afraid of what would happen. I was no longer afraid of what I would find out. She was magical, even although she didn't know it. Sophie was the person I had been looking for my whole life. I knew it instinctively, from the center of my being.

"You are the one I have been waiting for."

"What. Whoa Mister. It was a kiss. Just a kiss. Don't go crazy on me."

I stood up to regain my composure.

"I'm sorry. Yes. It was a kiss. Just a kiss. A very pleasant kiss."

"I would say an amazing kiss actually. But then . . . maybe we need to try it again."

"Again?"

"Sit doctor." She pointed to the sofa.

I took my seat again and she touched my face with her fingertips, tracing the line of my nose, the contours of my eyebrows, and my lips. Tiny electric pulses danced over my skin. She edged closer. I closed my eyes and allowed her the freedom of exploration. I felt her warm breath on my skin. Her lips touched mine, and the zap of electricity was milder this time. I had begun to relax, to enjoy this sensation when the addition of her tongue sent me over the edge. I actually moaned aloud, which encouraged her to be bolder. She climbed onto my lap and wrapped her arms around my neck, her warm breasts pressed against my chest. Sensory overload had reached maximum level. The erection I could feel was no doubt felt by Sophie as she squirmed against me. There was no stopping it now. She didn't appear to mind. In fact, I was sure she was smiling.

"I can help you with that. Although I must point out that I don't normally do this on a first date." She reached down and grasped me firmly. I rose from the sofa as if catapulted, with Sophie's arms still around my neck, and her legs now wrapped around my hips.

"No. Not happening."

"Why?"

"Your house-mate might come back. It's not appropriate." I placed my hands on her waist and extricated her from my body, to stand on the floor.

"Well, let's go to my room. Do you have a condom?"

"No. I don't carry condoms. I don't do this."

"I've never met a man who didn't have at least one in his wallet. Are you sure?" She patted the pocket of my trousers, searching for my wallet. The bulge in the pocket was nothing compared to the bulge in the front.

She looked up, staring at me. Staring right through me to be exact. Staring into my very soul. Her eyes grew wide.

"Oh my God. You're a virgin. I'm so sorry. I've just made a complete idiot of myself. You must hate me."

"I don't hate you."

"Is it for religious reasons? Because I'm Catholic, but not really practicing Catholic if you know what I mean."

"No, not for religious reasons. It's been by choice. I have an issue with close proximity, and I've never connected with anyone before that has made me want to take that step."

"And now you think I am throwing myself at you." Sophie covered her mouth with her hands.

"No. I don't." I laughed. I had relaxed with Sophie more than I had ever relaxed with anyone other than my family. "Please don't stress. I've had a wonderful evening." I pulled her to my chest. I knew she could hear my heart thudding against my ribcage.

"Would it be okay to just sit on the sofa for a while with your arms around me?" Sophie asked.

"I'd like that." We sat down, Sophie pulled her legs up under her, and she began to talk. I think she was trying to make me feel more comfortable, and I admired her for that.

And that was how we ended the evening. With Sophie curled up by my side, my arm around her shoulder, while she told me about her youth and her love of Irish Dancing. And I told her a little of my family history, and my father's heritage, and my love of Vikings. Of course, I didn't mention my Godfather Luc. He would be the topic of a whole other conversation. And I knew there would be other evenings, and other conversations.

When I left, I sat in the car for a few minutes before I started the engine, marveling that I have never felt more comfortable with anyone in my entire life.

11

LUC

I watch from the shadow land. My family, the humans I have come to love, were going about their day to day lives without me. They were managing. If I was honest with myself, they were thriving. An unfamiliar ache took residence in my chest, because I wanted to be missed. I wanted to be needed. I was the all-powerful, the majestic, the Satanic Lord of Hell. And yet, I just wanted to be a partner, a lover, a father, a constant member of the family. Not someone watching from the wings.

Rourke, my second in charge, called me back to the depths of Hell. Back to the underworld where at the moment, the masses were pushing all limits, straining resources, and the fighting, and uprisings were common occurrences. The fools who tried to revolt were quickly eliminated. It always amazed me that they would even contemplate rising against me. Did they think I would just slap them on the wrist and send them on their way? They were obliterated, their ashes scattered in the bowels of the earth, trodden on, mixed with the damp, black soil, never to be recreated into anything remotely human in appearance again. Their souls would never achieve restoration or rebirth. I guess it was the Big Guy's way, culling the numbers from up above, because there were only so many cells in Hell for the wicked.

Yet the human race seemed to be getting worse, pushing Hell to its limits.

"You paged me?" I strode into my office and sat behind my desk. Rourke appeared before me.

"I have intel about a likely explosion on Earth. It's going to be in the underground railway in London. Many people will be killed, the wrong people will be blamed, and chaos will start a chain reaction for retribution. I'm letting you know because we are about to get busier, and I could use a little extra help. I've had my eye on a demon who has shown promise. He's young, and untrained, but he has what it takes to work for you, alongside me. If you will allow me, I would like to take him under my wing and teach him."

"What is this demon's name?"

"Drake."

"If you think he's worthy, you have my permission. But on no account are you to give him any powers. He has to earn them just as you did. And I will be the judge of his ability."

"Thank you. I appreciate your trust in me."

"Bring him to me. I want to meet this demon you think so highly of."

Rourke left the room and returned with a young, virile demon, who I guessed would have to be only a few hundred years old. Very much Rourke's junior, but surprisingly similar in looks. Both had black shoulder length hair, both were wearing the traditional black, fitted guard's uniform with a red shirt, and black leather boots. Both had leather whips holstered on their belts. They stood to attention. I got up and walked around Drake, taking him in from all angles. I estimated he was about six feet and six inches tall, and he had the body and the build of a fighter. His bicep muscles filled out the sleeves of his shirt, the expanse of his chest strained the buttons. He kept his eyes forward, but I knew that he was assessing me, just as much as I was assessing him. All of his senses were on high alert. His telepathic senses were weak, but they could be worked on, and would grow in time. He would be thought of as handsome in the human world. Arched eyebrows over dark eyes, full lips, high cheekbones, clean shaven and a firm chin. He would have been very popular with the females on earth when he was alive. And no doubt, some of the men.

"Rourke has requested you move up in the ranks. I'm assigning you to this floor, where Rourke will train you to be his assistant. As he is my second in charge, this role is a very big deal. If you are half the demon Rourke thinks you are, there will be a promotion in your future. And of course, more powers assigned to you."

"Thank you, my Lord." Drake stood tall, back ramrod straight, shoulders back. His expression had not changed. However, his eyes had widened at this news.

"You are dismissed."

He left the room and I walked across, took my seat and put my feet up on my desk, ankles crossed.

"I hope your faith in him is warranted."

"I feel confident he can shoulder some of the load when you're not here."

"I am aware that there's more pressure on you when I'm on Earth. Which is why I'm agreeing to this plan of yours. Don't let me down."

"I will do my utmost to make this work. I know where you would rather be, and I do not blame you for that, my lord."

Rourke was right. I would rather be on Earth gathering souls and returning home in time for dinner. But my job was not that easy, and no matter how much I wished I could change things, I had to face facts.

Hell was where I belonged.

1 2

DOMENIC

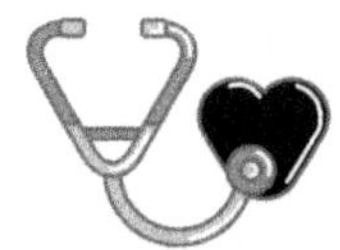

20th April 2017

I hadn't been to visit the family for a few weeks. The days had gotten away from me, and I wasn't surprised to find a text message from my mother, when I switched on my phone after surgery. Time to bite the bullet. I called her.

"Hey Mom. How are you?"

"I'm fine. But I've been wondering why we haven't seen more of you lately?"

"Work is busy. I've been settling into my apartment. You know."

"I have a feeling you're avoiding us?"

"No."

"Then you won't mind checking your schedule and adding dinner with the family on Saturday night. Luc promised he would try to make it."

"Saturday? I've got plans for Saturday."

"Really? What are you doing?"

"I'm meeting a friend for dinner."

"Bring him along. I would love to meet your friend."

"I don't know if that's a good idea."

"Why? Oh . . . wait a minute. This friend is not a 'he', but a 'she'. Am I right?"

"Yes, you're right. I don't want Sophie to be interrogated by the family."

"I promise I will make sure to let the family know, to take it easy on Sophie."

"Why do I get the feeling that you are grinning from ear to ear?"

"This is the first time I've heard you talk about a girl, with that tone in your voice."

"What tone?"

"You really like her. I can tell."

"You can tell by the tone of my voice?"

"I'm your mother. I know all your little idiosyncrasies. I can tell by your tone of voice, and the way you say her name, that you really like her."

"She's a friend."

"If you say so. Please bring her. I would like to meet your 'friend'. You've never brought a girl home . . . "

"Mom!"

"Okay. I promise to be on my best behavior. Please, Domenic, make your mother happy and bring her along. I want to see my first-born. Lucia's been auditioning for a part in a school play, and she is driving us all crazy reciting lines every chance she gets. I'm sure she wants to tell you all about it. She's actually excited about something other than boys. Which gives me hope for her future. Aimee will cook a delicious meal and it will be wonderful to have Luc join us."

"Alright. I'll ask her. But if she sounds even the least bit uncertain about it . . . "

"I'll take it on the chin. Promise."

"I have to go. It's been a long day, and I'm looking forward to having a hot shower and bed."

"Have you eaten? I'll get Cameron to drop off some leftover roast beef . . . "

"I'll pick up something on the way home. There are plenty of restaurants in town, you know. But thank you for the offer."

"Take out is not the same as a home cooked meal, or as nutritious. You need protein and healthy greens, not saturated fats in meals which will clog your arteries."

"Mom, I won't be eating a burger and fries. I can pick up a healthy salad and vegetarian meals just as easily. I do look after myself. I'm hanging up now."

"I'll see you on Saturday... I hope."

"Bye Mom."

My mother means well, but she underestimates my ability to look after myself. We were lucky to have meals cooked for us, and the cleaning taken care of, but that doesn't mean I am incapable of cooking basic meals or cleaning my apartment.

I'm still not sure that taking Sophie to meet my family is a good idea. And she was right, I do like this girl. I don't want to frighten her off. But it would be good to see how comfortable she is around my family. And Luc. He is a very commanding presence. It will be interesting to see if he gets the same impression of Sophie's abilities.

Hey big brother!

Hey yourself.

I hear you have a girlfriend. Way to go!

She's not my girlfriend.

That's not how Mom pitched it.

She's a friend I've spent some time with. That's all.

Have you done the deed yet?

Lucia!

What?

I'm not going to answer such a personal question, especially to my little sister.

You haven't. I can tell. Although I guess she must be something special if you've let her anywhere near you. I know you don't like being touched.

It's not as simple as not liking being touched. You, of all people, should know this.

It blows me away that you cannot stand physical touch. If I had to live

66

like that, I don't know what I'd do. I adore being touched . . . if you know what I mean.

We are not having this conversation, Lucia. Especially not about your sex life.

What can I say? Men find me attractive. I find men attractive. It's a win/win.

I'm stopping this now. Goodnight Lucia.

See you Saturday. I promised Mom I would behave. I'll try to keep my promise.

I might see you Saturday. If Sophie agrees.

Oh, she'll agree. If she likes you enough to go out with you, she'll want to see where you came from. It's another piece of the puzzle.

The puzzle?

You're the puzzle. She'll want to know as much about you as possible if she is going to keep on dating you.

I see.

Ask her if she'd like to have dinner with the family. If she says yes, you'll know she really likes you. If she says no, or makes an excuse, you'll know you're on the short list, and you're not impressing her.

Thanks

Any time big brother. Ciao.

Maybe I should get it over with, instead of worrying about it. As I walked to the car, I dialed Sophie's number.

"Mmmm hello?" she croaked.

"Sophie?"

"Sorry I was asleep. Early shift this morning. How are you?"

"Fine thanks. Just finished surgery and I'm heading home."

"I'm pleased you called. I was hoping to hear from you before Saturday."

"I'm calling about Saturday night."

"Oh."

"Do you mind if we don't go to dinner at Franco's?"

"You're pulling out?"

"Not from seeing you. My mother has invited us to dinner."

"Whew. I thought I was being dumped." Sophie laughed.

"Not at all. I wasn't sure if you wanted to join my family for a meal, they can be pretty intense"

"Hey, I'm Irish. My family can outdo your family for being "full on" any day of the week. I'd love to have dinner with your family."

"You would?"

"Sure."

Lucia's words sprung into my head. *"If she says yes, you'll know she really likes you."*

"Go back to sleep. We'll talk tomorrow."

"Okay. Goodnight."

I hung up and realized I had a smile on my face. She likes me! Now all I had to worry about was how she would react to my family. Especially Luc.

22nd April 2017

I pulled up outside Sophie's house. She'd been waiting on the step, and she ran down the path and hopped into the car before I had a chance to turn off the engine. Or even get out and open the door. I had an image of my mother frowning at me, and shaking her head, as she brought me up to be courteous.

"Hey, don't you look smart." She leant over and gave me a peck on the cheek. The zap of electricity was still there. She touched her lips with her fingertips and smiled.

"You look beautiful." Her pale green shirt dress was charming. It suited her coloring so well. She blushed and beamed at me.

"Is that going to happen every time we kiss? We sure have chemistry. I've never known that to happen before."

"I don't know. Maybe. Will it bother you if it does?"

"No. I kinda like it. It's just unusual."

"Your hair is different."

"I thought I would try and straighten it. To look a little more sophisticated."

"You don't need to try to be anything other than you, Sophie O'Connor."

"But I'm meeting your mother. I want to make a good impression. I've heard about her, and the charity work she does for the hospital. And the fact she was a stunt woman when she was my age. I've watched the movies. She's a bit of a legend."

"You've watched the movies?"

"Yes. I googled her when someone told me who she was, so I went looking for them."

"I think she'll be impressed with that."

"She was beautiful. She looked like Mindy Michaels, and she's a big star."

"She's still beautiful. Just older and wiser."

"So, who will be at dinner tonight?"

"My Godfather will be there, I hope. Unless business calls him away. Luc is quite a character, but sometimes he is a little scary, so I thought I would prepare you."

"Duly noted. Who else will be there?"

"My sister Lucia."

"The one from the club?"

"Yes."

"And I'll get to meet the famous Aimee, who cooks and delivers delicious meals."

"And Cameron who looks after the family. And Max of course."

"Of course. We can't forget Max. Lisa hasn't forgiven you. She's expecting a visit from you with Max. She's a dog person."

"What about you? Are you a dog person?"

"I've had dogs and cats growing up. I want a dog when I've got a place of my own. Although I can't see that happening with my student debt. I think I'll be sharing with Lisa for a few years yet. Dogs are great companions. How long have you had Max?"

"Forever." I smiled. Max was a phenomenon I wasn't going to explain anytime soon.

"A faithful dog is like a best friend."

"Max is a member of the family. Nothing happens in that house without Max."

"That's lovely. Will he let me pet him?"

"I've told him about you. He's looking forward to meeting you."

Sophie laughed. She thought I was making a joke, but I had actually had a long telepathic conversation with Max, and I hoped he would take to her. He's very protective of the family, and only tolerates those he trusts.

"We're here." I brought the car slowly to a halt by the gate. The security camera would have tracked us from the street. The gate slid open, and Cameron stood by the Gatehouse door. He had been waiting for us. I slid my window down.

"Cameron, I'd like you to meet Sophie O'Connor. Sophie I'd like to introduce Cameron Crawford. General factotum and all-round-good-guy."

"I'm very pleased to meet you, Cameron." Sophie leant forward and waved.

"Likewise, Miss. Have a lovely evening." Cameron gave a mock salute.

Aimee stood on the front step to greet us, and introductions were made. She directed us to the deck by the pool, where my mother was waiting for us. She had picked a place to meet Sophie, which was close to my heart. The trees in this part of the garden were festooned with small twinkling lights, and in the evening light, the glossy white painted wood of the pool house reflected their warm glow. Underwater lights illuminated the pool, turning the crystal-clear water into a shimmering aqua blue. The bright scatter cushions on the deckchairs, and the colorful ceramic pots filled with shrubs and plants, always made me think of summer. As a young teenager I would set up camp in this corner of the estate on weekends. Aimee would make me a picnic lunch, with a bottle of chilled apple or orange juice, and I would pull a deckchair into the shade and read to my heart's content. Max would lay by my feet. Lucia would sometimes splash about in the pool with Aimee or Cameron on watch if my mother was working. I would disappear from whatever was going on around me, into my own world of fantasy. Books about superheroes or aliens or other worlds were an escape from the reality of my academic life, which was filled with facts and figures and medical information.

My mother was sitting on a pool chair. As we approached, she stood and held out her hands to Sophie. She was wearing a sleeveless long white linen dress, which stopped above her ankles, and sandals the same vivid aqua color as the pool. Her blond hair streaked with silver was swept up and pinned with ivory combs. A colorful shawl with swirls of the same aqua hue lay across the back of her chair. She looked elegant and relaxed, and I was grateful she had chosen this informal setting to meet Sophie.

"Welcome Sophie. So lovely to meet a friend of my son." She kissed Sophie on both cheeks in typical European fashion.

"I'm pleased to meet you Mrs Ericson. You have a beautiful home, and an amazing yard. I feel like I'm on a movie set. It reminds me of a scene from the movie 'Dance With Danger' you were working on in Monaco."

"My goodness. You've seen that movie?"

"Yes. I loved it."

"I'm sure it's not playing in theatres, where did you see it?"

"I watched it online."

"Sophie was interested in your stunt work, Mom," I explained.

"I see. Please sit down." My mother sat down again and gestured to the chair opposite.

"I'm such a fan. You must have been very fit back in the day. I bet there were lots of injuries on that movie." Sophie perched on the edge of another sun lounge

"I was certainly fitter than I am now. No more injuries than on any other set. It feels like someone else's life. Although I haven't watched those movies in years."

"I've never been to Europe, although I'd love to go to Monaco one day."

"I think the Monaco of the nineties would be a far different place now in twenty seventeen. The world has changed a lot since then.

"Yes, but I have no comparison. To me it would be exciting."

"Let me pour you a drink. What would you like?" My mother stood again.

"I'll do it Mom. Sit please." The drink cart adjacent to my mother's chair was loaded with an ice bucket full of a variety of sodas, and small bottles of fresh juice and sparkling water. Another ice bucket contained white wine. I extracted the bottle of wine from the ice and showed the label to Sophie. "Would you like a glass of this Sauvignon Blanc, or shall I open a red? Or perhaps a soda or fresh juice?"

"I'll have a white wine please. I must admit it's nice to be able to have a drink and not have to worry about working tomorrow," Sophie said. She accepted the glass I handed her, with a smile, and took a sip.

"I believe you work at the same hospital as my son?"

"Yes, I'm a nurse."

"You must be very dedicated. Nursing is a hard life."

"The shifts are long, and there's certainly some heartache involved with the job. But the joys outweigh the bad stuff that happens."

"I admire you. Did you always want to be a nurse?"

"Yes. It was my calling. I've never thought about being anything else. Other than a mother. I want to be a mother one day, with God's grace."

"Are you Catholic Sophie?"

"Yes. But not fanatical about it. Are you religious Mrs Ericson?"

"No. Ah . . . here's Domenic's godfather. Great timing."

Luc appeared from the house, and Lucia skipped up behind him, and gave him a peck on the cheek, and tucked her arm through his. They were laughing as they approached the pool.

"Luc Nightingale, may I introduce Sophie O'Connor," I said. Sophie stood to be introduced.

"Charmed." Luc walked forward, lifted Sophie's outstretched hand to his lips and kissed the back of her hand.

"Lovely to meet you." Sophie blushed. Luc had turned on the charm, and to be honest it was a better outcome than the angry or argumentative mood he brought to the house on occasions.

"I'm so glad you could make it for dinner," Mom said to Luc.

"I wouldn't dream of being anywhere else tonight." Luc kissed my mother on both cheeks and sat down beside her on the sunlounge.

"Lucia, this is . . . " I began, but Lucia jumped in.

"Hi Sophie, I'm Lucia. The black sheep of this family. Domenic is the good child. I'm the naughty one."

"I'm pleased to meet you. I love your dress."

"Thanks. I found it in a little boutique in town. It's a designer knock-off but it was marked down. Such a bargain." Lucia twirled and the pretty pink skirt fluttered like petals in the wind. Her long dark ponytail swung over her shoulder. She looked wide eyed, adorable and very young, but I have learned that you should never judge Lucia by her childlike appearance. She can change in an instant and be very grown up and very sharp tongued. Lucia is a chameleon and an enigma that most people cannot work out. She prefers it that way. I have found she likes to keep you on your toes always guessing.

"I love a bargain. You'll have to share the location," Sophie said.

"Sure. Maybe we could meet for coffee sometime and I could take you there."

"That would be lovely."

For some strange reason this meet-up did not fill me with happiness. Lucia does not take to people this quickly. What was she up to? Lucia had her back to me and was pouring a bottle of sparkling water into a glass. Telepathy has its advantages in situations such as this.

Lucia what are you doing?

I'm making your girlfriend feel welcomed.

This is not the Lucia I know.

I like her.

She's not a toy for you to play with.

Seriously big brother. I like her. There is something about her. I want to get to know her.

If you do anything . . .

I promise I will not mess with her head. You have my word.

And no embarrassing stories about when I was growing up.

You're taking all the fun out of this.

Lucia!

Okay. No stories.

Luc was engaged in conversation with Sophie. My mother glanced over at me and smiled. I knew that smile. It was the one that said, "See I was right. I knew you liked this girl."

Aimee appeared on the patio and rang a small bell to announce dinner was ready.

Luc took my mother's arm, Lucia followed them, and headed for the house. I held back a little. I wanted to see how Sophie was feeling now she had met everyone.

"All good?" I asked.

"Your family's lovely. I'm having a nice time. Relax."

"Would you be nervous if this was your family and I was meeting them?"

Sophie laughed. She linked her arm through mine. We walked toward the house.

"Oh yes, I would be nervous. And there are far more in the O'Connor family than in the Ericson family. You wouldn't know if you were coming or going, they would have a million questions for you."

"You can understand then."

"I can. But it's fine. Honestly."

Max appeared from the house. He stopped abruptly on the edge of the patio when he saw us and cocked his head to the side. He sent me a telepathic message. I asked him to play nice.

"Oh, this is the famous Max." Sophie walked forward and stopped in front of him. She held out her hand.

"Put your hands down at your sides. Max will come to you."

"But I thought you should offer your hand to a dog to sniff."

"That's a misconception. Allow the dog to come to you. If he wants to be touched, he will approach you and nudge your hand. Some dogs do not like being petted by strangers."

Max did approach and walked around Sophie, sniffing and never taking his eyes off her. Satisfied she was worthy, he sat beside her left leg, his head only a fraction of an inch away from her hand. He nudged her.

"You can pet him now."

"I've passed the test." Sophie grinned and gently patted Max's head and stroked down his back. He stayed perfectly still and allowed this introduction.

"Max heel." Max walked around to my side and accompanied us along the alfresco to the door of the house. Then he peeled away into the garden.

"He's a very well-behaved dog. Where is he going?" Sophie peered into the evening gloom.

"He has a job to do checking the grounds, and he knows what he's doing."

"Will he come back?"

"Much later. Unless he finds something interesting."

"Interesting?"

"Yes. There might be an animal out there or a burglar scaling the walls."

"And what would he do if he found someone?"

"Max is a guard dog. He would kill them and bury them in the garden."

"You have a very droll sense of humor, Domenic."

"I'm not laughing."

"Stop teasing me. Let's go inside before they send out a search party for us."

The table was set for five. My mother and Luc sat on one side and Lucia, Sophie and I sat opposite.

"Why does no one sit at the head of the table?" Sophie whispered to me.

"In our house that place remains for my deceased father. My mother thinks he watches over us."

"I see."

"Does that bother you?"

"Not at all. My grandmother is psychic. I believe there's more going on in this world than the average person is willing to believe."

"Was she a descendant of the witch in your family?"

"Yes, she was. There's a long line of interesting women in our family back in Ireland."

"Every family has their skeletons in the closet."

"Actually, funny you should mention that. We found human bones inside a wall cavity of our house when I was a small child. That was one of the reasons we moved to this country."

"What are you two whispering about?" Lucia asked.

"Family history." I offered in response.

"Lucia managed to land the leading female role in the school play. Isn't that wonderful," my mother said.

"Well done." I knew she would be happy to have scored the lead.

"What's the name of the play?" Sophie asked.

"It's Macbeth. I play Lady Macbeth."

"That's a dramatic role," Sophie said.

"I'm quite excited. I'm new to the Drama Club. This is the first time I've gone for a role."

"Getting the lead is quite an accomplishment. There will be a lot of lines to memorize," Sophie said.

"I have a pretty good memory, so I don't see that as a drawback." There was a twinkle in Lucia's eye that I had not seen very often. This time it wasn't because she was planning mischief. I sensed her excitement. I was genuinely pleased for her.

Aimee arrived with the first course of gnocchi smothered in a delicious gorgonzola cheese sauce. Which was followed by a main course of mouth-watering beef wellington, flavorsome gravy, duchess potatoes and roasted garden vegetables. If Aimee was trying to impress Sophie, I think she had achieved her mission. There wasn't a crumb left on Sophie's plate, or anyone else's actually.

"Shall we adjourn to the living room for coffee?" my mother asked. "I think we're all too full for dessert at the moment."

"Good idea," Luc said. He walked around the table and offered his arm to Sophie. "Let me show you something I think you might like."

Sophie took his arm and they walked down the hall to the library. Luc sent me a telepathic message.

Don't worry Domenic, I only want to get to know her a bit better.

I'm not worried, Luc. I would actually like you to tell me if you have the same feeling about her hidden talents.

She definitely has secrets locked up inside her, that I can tell you.

My mother took my arm and we walked to the living room.

"I like her. She's engaging and quite charming."

"She's enjoying herself I think," I said.

"I would be surprised if she wasn't. Everyone's on their best behavior, even Lucia."

"Good for her in landing the lead role. I think she's genuinely pleased about this."

"As I said on the phone, this is the first time I have seen her as enthusiastic about something, other than boys." I could tell my mother was relieved. Lucia was finally taking something at school seriously.

"I heard a whisper that you would be donating one of your paintings to the hospital auction. Which one?"

"Really? News travels fast. I only confirmed it yesterday. I'm donating the sunset."

"But that's Luc's favorite."

"He has a master plan. He's planning on bidding for it. That way the hospital can get their donation and he can get the painting."

"In other words, you're giving it to him."

"Yes, but don't tell him. This way the hospital gets some well-deserved funds."

"I think he's taken Sophie to show her the painting."

"To show off more than likely. He thinks he masterminded the whole thing."

1 3

LUC

There was something familiar about Sophie O'Connor that I could not quite put my finger on. It was in the way she held herself, the angle of her head when she listened to someone talking, a faint Irish lilt in her speech when she was discussing her chosen career. I felt I had met Sophie before. Yet she showed no signs that she knew me. As we walked down the hall to the library, her arm still linked with mine, I had no sense of her being uncomfortable or unsure of herself, being steered away from the only person she actually knew at the dinner table. The opposite was the case, her confidence grew, the further we walked away from Domenic.

No denying she found Domenic appealing, you could tell by the warmth in her eyes when she looked at him. It seemed the feeling was mutual. Domenic gave her his total attention during dinner, passing her serving dishes of food, topping up her glass with water or with wine. But Domenic wanted my opinion and the only way I could do that was to have her undivided attention.

"I wanted to show you the painting that Harper will be donating to the hospital fundraiser. Isn't it wonderful?" I turned on the downlights so that we could get a better look.

"Wow. I didn't know Mrs Ericson was such a talented artist."

78

"It started as a hobby when Lucia was small. I've been encouraging her to have an exhibition of her work, but she doesn't think she's good enough yet. This is my favorite, and I'll be bidding on this one at the auction."

"Good luck."

"Luck has nothing to do with this. I want it, and it will be mine."

Sophie threw back her head and laughed. And it was the laugh that suddenly hurtled me back in time to Ireland, many, many, years before. To another beautiful red head, who had all the men in the small village bewitched. Much to the dismay of the women.

I looked Sophie in the eye, snapped my fingers, which froze Sophie on the spot. Time stood still all around us. "Maggie Mae, is that you?" I took a step back. "Come on out Maggie Mae. I know you're in there."

A ghostly female figure shimmered and detached from Sophie's body to stand before me. The image solidified into an older attractive woman with long red curls, darker than Sophie's, cascading down her back. She wore the hand-made clothes of her era. The skirt of her long black dress was covered with a white apron. She had a black woolen knitted shawl around her shoulders, crisscrossed over her breasts and tucked into the waistband of her apron, tied at the back. Her piercing blue eyes danced with delight.

"How did you know, my Lord of Darkness?" Maggie Mae asked.

"Your laugh. It took me back to a time long, long, ago, when you laughed at the villager's concerns. You said you would move heaven and earth and called upon me to save Damon."

"He was my heart and soul. I couldn't let him die without trying to save him."

"But you were not prepared for what that would cost you. You had good standing in the village before that. Once they linked your name with the Devil . . . "

"I worked hard to rid myself of the label they gave me."

"I know"

"But at that time when Damon was dying, I had a child growing in my belly. When she was born, I had a part of Damon that no one could take away from me. I have no regrets."

"Hiding your pregnancy was one thing. Hiding a growing child was another thing altogether. They saw that child as a threat to their Christian beliefs."

"And yet I brought her up to be a Christian and to know what I knew about healing. I taught her my life's work."

"They were afraid of you, and what you could do."

"I was no threat to them. I only wanted a peaceful life. I cured their ills. I birthed their children and laid out their dead. But they wouldn't let me forget trying to save Damon."

"The villagers had long memories. They turned on you in the end. Trying to save him was your undoing. Damon's body might have been cured, but you could do nothing for his mind. He drank himself to death because of the taunting."

"I thought he was stronger. I was wrong."

"What do you hope to achieve with Sophie?"

"My legacy lives on. I said I would be back. She was perfect in every way. Same hair color, same complexation, and the same blue eyes."

"Your healing talents have been passed on. She is a dedicated nurse."

"I have no doubt. But there is more she has yet to discover. I wanted to wait until the time was right to show her the way."

"She has become friends with my Godson. Should I be worried about your connection to this family?"

"To be sure Luc, there's no need to fear me. You should know that." Maggie Mae's Irish accent was stronger now that she had been separated from Sophie for a few minutes.

"It's not me I am afraid for. It's Domenic. I think he really likes this girl."

"Aye. She likes him too. Don't worry I am only here to guide her as a healer, nothing more."

"When the villagers burnt down your cottage, with you inside it, I thought I might see you in Hell. You surprised me. I never imagined you up above in the land of the angels."

"I've been rewarded for all the good I did, the children I brought into the world, the people I healed, and forgiven for the few incidents when I called on your help for a curse."

"That was big of Him."

"You of all people should know we are not all good or all bad. There is light and shade in all of us. I was given another chance to come back and do some good. I chose Sophie O'Connor because she is blood of my blood. She is the spitting image of me as a girl. My spirit lives within her."

"I'll trust you know what you're doing. But if you harm Domenic . . ."

"I know. I will pay the price. I've already faced the fires once. I never knew pain like that existed. I have no desire to go to Hell where that form of daily torture resides."

"Time to return to the others. I'm sure we'll talk again Maggie Mae."

She faded to a ghostly presence and shimmered back into the body of Sophie. I snapped my fingers, time resumed, Sophie returned to normal and continued her conversation as if nothing had interrupted her.

"And do you always get what you want?" she asked.

"Most of the time," I replied.

"I heard that when you imagine you have it, when you can already see it hanging on your wall, the laws of attraction will make that happen."

"Do you believe in the laws of attraction?" I asked.

"I do. I spent many years manifesting my career as a nurse."

"Why a nurse? Why not a doctor. They make more money."

"I don't do what I do for the money. I care about helping people. Nurses spend more time with the patients than the doctors who rush in, prescribe medicine, and rush out again. I give my patients a lot more time and attention to get them on the road to recovery."

"What about Domenic. Don't you think he gives his patients something more than medicine."

"I'm not talking about surgeons, who basically save lives. I admire Domenic for the work he does. I've watched him operate from the observation platform. He's focused and controlled and seems to know exactly what to do to fix his patients. The OR staff all think he's wonderful."

"I get the feeling you think he's wonderful too."

Sophie blushed, and lowered her eyes. Then she raised her head and looked me in the eye. "I do think he's wonderful. He's very young to be a surgeon, but I know he was gifted as a child and was fast-tracked through medical school. He's kind and generous . . . and a bit naïve. Don't worry, your Godson is safe with me. I won't take advantage of his naivety."

"I have no doubt my dear. No doubt at all." I switched off the overhead light. "Let's get back to the others."

Domenic, your young lady is charming. She does have hidden healing talents, but they will come to pass when she's ready. I like her. You have my blessing to pursue her.

Thanks Luc. But we've only just started to see each other. I think you're jumping the gun here. I'm not sure if she really likes me.

Mark my words, she likes you. And you're in the very lucky position of having me to look out for you. So, if I can do anything to help speed up the process . . .

Please don't. No hocus pocus. I want her to like me without magic tricks.

Magic tricks! I'm offended you think of my powers as magic tricks.

Let me work this out by myself. Please.

As you wish. We are on our way back.

I had learned a bit about Sophie, and a bit more about Maggie Mae. I have a feeling I am going to see both of them a lot more in the future. The laws of attraction might be working in favor of Domenic and Sophie. He needs someone he can trust in his life, someone kind and caring and not judgmental. She needs someone in her life who will protect her and allow her to grow to be the person she was meant to be. I think they are very lucky to have me watching over them. I want the best for my Godson. It stands to reason I want the best for my family.

HARPER

*L*uc and Sophie appeared from the library and joined us all in the lounge. Aimee brought a tray with a pot of coffee, cups, and some of her special devilish chocolate chip cookies.

"Luc showed me the painting you've donated to the hospital auction. It's really beautiful. You have many talents Mrs Ericson."

"I have always had a creative streak, but I really never found a way of expressing it in art until after Lucia was born. I find painting relaxing. It is especially good when I am stuck in a scene or a need to be a bit more adventurous with the script. When I paint, it allows the ideas to flow naturally, and the scenes take form in my mind."

"I'll arrange for your donation to be boxed up and taken to the hospital tomorrow," Luc said.

"Have you found out what other items are going to be auctioned?" I asked Luc.

"There are tickets to live theatre, and a gift certificate for a weekend getaway. There are a few spa gift certificates, more paintings I believe, and a dinner created in your home by a personal chef. Of course, I am certain the other pieces of artwork offered for auction are nothing in comparison to yours," Luc said.

"I'm sure they are all gratefully received," Sophie said.

"I've bought dinner tickets for a table of eight. We can all go together," Luc announced.

"Can I bring a date?" Lucia asked Luc.

"If your mother approves," Luc said.

"That depends on who you're going to ask," I said.

"I'll let you know." Lucia had a mischievous look on her face. I wondered what she was planning.

"Would you like to go?" Domenic asked Sophie. "Don't feel you have to."

"I would, thank you," Sophie replied.

"I'll pick you up at six o'clock. Dinner is at seven, and then the auction is planned for eight thirty after dessert is served," Domenic said.

"It should be a nice evening, Sophie. The hotel and restaurant are five-star. I imagine the dinner will be delicious," I said.

"I'm looking forward to it. I've never attended an art auction before," Sophie said.

Sophie talked about the auction, but I could see that all she was interested in was spending time with Domenic. There was a very strong connection between the two of them, I could sense it. I hadn't had the opportunity to see Domenic around many women, but there was no doubt that they found each other attractive. He was attentive to her needs and hung on her every word.

My son had grown into a caring individual, and I'm very proud of him. If only Richard had been able to see him now. I know he would also be very proud of the man Domenic had become.

I raised my eyes to the heavens.

Can you see our boy, Richard? Are you helping to guide him?

1 5

DOMENIC

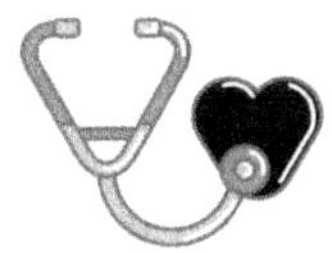

5th May 2017

*S*ophie descended the stairs and surprised me with her choice and the elegant simplicity of the knee length black dress and rose gold high heels and jewelry. Her hair was pulled up on her head and twisted into a style not unlike Audrey Hepburn, in Breakfast at Tiffany's. I wasn't used to seeing her in anything other than bright jewel colors.

"You look beautiful."

"You can never underestimate the LBD," Sophie said, turning around to show off the back view. I had an appreciation of how the dress clung to her curves.

"LBD?"

"Little black dress. Your sister helped me find it. She thought it would be appropriate for the fundraiser."

"You went shopping with Lucia?"

"Yesterday. A connection put her onto designer clothes, at reduced prices. Wait till you see what she's wearing."

"I can only imagine." I shook my head

"No, it's not what you think. She will look gorgeous. Very grown up. You'll see."

Cameron opened the rear door of the car for Sophie, and I walked around to the other side.

"I thought it best to have Cameron drive us. Luc has arranged another car to pick up my mother and sister."

"I thought Lucia was bringing a date?"

"Apparently he's meeting us at the venue."

"I see. Your mother approved then?"

"She hasn't met him. But he's a young artist and he's donating a painting, which he needs to transport tonight. That's why he's meeting us there. I think she's worked out he is safe. For now."

"I'm looking forward to tonight. I haven't had a chance to get this dressed up in a while. There will be a lot of hospital big-wigs there, and I heard there will be a couple of Hollywood B grade movie stars there too."

"Good, we may get some decent donations for the hospital after all."

We pulled up at the convention center. There were parking valets waiting to move cars, but we had no need of that. Cameron pulled up parallel to the sidewalk, and a valet opened the door to allow Sophie to step onto the red carpet. I joined her and she linked her arm through mine to walk to the door. Cameron drove off. We stopped when requested and allowed photographs to be taken for the local media outlets. Inside the building we saw Luc and my mother talking to someone from the Hospital Board of Directors. We followed them into the ballroom. The table Luc had been appointed was in the front section, near the stage.

"This is a great table," Sophie said.

"It should be. I paid double the asking price for this one," Luc answered.

"You bribed the staff?" Sophie looked shocked.

"I don't call it a bribe. I call it an extra donation. I wanted to be front and center to bid for Harper's painting." He produced a paddle with number 666 engraved on it.

"You brought your own paddle?" I smiled in spite of myself. Luc was a cliché.

"Yes, it's my lucky number."

"The auction isn't until after dinner." My mother took the paddle from Luc and patted his cheek affectionately. "Let's not get too excited yet."

I turned to see Lucia walk in with a tall, slim young man at her side. He was clean shaven and smartly dressed in a dark suit and bow tie, and had his blond hair pulled back in a small ponytail tied with black ribbon. He was definitely a step up from the wild boys and musicians she had been hanging about with over the last couple of years.

"Mom this is Karl Jager. Karl this is my mother, and my brother Domenic. His girlfriend Sophie. And this is Luc, our Godfather."

"I am honored to meet Lucia's family. And to join you as your guest. Thank you." He helped Lucia by pulling out her chair and sat down beside her. He was clearly besotted with her. If he had to answer a question, he didn't take his eyes off Lucia for more than a few seconds.

My sister had surprised me tonight. Sophie was right, she looked beautiful and very grown up. Her hair was pulled up on top pf her head and elegantly coiled and styled. The long wine-colored velvet dress with a high neck and long fitted sleeves was modest and not at all her normal attire. It clung to her shapely figure, and not a bit of skin was showing. But strangely enough all the males in the vicinity were drawn to look at her. I think my sister exudes a sexual vibration that men pick up. To me she is my little sister, but to the male population she is sexually alluring, and a challenge. Karl sat very close to Lucia and took her hand under the table. I think he also sensed what was happening around us, and lay claim to her.

"See I told you Lucia would impress you tonight. She looks very grown up and elegant," Sophie whispered to me.

"I admit I am impressed." But I wasn't letting my guard down yet.

Dinner was enjoyable, conversation flowed around the table. When it was time to auction off the various pieces donated by some of Hollywood's elite, the waitress filled everyone's glass and discretely returned to the back of the ballroom. The Master Of Ceremonies was a local well known comedian, named Pete Stevens. He was doing an outstanding job tonight, and the audience were relaxed and enjoying the show he provided with one liners and funny stories, just as much as the bidding.

My mother's painting "Sunset" was up next. As the artist, she was asked to come up on the stage to stand beside her work as they unveiled it. Luc appeared to be relaxed, but I could tell by his ramrod straight posture that he just wanted this auction to begin, so the painting could be his.

The bidding started at one thousand. There were a few interested people bidding around the room. Luc's paddle didn't stay down long, for as soon as someone outbid him, it was up again. The bid was at ten thousand dollars now, and there seemed to be someone at the back just as interested as Luc in procuring it. I could tell Luc was not enjoying this game of cat and mouse as much as he thought he would. The bidding continued. The last bid was twenty thousand dollars, by the man at the back of the Hall. Luc probably thought people would have given up by now.

"Let's just cut to the chase. Fifty thousand dollars!" Luc announced. There was an audible gasp from around the room. My mother looked shocked.

"Any advance on fifty thousand dollars?" Pete asked. "You sir. . .at the back. . . do you want to proceed? No? Going, going, gone! Sold at fifty thousand dollars to the handsome man in front dressed in black."

Now Luc relaxed, took a swig of his wine and beamed at my mother, who simply shook her head in amazement. He jumped up to offer her his hand to descend the stairs.

"He looks pleased with himself. That's an awful lot of money."

Sophie whispered to me, as Luc pulled out my mother's seat, and sat down beside her, smiling from ear to ear.

"It's for a good cause. Luc donates money all the time. He could easily have handed over a cheque to the hospital committee raising the funds, but this way he gets my mother's painting, which he has coveted for some time. My mother knows Luc has gone the extra mile for her and supports her work. It's a win/win all round." Money is always in plentiful supply for Luc. Most people are not aware of Luc's philanthropic side, preferring to always have a negative view of someone they don't take the time to understand.

The next piece was painted by Lucia's date, Karl. He squeezed her hand as they announced the name of his artwork "Lady In Red". He happily joined the auctioneer on the stage.

The curtain in front of the painting was pulled back. Karl stood to one side and looked directly at Lucia. He failed to see the shocked expression on my mother's face, or the fury on Luc's.

The painting was of a beautiful young woman, dark hair cascading down over her shoulders, her face turned towards the audience. The scene was a bedroom, and she sat perched on the edge of a bed. Clad only in a red silk sheet, partly covering her modesty, enough of her left breast was on display and all of her left leg up to her thigh to indicate her nudity under the drape. The story depicted by the rumpled bedding in the painting was very clear. The swollen luscious red lips, the flushed face and the satisfied expression had captured every man's imagination in the room. Lady In Red was every man's fantasy.

Luc erupted out of his chair and drew the curtain over the painting once more. The look he gave Karl would have crumpled a lesser man. Karl stood tall. What was wrong with him? Didn't he realize he had just made an error in judgement and probably one of the biggest mistakes of his life. To tell the truth, I was amazed he was still standing.

"This painting is not for auction. Name your price and remove it now." Luc spoke to Karl through clench teeth.

"I don't understand. It is beautiful, and so like Lucia."

"Lucia is seventeen. She is a minor. You did not get her mother's permission to paint her *in the nude*. Do you know what you have done?"

"Lucia told me she was twenty-one. She does not look or act seventeen. She has the body of a woman. Not a child." Karl appeared shocked.

"This conversation is over. Deliver the painting to my home tomorrow and I will donate your asking price to the hospital. Remove the painting. Now!" Luc's voice had risen. Glasses on our table jittered. Karl removed the painting and left by a door near the stage. The auctioneer called a short intermission for everyone to refill their glasses and settle down again.

Luc returned to our table. Lucia was gone. Luc did not seem surprised, he was probably talking to her now telepathically, telling her she is grounded for the rest of the year. I had not noticed her leaving. There was going to be a big argument in the house tonight.

"Time to go I think." I helped Sophie with her wrap and leaned in close. "We can go back to my apartment for a nightcap if you like. It's a shame to end the evening so quickly."

"Yes, I'd like that," Sophie replied. She looked shocked by the turn of events.

"Mom, Sophie and I will take a cab back to my apartment for a nightcap. Cameron can pick you up."

"Luc has a limo waiting downstairs. I'll call Cameron to tell him he won't be needed." My mother stood to kiss my cheek and then Sophie's cheek.

"It was lovely to see you again Sophie. I apologize for the abrupt ending to the evening. But we have to find Lucia and have a little chat." Luc took my mother's elbow and they hurried out of the ballroom.

The whispering around us grew in volume. Sophie started to walk toward the exit. I began to follow, then noticed something left behind. I returned to the table, picked up my mother's wrap from the back of the chair and turned to see Luc striding through the double doors of the ballroom. He snapped his fingers. Everything stopped and froze in place. I seemed to be the only one still able to move, along with Luc. Even Sophie was a statue.

"Luc what's going on?"

"I decided to remove the last 15 mins of their memories. No one is leaving this ballroom with an image of Lucia implanted in their brain."

"Do you know where she is?"

"Yes. I found her. She should be sitting in the back seat of the Limo with your mother by now, waiting for me. She has some explaining to do."

"Go easy on her. Karl was unaware she was a minor, and I think she's struggling with the fact that she's growing up very fast. I notice a big difference in her physical appearance and her mental state of late. Even her face is changing. I think she's had a surge in development in the last few months. She doesn't have the appearance of a child Luc. I also think she has your ability to change her appearance, to what extent I'm not sure. Perhaps she's experimenting with that side of her nature."

"I guess you're right. She gave false information to Karl. He's very lucky I didn't reduce him to dust on the spot." Luc smiled. I could see he was calming down. I gave him my mother's wrap. He snapped his fingers, disappeared into thin air, and the room returned to normal. There was no whispering now, no heads together discussing the semi-naked woman's attributes. Just people enjoying their wine and waiting for the next piece of art to be auctioned. Pete consulted his running sheet, with Karl's painting conveniently removed from his paperwork as if it never existed and returned to the stage ready for the next auction to begin. No one paid any attention to the empty table at the front. I joined Sophie, took her arm and led her out of the building to a waiting taxi.

I switched on the table lamps in the living room. The subdued light reflected in the glass of the unadorned windows and cast shadows around the room. Music played softly in the background. I poured two shots of Hennessy cognac into crystal brandy balloons and handed one to Sophie, who was standing by my side. She lowered her eyes and swirled the golden-brown alcohol around in the base of the glass, allowing it to warm against her palm before taking a sip. Her cheeks flushed pink. She took another sip of her drink, and I enjoyed the warmth of the alcohol as I swallowed. The eyes that lifted to meet mine had a question. I lowered my head and delighted in the taste of the cognac on her lips, and the zap of electricity when we touched. As I sucked her bottom lip between mine, her sharp intake of breath and her hand which reached out to grip and steady herself on my upper arm, gave me some indication that inexperienced as I was, whatever I was doing, I was doing to her satisfaction.

Her heart thudded in her chest, which was pressed against mine. Her hand slid up and snaked around my neck. We were standing as close as any two people could be. Or so I thought. Sophie had other ideas. She took hold of my tie and walked backwards to the sofa taking me with her. We perched on the edge of the sofa. Still holding the drinks and with only our lips touching, we kissed some more. I was becoming more familiar with the way she liked to be kissed. The small moans and quick flicks of her tongue encouraged me. I took the glass from her hand and put both our glasses on the end table. Time to find out if I was capable of more. I slid an arm under her knees and stood, lifting her to be cradled against my chest. The smile she gave me warmed my heart. The walk to the bedroom seemed to take forever. Was this a mistake? Could I handle such close proximity? I was about to find out. If the kisses we had shared were any indication, our compatibility was extremely likely. I hadn't done this before, but the Sophie I knew was kind and patient, and she would be understanding. Of that, I was sure.

I lowered her to sit at the bottom of the bed and began to remove my tie and shirt. Her hand reached up and touched my bare chest. The shirt slipped to the floor. Heat seared through me. Everywhere her hand moved, fire followed in its wake. I unclipped my belt and began to unzip my suit pants, but Sophie reached out and pushed my hands away and helped me to undress. When she pushed down my boxer shorts and the cool air caressed my skin, I was not embarrassed or ashamed by how proud I stood for her. Her eyes grew wide, but the smile stayed. I toed off my shoes and socks and stepped out of my clothes.

She pulled the dress up and over her head and quickly discarded her underwear. I smiled at how eager she was, with no hang ups, no shyness, simply joy at being able to be together. I took a minute to appreciate her petite figure, the swell of her breasts, her rose tipped nipples, the tights curls on her mound. I was glad she wasn't one to shave off all of her body hair. She was Venus de Milo, beautiful, tantalizing, and every inch a woman. She took my hand in hers. This was it. The next few minutes would tell if I was a man capable of loving another . . . or destined to be alone all my life, unable to be touched. I left momentarily, found the condoms I had recently purchased in preparation for this moment in the bedside drawer, sheathed myself and returned to Sophie.ƒ

I climbed onto the bed, between her legs and laid my body full length against hers. Instead of the sensory overload I had expected, joy coursed through me. Her lips found mine in an instant. Her hips rose up, her feet clasped around my buttocks, and before I even realized it, I had entered her, and we were rocking against each other. Electric pulses were going off everywhere she touched me. As the pace quickened, her hands roamed, and her mouth and teeth grazed my shoulder. Her feet tightened on my lower back bringing me closer to her than I thought humanly possible. And then everything slowed down to a point I could see and feel even the slightest movement. Sophie's head was thrown back, her eyes tight shut, her blackened eyelashes dark against her skin. Pleasure flushed her cheeks. Her fingers dug into my shoulders, her lips clamped tight in concentration, and she rose to meet my body. When I sensed her time was near by her heart rate and her breathing, I held back watching, waiting. As her body closed around me, gripping me tighter, I allowed the exhilaration of release to take over. I lost myself in pure bliss with another human being. No one could have explained the sensations. No medical knowledge could have prepared me for the heady pleasure I experienced buried deep inside Sophie. Her heart had opened to me, accepted me, and what I was feeling was far more than gratitude. I loved her.

Sophie was the one.

1 6

DOMENIC

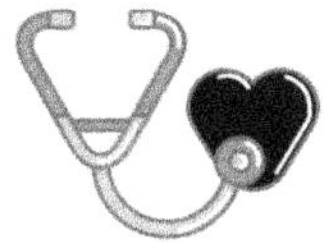

6th May 2017

When I awoke in the morning, the bed was empty. I got up, pulled on some jeans and a sweatshirt and walked down the hall to the living room. Sophie was curled up on the chair on the balcony, wearing only the white shirt which I had removed last night. Her head was bent forward resting on her arms, which were in turn resting on her knees drawn up to her chest. Her abundant red curls cascaded over her shoulders and arms obscuring her face with only her bare legs and feet on show. I was unsure if she was awake or asleep. I pulled back the sliding door and she looked up at me. Her face was tear stained.

"What's wrong. Did something happen? Are you hurt?"

"No nothing's happened. I'm not hurt. Well not physically anyway."

"Why the tears? Are your regretting coming home with me?"

"Oh no!" Sophie untangled her legs and stood up facing me. "I am not regretting anything. I feel so at home here, with you. It's as if I've

95

found another part of me, the missing link, but I'm confused, and worried now you'll think me mad. There was a woman in your room early this morning, standing at the foot of the bed, and she was smiling."

"A woman?"

"Not a real woman. More a ghostly image of a woman. I think it was my great, great, great, grandmother, Maggie Mae."

"Why do you think it was her?"

"Because she looked like me. But older. With old fashioned clothes."

"You said she was smiling."

"She didn't talk to me, but I had the distinct impression she was pleased we were together."

"How long did she appear to you?"

"Not long. Maybe a few minutes. Why are you so calm? Don't you think this is strange? Or that I'm crazy? Or do you have ghostly figures popping up in your apartment regularly?"

"I believe all things are possible. It doesn't shock me to know we have had a ghostly visitor. I wonder what she wanted."

"You wonder what she wanted? You don't think I'm crazy?"

I pulled Sophie into my arms. "I don't think you're crazy. Believe me I have seen some very strange things in my lifetime. This episode doesn't even come close." Sophie shivered. "Come on inside you're freezing. Why don't you have a nice hot shower and I'll take you out for breakfast."

"I can't go out. I literally have nothing to wear. Other than the dress I wore to dinner, which is crumpled from laying on the floor all night."

"Go have a shower at least to warm up. Help yourself to towels, product, shampoo. There's a packet of new toothbrushes in the drawer. No pink ones though, sorry. Open cupboards and drawers till you find what you need. I'll be right back."

The good thing about living in town, is that there are boutiques and shops on the ground floor of my building. I called my neighbor Louise who lived in the apartment downstairs and asked her to come and open up her boutique in the building, just for me. I had saved her father's life, in this very building when I moved in, and she offered to help me whenever I needed anything. I hadn't thought I would need her assistance picking out clothes, but she was really good about it. She turned up within five minutes and helped me select some casual clothes for Sophie. I showed her a couple of photographs we had taken the night before at dinner on my phone so she could estimate the size I needed to buy. When I returned to the apartment, I laid the clothes on the bed. The master bathroom door opened, and Sophie stopped dead in her tracks when she saw me. She had a bath sheet wrapped around her, and her hair gathered up on top of her head. She looked deliciously fresh and appealing, and it took a few seconds to get my thoughts back on track.

"Oh. What have you done?"

"Pick something to wear for breakfast. There are a couple of sizes. I'll return the ones that don't fit."

"Where did you get these? Did you break into a boutique? No one is open at this time of day on a Saturday."

"I have a friend in the business. I called in a favor. Please try on the clothes, pick whatever you like. On me of course. I'll have a quick shower."

"I can't accept these."

"Why not? You would accept dinner or flowers from me. What's the difference?"

"The price tag!" She held up a garment and a tag to show me.

"A gift is a gift. No matter the price tag. Please try them on. I want to take you to breakfast. I want to spend more time with you today, and I want you to be comfortable."

"Okay. I'll try them on. Thank you."

I turned back at the door of the master bathroom and caught sight of Sophie's delighted expression when she selected a pretty top and skirt from the variety in the bed. I knew that look, as I had seen it on Lucia's face many times when opening gifts of clothing from our mother. She was imagining herself in the clothes already.

The fresh faced and excited woman waiting for me in the kitchen after I'd showered and dressed, was vastly different to the woman on the balcony this morning. The knee length fitted skirt she had chosen in emerald green and the short-sleeved top in pale peach with splashes of cream and the same emerald green were a great match. The colors worked wonders with her vibrant red hair, which was a halo of riotous curls, pinned back from her face and tumbling over her shoulders and down her back.

"You look adorable. Like a spring garden."

"And my shoes are perfect to wear with these colors too." Sophie posed like a model, hand on hip, one foot forward and toe pointed in my direction to show off her rose gold shoes from last night.

"Oh, I forgot about shoes. But I agree those are perfect."

"Thank you again. I love this." Sophie twirled around. The fabric of the short sleeves fluttered against her arms. "So pretty and soft." She ran the hem of her top between her thumb and forefinger.

"Yes, she is. So pretty and soft." I bent and kissed her lips. I wasn't talking about the clothes. "Breakfast and then maybe a drive down the coast?"

"I'm all yours. It sounds wonderful."

I pulled her into my arms and enjoyed the freedom of being able to hold her without fear of the intrusion of a download of data in my head. I don't know why it's not happening with Sophie, but I'm not about to question it today. It was wonderful at last, to be spontaneously affectionate.

"You do realize now that I have you, I'm never going to let you go."

"I could think of worse fates."

I stood back and held her at arms-length. "I'm serious Sophie. I've never felt more myself with anyone. Consider yourself being courted."

"Wow, that's an old-fashioned term."

"I'm an old-fashioned guy, what can I say? Do you approve of me as a suitor?"

Sophie giggled and curtseyed. "I feel like I've stepped back in time."

She looked into my eyes, suddenly serious. "Yes, kind sir, I approve of you as a suitor."

"Wonderful. Let's go." I took her hand in mine and made a vow I would make her happiness my first priority.

Today will be the first day of my campaign to encourage Sophie O'Connor to fall in love with me.

17

SOPHIE

7th May 2017

I opened and closed the front door as quietly as I could and tiptoed around in the dark so as not to disturb Lisa. I wasn't sure if she was on the early shift at the hospital in the morning. I hadn't seen her since Friday, and I didn't get a reply late on Friday night when I sent a text to say I wouldn't be home. My head was full to bursting with all the thoughts and emotions clamoring for attention. Was I ready for a full-on romance with a gorgeous, courteous, articulate, interesting, kind and thoughtful man, who happened to be an exceptional surgeon? *Hell yes!* Was I kidding myself that he would still find me attractive when he realizes all of my family are slightly mad, believing in witches and messages from the "other side", and seances? I'm not convinced he can ignore all that. Although he did say that he had seen some amazing things in his life, so maybe he's open minded.

The light from the table lamp suddenly switched on and I gasped when I saw Lisa huddled under a blanket on the sofa.

"You scared the crap out of me! Why are you sitting here in the dark?"

"Pete and I broke up. I was feeling miserable. Drowning my sorrows." Her hand clasped the neck of a half empty bottle of red wine. She took a swig.

"It must be bad. No glass?"

"Who uses a glass at a time like this. I feel like shit."

"I didn't know you and Pete were exclusive. I thought you just hung out together."

"Obviously Pete had the same idea. I caught him with someone else in the alley behind the bar. It's funny really, cos one minute he was laughing and flirting and buying me drinks and kissing me. The next minute he goes off to the bar and when he didn't come back, I got worried. Someone said they saw him leave through the door to the parking lot, and there he was, with some hussy, getting down and dirty in the back alley."

"Oh God. I'm sorry Lisa. I know you probably don't want to hear it but he's not worth your misery. If he does something like that with you only a few feet away, he doesn't deserve your tears. Fuck him!"

"Yeah. Fuck them all. Men are bastards."

"Not all men."

"You gonna rub it in now that you're dating a doctor?"

"I'm not going to rub it in, but I can defend the man I care about."

"Oooohhh *care about*. Things have progressed from the last time we talked about the doctor." Lisa pushed down the blanket and sat up straighter. "Come on, spill it. What happened? Was he good? Was he better than good? Does he have a huge . . . "

"Stop it! You're making this . . . dirty . . . and it was so far from dirty that I don't want to talk about it and spoil the wonderful weekend I've had."

"Well, well, well. Look who has herself a boyfriend." Lisa took another swig of the wine.

"Maybe Domenic could set you up with a friend. Maybe another doctor."

"I don't think I'm doctor material."

"You know, I figure someone, somewhere has definitely done a number on you. Why are you always so down on yourself? I think the reason you end up with losers is that you think that's all you deserve."

"You don't know me as well as you think you do."

"I know you well enough to know you're a caring woman, a dedicated nurse, and a good house-mate. You do your share of the cooking and cleaning, pay your bills on time, and you help the neighborhood children. Yes, I've noticed the homemade muffins and cookies you hand out to the local kids shooting hoops in the park. You adore animals. Especially dogs. And most important of all, you are my best friend. So, ditch the wine, dry the tears and let's go to bed. I'm exhausted."

"Okay, but you are going to tell me about your weekend. I need to live vicariously through you for a while."

"Maybe tomorrow, after work. I just want to hold onto it, hold it tight, for a little while. Not ready to share yet."

"I get it." Lisa got up from the sofa, put the wine in the kitchen, and followed me up the stairs. We hugged each other tight at the top, before going our separate ways to our own bedrooms. "Goodnight."

"Goodnight. . . . and Lisa." I stopped at my door.

"Yes?"

"It's going to be okay. I feel in my waters."

"Hahaha. You and your predictions. You're a nutcase, you know."

"Yes, but I'm *your* nutcase, on *your* side. Goodnight."

Domenic messaged me to meet him in the cafeteria at lunchtime. He had managed to get a table and was chatting to another well-dressed man in a navy business suit.

Domenic stood and pulled out a chair for me. "Andrew Campbell, this is Sophie O'Connor. Andrew and I were in med school for a year together."

"Nice to meet you," I said, reaching out to shake Andrew's hand.

His handshake was firm, and his smile was genuine. Little laugh lines around his eyes indicated he smiled a lot.

"Likewise."

"Are you new to the hospital?"

"I've opened a clinic near here. I stopped by to see Domenic and give him my card, if he hears of anyone in need of my specialty."

"What do you specialize in?"

"I'm an audiologist. I specialize in hearing issues. I decided to concentrate on technology to help my patients with hearing issues."

"Interesting. May I have a card? My father has hearing problems."

"Certainly. I must go. Nice to see you Domenic. Nice to meet you Sophie. Perhaps we'll meet again."

Andrew left, and I glanced at his business card.

"He seems nice."

"Salt of the earth."

"Maybe we could have a drink with him one night. Is he seeing anyone, do you know?"

"I don't think so. Are you ditching me for Andrew?"

"As if. No. I'm thinking of Lisa. She could do with meeting a nice man. It would do her good to get dressed up and go somewhere fun. I've been worried about her."

"I'll ask Andrew. He may not appreciate being 'set up'."

"It's only a drink. If there's any chemistry, they can take it from there. Here let me send you a photo of Lisa to show him." I pulled out my phone and sent him a nice photograph with Lisa smiling and happy.

I had a good feeling about this. Now all I have to do is convince Lisa to ditch the sweatpants and the swearing and make a good impression.

18

DOMENIC

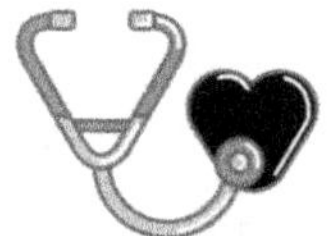

"I want to marry Sophie."

My mother and Luc were sitting across from me at dinner. They glanced at each other, and my mother stopped eating and laid down her knife and fork on her plate.

"Domenic you've only known Sophie for a short time. You don't really know each other that well."

"I know her well enough. She's a good person, with a big heart. She is kind and clever and funny and smart and she makes me feel as if I have a future. A purpose other than medicine."

"How does she feel about this?" Luc asked.

"I haven't asked her to marry me. But she does know that I am courting her, and what that means to me. She approves."

"Sophie is a lovely girl, I agree, it's just that you're young, and you haven't had much experience with this sort of thing." My mother's concerned expression implored me to think this through.

"You know why I've never had experience. But with Sophie, I don't have the voices in my head determining her stats and her medical history when I touch her. This is monumental. It has never happened before, and I feel there is a reason for that. She is the one I want to spend the rest of my life with, have children with, grow old with."

"Do you know her history? Has she told you about her ancestors?" Luc asked.

"I know a little bit. Why? Is there something I should know?"

"I have had dealings with a relative of hers, many years ago," Luc said.

"Why does this not surprise me. Was her name Maggie Mae? Are you the reason Sophie has started seeing visions of her dead ancestor now?"

"No, I'm not the reason she's seeing her. I don't know this woman's agenda, but I do know she feels very strongly about Sophie, and she has attached herself to her."

"Care to tell me how you know this?"

"I recognized something familiar about Sophie the night you came to dinner. When I took her to show her the painting, Maggie Mae materialized. Sophie was not aware she had been 'tagging along' I am sure. Maggie Mae assured me she meant no harm."

"What is she doing here? Don't you think it is very coincidental that she is someone you knew, and now she is someone who is involved in our lives?"

"I agree it is puzzling. Bring Sophie to the house and I'll talk to Maggie Mae."

"Are we going to tell Sophie what's going on?"

"Not until I can figure out her agenda. We don't want to frighten Sophie, do we?"

"I guess not. Okay I'll bring her to dinner. I want her to get to know you all better, and it will give you a chance to see how wonderful she is."

"Tomorrow night then. I'll let Aimee know we'll have a guest for dinner," my mother said.

"Where's Lucia tonight? I thought she was grounded."

"Rehearsals for the play. She'll be home soon. Cameron is waiting to bring her home," my mother said.

"I was hoping to see her to thank her for helping Sophie pick out a dress for our dinner the other night. It was kind of her, and it surprised me. I guess my little sister is growing up and being more thoughtful."

"Lucia can be very thoughtful when it suits her. I guess we're used to Lucia having another agenda." My mother stood and came around to my side of the table. She gave me a hug. "I'm thrilled you've found someone you can have a normal physical relationship with. We all take it for granted, but I am aware it has not been easy for you growing up without physical touch. If Sophie is the one you want, and she makes you happy, you have my blessing. Can I ask that you take it slow, and really get to know one another first?"

"Can I also mention that coming into this family means she will have to be aware of certain things. Things she may not be able or willing to embrace," Luc said.

"I understand that. But knowing she has members of her family who were witches and clairvoyants means she's open minded. I want her to get to know the family, so that when the time comes to share with her, it won't be such a shock," I said.

"We're not an ordinary family, that's true, but we do have the same problems and family dynamics as other families do." My mother took a sip of her wine and placed her hand on Luc's on the table. "We should give her a chance to get to know us."

"All I ask is that you accept that I see a future with Sophie. There's a reason we have been brought together. I'm sure of it."

19

LUC

8th May 2017

I strode into my office in the bowels of the earth and summoned my second in charge, Rourke. I wanted all the intel I could get on the ancestors of Sophie O'Connor.

"I have a job for you. Here are the details I have already." I handed over a manilla envelope. "I need you to investigate the history of the O'Connor family, from the time they lived in Ireland to the present day."

"How far back would you like me to go?"

"Say three hundred years."

"Can I ask why?"

"Domenic is planning on marrying Sophie O'Connor, and an ancestor of hers called Maggie Mae is materializing in her presence. I want to know why she has decided to reveal herself now."

"I'll get right on it. How quickly do you need this?"

"As quickly as possible. I would prefer you did this yourself, but if you need help . . . "

"I can manage this task alone. I'll do my best, my Lord."

"I can always count on you Rourke."

He left and I sat in the black leather wing-backed chair, behind my oversized mahogany partners desk, and looked down on the multitude of sinners in the cells and torture chambers below. I glanced at the books, files and stationery on my desk. At the stack of admission papers arranged neatly, awaiting my signature. I wondered how long I could go on neglecting my responsibilities with Harper, Domenic and Lucia in favor of the inmates of Hell. I had longed for someone to take my place for centuries. If I examined my feelings, that has not changed.

Where do I go from here? The last time I left Hell to pursue a life with Harper and Domenic and Lucia, it started an uprising, which threatened the ones I love. Yes, I returned to Hell nearly seventeen years ago, as was my duty, but my heart is not here. I've lost the pleasure I once had for torture and maiming. The buzz I received out of changing my appearance and making deals to trap mortal souls has fizzled out. I am tired of watching my family live their lives from the other side of the veil, and not being a part of their everyday decisions.

Now Domenic wants to get married, live a normal life, or as normal as someone who carries the Devil's DNA can live. He wants a wife, children and the whole "white picket fence" deal. Not the "shake my hand and come to replace me in Hell" deal I once considered he would be able to handle. He was gifted with the ability to read a patient's medical history by laying his hands on them, thereby saving many lives on the operating table. I had no idea that the combination of genes from his father, his mother and me would bring about such a talent. I have the feeling that he does not always consider it a blessing though. If Sophie can give him the normal life he desires, who are we to stand in his way?

I cannot deny him the right to have the normal life I long for. I wonder if his children will have the same heightened sensory ability. The thought of Domenic having children is appealing. I remember Lucia the night she was born holding on to my finger and looking into my eyes, instantly knowing who I was, trusting me to guide her.

And I have, as best I could, through the guise of her Godfather, but all the time loving her. Loving her as her father, and loving Domenic. But Harper. Harper is another love altogether. Deeper, binding, and long lasting. Breathtakingly beautiful Harper is my one and only love through all the centuries.

I have seduced, beguiled, cajoled, enticed, and lured many, many women . . . and men . . . into my bed. But I have never loved with all my heart, until Harper.   Making love to Harper was the most connected I have ever been with another soul. And from that love we created Lucia. The one and only time I fully allowed myself release without fear of consequence.

Lucia has powers locked inside her. I can sense it. But for her own sake I will not show her how to release them. She's too young, she doesn't have the maturity to make good decisions, and she could be manipulated.

Time now to focus on other things. If Domenic wants to bring Sophie into this family, I want to know who else is tagging along. Is Maggie Mae the only dead relative hitching a ride?

And what does she intend to gain from this connection?

2 0

DOMENIC

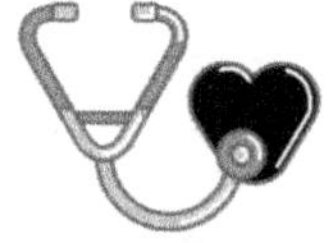

10th May 2017

I had promised Lisa I would bring Max to visit. I pulled up at the Gatehouse and informed Cameron I was borrowing him for an hour or so, and opened the back door to allow Max to hop in. We had a nice chat on the way to explain just how I wanted him to behave. No sudden moves, no slobbering on the furniture, no disappearing into thin air, and no bad manners. Lisa had said she loved dogs, but Max would be the better judge of that. Max is a lot to handle and being a large dog with huge paws and sharp teeth makes people anxious. He has an uncanny ability to pick out a fraud.

I had called ahead to make sure Lisa was going to be home when I picked up Sophie to take her to dinner with my family. When I pulled up, the usual group of young men were standing around their cars across the road. Max joined me on the sidewalk and turned to look at the group. He wasn't wearing a leash, which wasn't lost on the men. I sensed their nervousness. Max gave a low growl to let them know he was keeping his eye on them. I gave the command to follow me to the house. He took one long last look at the men and followed me up the path. I glanced back and noticed they had moved closer to their front doors and were not venturing anywhere near my car this time. I gave the command to sit and Max turned around and faced the street and sat still. But anyone who would have moved even an inch in our direction would have witnessed how fast he could run. I rang the doorbell.

"Come in. Oh, you brought Max. Lisa, Max is here," Sophie called up the stairs.

"Maybe we should stay out here and wait for Lisa," I suggested.

Lisa ran down the stairs, got on her knees, threw her arms around Max's neck and hugged him before I had a chance to say a thing. There was a moment when time stood still. Then Max turned his head and licked her face with a huge slobbering kiss.

"You're just a big teddy bear, aren't you Max. I don't know what they're frightened of, you're just a big ball of fur." Lisa was scratching behind his ear and Max was leaning in and loving all the attention. The men across the street were looking on in awe. Max wasn't looking so scary now. He was bounding about like an excited puppy.

"He likes you. He isn't usually this affectionate with new people."

"He can come to visit any time. You're a good boy, aren't you Max?" Lisa said, scratching his stomach.

"Time to go. Heel." Max jumped up and came to stand by my left side. His demeanor changed abruptly. He was once again the guard dog I was familiar with, not the slobbering puppy I had just witnessed. I spoke to him sternly.

Get a grip man. What are you doing? I've never seen you behave like that before.

Max had no answer. I think he was just as surprised as I was at the outpouring of affection and reacted to it accordingly. He was usually feared without question. It was probably a nice change to have someone touch him without fear of him biting their face off.

As we drove off Max lifted his head to the window and bared his teeth to the young men. Showing them that he was still in charge, and not to be challenged at any time in the future.

&a,

"Sophie, how lovely to see you again. You look so pretty in that color. Green suits you so well. Come sit beside me."

"It's lovely to see you too Mrs Ericson."

"Please call me Harper. I think we have passed the Mrs Ericson stage."

"Okay, Harper it is. Thank you for inviting me to dinner," Sophie said.

"You are very welcome. I have seen more of my son in the last few weeks since you two have been together, and that makes me very happy. You should expect more invitations in the future."

"Hi there, big brother. Hi Sophie. Good to see you." Lucia didn't seem to be her normal buoyant self.

"I meant to thank you for helping Sophie to find a dress for the auction," I said.

"No problem." Her eyes took on a look of sadness.

"How are rehearsals for the play going?" Sophie asked.

"Dress rehearsals are coming up. Everyone is a bit nervous. Including me."

"We have to come to the play. Where can we get tickets?" Sophie asked.

"They go on sale next week. You really want to come?"

"Of course. We want to support you. Don't we Domenic?"

"I wouldn't miss it," I replied.

"Wouldn't miss what?" Luc asked, as he walked into the room. Lucia looked even more unhappy when Luc arrived.

"Lucia's opening night."

Aimee arrived to tell us dinner was ready. As we made our way to the dining room, I took the opportunity to talk to Lucia.

What's wrong little sister? You look so sad.

I'm grounded. Apart from school, and rehearsals, I'm not allowed to go anywhere.

You might have guessed that would happen.

I've never seen him so angry. He's still not talking to me. I thought he was going to explode.

You're a minor. What did you think he was going to do?

I didn't think it would be so bad. That he would be that ashamed of me.

Oh, little sister, he's not ashamed of you. He's fearful for you. You are a beautiful young woman. You were exploited, and he didn't want men looking at you in that way. He loves you and is trying to take care of you.

I can take care of myself. I'm not a baby. When is he going to see that?

21

SOPHIE

12ᵗʰ May 2017

"*I* don't think this is a good idea." Lisa said, peering at her refection in the mirror.

"It's a wonderful idea. Stop being so negative."

"Does he know I'm going to be there?"

"Yes, Domenic told him. It's a group of friends meeting at a bar for a drink Lisa, nothing more. And some pleasant conversation."

"What if I don't like him? What if he takes one look at me and runs?"

"He won't run. He's too well mannered." I laughed at her shocked expression. "Look, I'm not asking you to marry the man and have his children. Just meet him, enjoy an evening out with me and Domenic. If you don't like Andrew . . . although you'd have to be blind and crazy not to, because he's cute . . . then we'll all go home, and you never have to see him again."

Lisa finished applying her coral lipstick and stood up to let me look at the finished product. It had taken a few hours trudging

114

through shopping malls, but I had finally convinced her to dress conservatively, and allow her personality to shine tonight. Lisa was accustomed to wearing low cut tops and short skirts but was amazed when the men she attracted were only interested in her body. She was intelligent and sassy and funny and had a huge heart. I wanted Andrew to see that view of Lisa tonight. The royal blue cocktail dress she had bought at a bargain price, accentuated her small waist and skimmed over her hips to end at her knees. Her black hair was pinned back from her face at the sides with pearl clips and hung in luscious waves over her shoulders and down her back. Her bangs stopped short of her arched eyebrows. But her big brown eyes stole the show.

"You look beautiful. Very elegant. He's going to be impressed, take my word for it."

"I don't recognize the woman in the mirror."

"Do you like her?"

"Yes, I think I do. I'm not used to . . ." Lisa waved her arms over the bodice of the dress.

"Covering up the *girls*? I know. But you want him to be looking in your beautiful eyes tonight. And listening to your voice. Remember that's his business. He's an audiologist."

"Well technically his business is about hearing, and loss of hearing . . . but I get the gist."

"Let's go, the car's here." I grabbed my purse, and Lisa's arm.

Cameron was waiting by the curb. He jumped out of the driver's seat and held open the back door. Lisa looked impressed and gave me a nudge in the ribs.

"Good evening Cameron," I said.

"Good evening Miss."

"Where's Domenic?" Lisa whispered to me in the back seat.

"He had an emergency surgery, so he sent a car for us."

"Are you sure he's going to be there? Do we pay this guy?"

"Of course not. Cameron is Domenic's family chauffeur."

"O.M.G. How much money does his family have?"

"Shhh. He'll hear you." I never felt comfortable talking about someone's financial position. Although I did wonder about this myself. Money didn't seem to be an object with this family. "Cameron, do you know what time Domenic will be arriving at the bar?"

"Domenic said he would be there to meet you, Miss. I estimate our arrival time will be in fifteen minutes, depending on traffic."

"I'm having second thoughts about these shoes. I'm not going to tower over him, am I? How tall did you say he was? Lisa asked.

"Don't worry, I think he's just under six feet tall. He's a bit shorter than Domenic."

"Six-feet tall, dark hair, a nice smile, a firm handshake. It's not much to go on. Haven't you got anything else you can tell me?"

"I was only with him for a short time."

"Yet you decided you would set me up with him."

"I've met some of the guys you've dated, and he's definitely a big step up from them. I have a good feeling about him. Trust me."

"I guess it's too late to make excuses and go back home."

"That's my girl." I checked my phone and saw a text from Domenic verifying he would meet us at the bar.

When we pulled up Domenic was standing on the sidewalk by the door of the bar talking to Andrew.

"Perfect timing. See. They're both here. Quick have a look and tell me what you think before Cameron opens the door." I nudged Lisa.

"You're right. Tall, dark and handsome." Lisa gave me a cheeky smile of approval.

Cameron opened the door and held out his hand to help me out of the car. Then he extended his hand to help Lisa. Domenic came over to the car and gave me a quick kiss on the lips. Andrew was right behind him.

"Lovely to see you again Lisa. Let me introduce you to a friend of mine. Andrew Campbell, this is Lisa . . . sorry I don't know your surname."

"Russo. Lisa Russo. Nice to meet you, Andrew." Lisa smiled and nodded in Andrew's direction.

"And you, Lisa." Andrew returned the smile.

Cameron tipped his hat to Domenic, gave us a wave, slipped in behind the wheel and drove off.

"Shall we go in?" Domenic herded us all toward the door.

We entered the bar and followed the waitress to a booth in the corner. She took our drink order and left.

"I wasn't sure if you were going to make it on time. Was it a difficult operation?"

"It was a difficult procedure. With complications arising from being in a motor vehicle accident," Domenic replied.

Goosebumps appeared on my arms and a prickling sensation along my neck altered me to a change in the atmosphere. My heart beat a little faster. My head throbbed. This was bad.

"Something's wrong," I whispered to Domenic, gripping his hand tightly. He turned to stare at me. "Something really bad is going to happen!"

Andrew leant in closer to talk to Lisa. "Domenic tells me you're a nurse. How long have you worked at the hospital?"

The piercing scream broke through the soft background music and the voices of the patrons in the bar. Everyone turned and craned their necks to see what was happening. A man with a red woolen ski mask had grabbed the waitress and was brandishing a handgun, waving it at anyone near him, and ordering them to get down on the floor. Another man, also carrying a gun and wearing a black ski mask, jumped up and over the bar, forcing the bartender to open the till, and demanding he fill a small bag with the takings. Men and women began kneeling or sitting on the floor. The few of us in the booth along the wall sat still. Red ski mask pushed the waitress down on her knees, moved toward us and yelled for us to get on the floor. As he came level with our booth, he yanked a folded canvas bag out of the front of his jacket and demanded we all put our phones, money, rings and watches in the bag. He was obviously high on something and extremely agitated because he was very twitchy and he was waving the gun about and pointing it at everyone's head, telling them to hurry up.

Lisa, Andrew and I knelt down on the floor. Domenic stood by the table trying to remove his watch. Red ski mask reached out, grabbed his hand and pulled Domenic's watch from his wrist.

"Get down. Now." He pushed Domenic down to kneel on the floor beside us and went through the crowd gathering possessions.

Domenic leaned in to whisper in my ear. "He's on a very strong prescription drug for health issues, plus he's taken other illegal substances which is making him reckless. He's desperate for cash for medication. He's probably going to have a melt-down shortly and that cannot happen here with all these people. I'm going to try to get him out of here."

"What? Are you crazy? You'll get yourself shot!"

"Hey. What's goin' on over there. Shut the fuck up. You! Get over here. Pick up this bag." He pointed the gun at Domenic.

Domenic stood and picked up the bag filled with wallets, jewelry and cell phones and put it on top of the bar as instructed. Red ski mask turned to watch Domenic, and Andrew took his chance, reached up and tried to disarm him. Red ski mask rewarded him with a vicious blow to the temple with the handgun. Andrew fell back into the crowd. Lisa inched forward and put her arms around him, pressed a napkin to his wound and applied pressure to try to stop the flow of blood from the cut in his forehead.

"I think you should take your bag of money and possessions and get out of here before the authorities come," Domenic said.

"Who the fuck asked you?"

"It stands to reason there's nothing more you can gain from being in here, we've given all we have."

"Shut up!" Red ski cap yelled, pointing the gun in the direction of Domenic's head.

"Hurting someone is only going to make it worse for you," Domenic announced.

A low growl could be heard coming from the door to the street. All eyes turned. The growl became louder, and Max appeared, walking slowly in between the patrons who shrank back. His lips were pulled back, nostrils flared, his vicious teeth were barred and gleaming with saliva. He had his sights set on red ski cap, immobilized on the spot, who blinked and shook his head to dislodge the image he no doubt thought he was imagining. The growl became a snarl. I glanced back at Max and blinked several times, because it looked as if Max was getting much bigger by the second.

Max launched himself at red ski cap. Women screamed. The gun went off.

2 2

DOMENIC

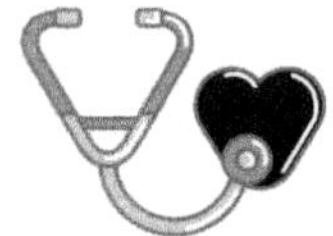

I had called on Max because I was worried for Sophie, Lisa, Andrew and everyone else in this bar. I knew I couldn't disarm the men alone. And of course, I knew Max couldn't get hurt. I hadn't factored in that Max would feed from the fear in the room. As he brushed against the patrons, he absorbed their fear. With each measured step he took, he became larger, more ferocious. By the time he launched himself at red ski mask and sunk his teeth into his neck, he was more the size of a pony. They both fell to the floor, and Max pinned his chest with a huge paw. The piercing screams around the room were deafening. I caught a movement out of the corner of my eye and turned to see black ski mask jump up on the bar and aim his gun at me, the only man standing.

Luc casually sauntered through the door looking suave and elegant in his usual black suit, shirt and tie and all eyes turned to him. "Put that gun down you stupid little man."

Black ski mask fired at Luc, who caught the bullet in his hand.

"I said put that gun down!" Luc yelled. People covered their ears. The frequency of his voice shook all the glass in the room. Black ski mask put the gun down on the bar with a shaking hand. Luc pointed a finger at him, and he rose to the ceiling where he appeared to be stuck

120

to the plaster. Shocked gasps and muttered comments of disbelief and fear could be heard from around the room.

You didn't think that one through, did you Domenic? How were you going to explain a very large dog to the police and the media who will no doubt be clamoring for a story? Never mind explaining him and my appearance to all these lovely people.

You're right I didn't. I was trying to protect my friends.

You had the right idea, but you should've called me first.

At least your trip isn't wasted. These two idiots are right up your alley.

I guess we'd better check on the one under Max. I think he's passed out. Oh no, he's dead. Good work Max. Good boy.

How are we going to fix this then Luc? Can you snap your fingers and remove everyone's memory?

It's not that easy Domenic. At what point would you like their memory to remain? Your friend Andrew was trying to be a hero, and that looks good in Lisa's eyes. Lisa is caring for Andrew and his sore head and that means a lot to him. Sophie thinks you're very brave for standing up to the drug crazed idiot and nearly getting shot. Let me think about this for a second.

Could you hurry up? People are getting restless.

I'm going to rewind this back to the part just before Max appeared. I'll have their getaway driver come in and tell them the cops are here. I'll deal with them of course, including the getaway driver, once they leave the premises. Then you're on your own.

They have a getaway driver!

Doesn't everyone?

But isn't the point of a getaway driver supposed to stay in the car ready to "get away".

Semantics Domenic.

Sorry. Your plan sounds good.

I'm so glad I have your approval.

Luc snapped his fingers, and everything ran backwards in fast motion to the point before Max arrived. Then Luc disappeared.

"Shut up!" Red ski cap yelled, pointing the gun at me.

"Hurting someone is only going to make it worse for you," I repeated.

The door burst open and another man in a blue ski mask appeared.

"The cops are comin' I can hear the sirens. Come on!"

"Okay, let's go. Grab the bags."

Black ski mask jumped the bar with the bag of money. Blue ski mask picked up the bag of loot and took off out the door. Red ski mask backed up to the doorway still waving the gun in the air. He shot a few rounds into the ceiling, everyone ducked as plaster fell around them, then he was gone. No one moved for a few seconds. Sobs of relief echoed around the room. People stood up, comforted each other, and dusted themselves off.

Domenic, I have all three gentlemen in the car, and we're taking a little drive out to the countryside. The bags of money and belongings are at the door, go get them before a homeless person picks them up. I'll let you take it from here, Domenic.

The sirens weren't real. The law enforcement's not on their way. Unless someone reported the gunshots.

By the way, good work. I'm proud of you.

I followed the men out of the bar, opened the door to the street, and sure enough the bags were there. I picked them up and carried them inside.

"Can I have your attention? I have our bag of possessions. If you form a line, I can give them back to you. Sophie, can you make sure this money goes back into the till?"

I was hailed as a hero, and they all wanted to know how I had managed to get the money and the bag of belongings. I told them they must have dropped the bag trying to leave in a hurry, but no one pursued it as their main concern was retrieving what belonged to them. Once we had established who the wallets belonged to by the drivers licenses and identification, the rings by the inscriptions, there were only a couple of items people were arguing over.

Someone did notify the authorities. Members of the county Sheriff's department eventually arrived to take statements. There was clear video footage on a security camera of a car parked at the curb, and three men leaving in a hurry. I was convinced Luc had a hand in that. The Sheriff put out a call, but they couldn't find any trace of the getaway car or the perpetrators. I knew they were never going to find anything.

·❧·

Back in my apartment, Andrew's headwound had been cleaned, dressed and tended to by a very qualified nurse, Sophie had made everyone coffee and I offered to top up their drinks with brandy. Andrew was laying back on the sofa with Lisa by his side. Sophie had taken off her shoes and was sitting on the oriental rug by an armchair.

"That wasn't the quiet night I'd expected." I poured a shot into Andrew's mug.

"No one will believe me when I tell them how I got the bump on the head." Andrew took a sip of coffee.

"You're lucky, it could've been a bullet wound. Maybe you should drop into Emergency on the way home and get checked out?" I suggested.

"He doesn't have concussion. I'm keeping my eye on him," Lisa announced. I topped up her coffee with some brandy.

"My own private nurse." Andrew gave Lisa a warm smile.

"It was an experience I don't want to have again," Sophie announced. She shook her head at the offer of brandy, covering her cup with her hand.

"Why do you think they dropped the bags?" Lisa asked.

"No idea, but lucky for us," I answered. I sat down in the chair beside Sophie. She leant back against my legs.

"Apart from the headache, I'm exhausted. Maybe I should take a cab home now," Andrew announced.

"Not without me," Lisa said.

Everyone looked at Lisa.

"I just mean you shouldn't be alone after a head injury," Lisa said, trying hard to look professional.

"You're welcome to stay here. Both of you. I have a spare room, and a comfortable sofa," I offered.

"I'll take the sofa. You take the bed. Be aware I'll be checking up on you." Lisa stood and held out her hand to Andrew.

"Anyone ever tell you how bossy you are."

"Duh. I have two brothers. Plus, I'm a nurse. It goes with the territory." She pushed him in the direction of the spare bedroom.

"Are you sure you want to do this?" I could sleep on the sofa, and you can have the bed with Sophie," I called out to Lisa. Sophie shot me a meaningful look.

"I'll be fine. That sofa is more comfortable than my bed at home."

"I'll get you both something to wear. And some blankets."

❧

I closed the bedroom door and turned to Sophie sitting on the edge of the bed.

"Your plan seems to be working. Although we could have had a less dramatic start to their blind date."

"Shhh she might hear you. I didn't tell her it was a blind date. I told her it was drinks with friends. Did you tell Andrew it was a blind date?"

"Sure. I found no reason to lie. And he was up for it when I showed him the picture of Lisa you sent to me."

"She likes him. I can tell. And it looks like he's equally as interested."

"He's lapping up all the attention. Let's see what tomorrow brings."

"I was so scared tonight when you were trying to be a hero. I could do with a hug."

"Let's go to bed, and you can have all the hugs you want."

"I mean it. I couldn't bare it if something happened to you."

"Nothing's going to happen to me." I took Sophie in my arms.

"I love you, Domenic," Sophie said.

I held her tighter, reveling in the fact that I could, without fear of receiving anything but positive endorphins flooding my senses.

"I'm happy to hear you say that. I love you too." I took her hand and kissed the back of her fingers. "'I'm so happy I found you."

I undressed her slowly, kissing each exposure of skin along the way until she stood before me, naked and glorious. I discarded my clothes as quickly as I could and we tumbled into bed and dove under the blankets to muffle our laughter, acutely aware of others in the apartment.

In our blanket cocoon I pulled Sophie into my arms, and we made slow, tender love. Afterwards, we talked about our lives, our work and hopes for the future in hushed voices, into the wee hours. My last thoughts as I fell asleep, arms and legs wrapped around each other, was that only a few months ago I would never have imagined such bliss.

23

SOPHIE

13th May 2017

The early morning sun streaming through the windows shows promise of a beautiful day. Domenic is asleep beside me, and I have a chance to examine his face in detail. He is so handsome. My heart aches when I look at the thick dark eyelashes fanning out against the fair skin of his cheeks, the dark stubble on his chin, and the strong, straight line of his nose. I control myself from reaching out to trace the contours of his lips. He has good bone structure. I remember seeing photographs of his father. The genes are strong in this family, from both his father and his mother. I wonder what our children might look like. Would they be redheads like me, or dark like their father. Our children. Butterflies flutter in my stomach at the thought. I've always wanted to be a mother, and he's admitted he wants to be a father. It's all happening so fast, but meeting Domenic was a gift from God, I have no doubt about that fact. I pinch myself to make sure I'm not dreaming.

His eyes open and his smile widens when he sees me. He stretches his arms, then pulls me close to nuzzle my neck. "Good morning."

"Good morning. Did you sleep well?"

"I did. I wonder if our guests slept at all."

"I'd like some coffee. Do you think it's too early to disturb them?" I asked.

"No."

"Let's go then."

"But first . . . the bathroom." Domenic rolled over and stood up. As he walked away, I had a great view of his naked physique and tight high butt cheeks.

"I do love your gluteus maximus." I giggled to myself as Domenic swaggered all the way to the master bath, showing off.

Domenic and I dressed and crept quietly into the living room. The sofa was empty, blankets pushed to the side. We peeped through the crack of the spare room door. Andrew was asleep under the covers, and Lisa was on top of the bed, on the opposite side, wrapped in Domenic's grey bathrobe, also sound asleep.

We closed the door and backed away to the kitchen.

"It feels wrong to wake them. Maybe we should take our coffee back to bed?" I suggested.

"Good idea. I'll come back and make breakfast soon, but there's no rush."

When the coffee was made, we picked up our coffee mugs ready to head back to bed when the spare bedroom door opened. Lisa appeared, tightening the tie around her waist.

"G'morning. Do I smell the elixir of life?" she asked.

"Good morning," Domenic said.

"One cup of java, comin' right up. Have a seat," I said.

"Your sofa is really comfortable Domenic," Lisa announced.

"Yes, we could see that you enjoyed it," I said.

"I spent most of the night on the sofa. I fell asleep talking to Andrew when I went to check on him early this morning."

"Of course you did," we both said in unison.

"I did!"

"We believe you." I laughed.

"Nothing happened," Lisa said through gritted teeth.

"Something did happen. I feel a lot better today." Andrew appeared wearing only a pair of Domenic's grey linen pajama pants. The beginning of a black eye had appeared under the dressing on his head. I noticed a really nice six pack, and a faint line of dark hair descending under the waistband. No doubt Lisa noticed it too. They exchanged a knowing smile. *Note to self, ask her about that later.*

"So glad you're feeling better," I said.

"Coffee Andrew? Pull up a chair," Domenic asked.

"It looks like it's going to be a beautiful day." He accepted the mug of coffee from Domenic. "What's everyone planning this weekend?"

"Chores for me," I said.

"Chores and study for me," Lisa said.

"I was planning on visiting my mother. Why?"

"I thought it would be nice to do something together since our night out was abruptly cut short."

"I thought you would've seen enough of us," I said.

"Not at all." Andrew was looking directly at Lisa.

"Sounds good, what do you suggest?' Domenic asked.

"Maybe a drive in the countryside?"

Domenic chortled.

"What's so funny?" I asked

"Nothing. Nothing at all. That's a great idea Andrew. I'm game," Domenic replied.

"Count me in," Lisa said.

"Looks like we're going on a road trip!" I said." We can't go in Domenic's car it's too small and cramped for all of us."

"Don't worry, I've got a plan," Andrew said. "I'll borrow a comfortable car. Bring something to swim in."

"I'll call an uber and Lisa and I will meet you back here in an hour or so."

"I'd better get moving then. Give me five minutes to grab my things." Lisa dashed off to the bathroom to get dressed.

"Are you sure you want to go somewhere with the start of a black eye appearing? Does your head hurt?" I asked Andrew.

"I'll wear sunglasses. It's throbbing a bit, but nothing that a couple of headache pills can't handle. I'm tough."

"I'll give you A for effort. I'm glad you didn't need stitches."

"In hindsight it wasn't the smartest move. I've been watching too many action movies."

Lisa appeared. "Well, you're *my* hero. I appreciate what you tried to do." She picked up her bag and shoes. "I'm ready, let's go."

"You're both heroes as far as I am concerned. And returning the money and everyone's belongings was a good outcome," I said.

"Do you think they'll catch them, before they try it again?" Lisa asked.

"Oh, they won't be trying it again," Domenic said.

"How can you be so sure?" I asked.

"Let's just say I'm psychic, and I see a very bitter end for those villains."

Andrew was true to his word. The restored 1965 Lincoln Continental, with whitewall tires, was the size of a boat. The black exterior was buffed and polished to a high sheen; the upholstered red interior was pristine. I settled myself in the comfortable back seat and I ran my hand in admiration over the butter soft red leather. We cruised down the highway with the music up loud, singing along, and leaving all our cares back in the city.

"I could happily stay in this car forever. Just pass some food in through the window now and again, and I'll be fine." Lisa stretched out on the back seat and leant her head on my shoulder. "And maybe the odd beer or tequila shot."

"Rule number one. No eating or drinking in the car," Andrew said.

"But how can you go on a road trip without food?" Lisa asked.

"Easy. You stop at a diner. Get out. Eat. Get back in the car," Andrew replied.

"*No!* You can't mean that. Snacks are life on a road trip."

"Rule number two. Feet off the seats." Andrew checked the rear-view mirror for compliance.

"You're no fun." Lisa sat up and put her feet on the floor.

"How long till we're there?" I asked.

Domenic, Andrew and Lisa called out in unison. "Are we there yet?" We all laughed.

We pulled off the road onto a long driveway leading up to a property surrounded by a very high brick wall. The red tiled roof of a building, and the tops of some palm trees in the distance, was all we could see from this angle. Andrew pressed a remote and the solid metal gates slid open to display a beautiful well-maintained garden full of shrubs and multi-colored plants. Directly ahead, to the right side of the sprawling ranch style home, a garage door tilted up. Andrew pulled into the interior of the building, and the door slid back into place. We gathered our bags and walked through the door of the dark garage into an oasis of palms and foliage surrounding a beautiful in-ground pool. A water feature set into the brick garden wall at the far end of the pool poured filtered water into the spa below. Lisa grabbed my arm. The lush green setting took our breath away.

The sounds of insects buzzing about in the plants around us and the occasional bird call, and water trickling into the spa below, had captivated us. I think I drooled a little bit. The hot sun beat down on the three of us, gazing lovingly at the sparking water. Andrew had disappeared through a sliding door off the covered patio. Lisa and I followed into a well-appointed kitchen, with a large two door fridge freezer dominating one wall. He was loading the provisions he had brought with him for a picnic lunch, into the cool interior.

"Who wants a cold beer? Or cider? Or Soda?" Andrew asked. "The wine I brought needs to cool."

"This place is fabulous. Is this yours?" I asked.

"No this is my parent's home, and they're travelling. I drop by and keep an eye on the place. They're both retired."

"What did they do. Before they retired, I mean?"

"My father was a doctor. Ear, nose and throat specialist. My mom was a psychologist."

"Brains run in the family then," Lisa said. "Is that why you studied medicine?"

"In part, yes. But I thought about how many hours my parents worked and wondered if I had made the right decision. Then I found out about the difference technology can make and changed direction and started my own business."

Domenic walked into the cool kitchen, pulled sheets of paper towel from a roll on the counter and wiped the sweat from his brow. "I've pulled the chairs back into the shade and put up the umbrellas."

"Good idea. It gets pretty hot out there. I've got sunscreen in my bag if anyone needs it," Andrew announced.

"I could do with a cold drink of water, thanks," Domenic said.

Andrew held a tall glass against the ice maker in the fridge door and chunks of ice and water tumbled into the glass. He handed it to Domenic.

"I can't wait to dive into that crystal clear water," Lisa said.

"Go for it. I brought you here to enjoy the pool." Andrew disappeared into the living room to turn on the sound system and music filtered out through speakers built into the patio roof.

Lisa and I found the guest bedroom down the hall to get changed into our swimwear.

"I'm impressed," Lisa announced.

"By the house?"

"By the house. By the car. But especially by Andrew," Lisa said.

"You can thank me later."

"You're feeling pretty pleased with yourself, aren't you?"

"I told you I had a good feeling about him. He's a sweetheart. And funny."

"Yes, I've noticed."

"And the best thing is, he likes you too. I see the cute little smiles you share. Don't think I haven't noticed."

"I just hope I don't blow it."

"I'd advise you to stop thinking like that. Think positive."

"Okay Miss Sunshine. I'll follow your example and keep a smile on my face."

"You know that wasn't what I meant. Just be your funny, kind and quirky self. No tricks, no games, no playing hard to get. Show him you like him. Andrew is not like those young idiots you work with. He's older, he's sophisticated, and he has travelled. I think a lot has happened in his life. And not all of it was pleasant. I feel a lot of sadness coming from deep inside him."

"How do you know all this?"

"I listen to him when he's talking. In the car he mentioned countries he loves. He would not have known the things he discussed with Domenic if he hadn't lived there or visited there for a reasonable time. I get a sense of the man, and I think I'm reading him clearly. Ask him. I bet I'm right."

"I'll ask him." Lisa twisted her hair up and secured it with pins. "Does this look alright? I haven't been swimming in a while. I think this suit is a bit small." Lisa turned to look over her shoulder at her rear view, in the full-length mirror on the bedroom door. The one-piece black suit was modest, but the back plunged down to the top of her rounded derriere. The front had a panel in cream and gold geometric design swathed across from left hip to disappear under her right breast. The suit had molded to her curves and there was no denying her full breasts stole the show.

"You look very sexy. You're going to knock his socks off," I said glancing down at my own small breasts and suddenly feeling inadequate. My white and navy polka dot bikini didn't look so sophisticated to me today. I pulled my hair up on top of my head and secured it with a stretchy hair tie.

"And you look so cute. Like a porcelain doll with your fair complexion. Better stay out of the sun. My Italian olive skin won't burn like yours."

We joined the men who were already in the pool, sitting on the swim ledge at the far end. A few inflatable pool toys bobbed about on the surface of the water. Lisa dove in first and disappeared under the water to appear at the far end without taking a breath. I took my time getting in via the steps and swam up to the safety of Domenic's arms. I wasn't a confident swimmer like the rest of them.

The dressing had fallen off, and Lisa was checking Andrew's forehead. I noticed her give his cheek a little kiss. I also noticed his hand lingered a long time in the curve of her waist when she examined the cut. They gravitated toward each other in the water, swimming around each other, often touching. You could see something had begun, only flirtatious, but at least both showed interest.

After a little while I got out, pulled on a sun hat and sat on the edge of the pool watching them showing off their swimming skills. I knew that Domenic had grown up with a pool, and Lisa has been a member of a gym for many years, which has a pool. As I rubbed sunscreen on my face, neck, shoulders and arms, I dangled my feet in the water. Out of nowhere the hairs stood up on my arms and neck. My heart rate increased, and I felt queasy. I began to worry because this usually heralded something bad about to happen. I jumped up and looked around. Maybe I had imagined it. *Relax, it's a beautiful day. There's nothing here to be worried about.*

After a while, splashing about in the water with the beachball and the pool toys, Andrew announced lunchtime. He pulled himself up and out of the pool effortlessly, dried off with a towel, and went inside to prepare lunch. I still felt queasy and out of sorts. Perhaps a cold drink, and a seat in the shade would help. I hung my towel to dry, over a shrub in the sun, and commandeered a seat at the table.

Andrew returned a short time later with a tray loaded with olives, pickles, salami, roast beef, and turkey cold cuts, some French brie, Jarlsberg and cheddar cheese, and a French baguette which he set out on the table under the shade of the umbrella.

He returned to the kitchen to pick up plates, silverware, a bottle of chilled white wine, and four glasses.

My attention was focused on the food, laid out on the table, and yet the hairs on the back of my neck stood up and shivers ran down my spine again. I shrugged it off this time, thinking it was because my suit was wet, and I was cold. Domenic and Lisa got out of the pool and dried off. As I poured the wine Domenic joined me at the table and laid out plates. I turned to see why Lisa was taking her time to come to lunch and saw she was drying off beside a shrub in the garden. I could not shake the feeling of foreboding.

I stood and walked toward Lisa who was now motionless, staring at her feet. She slowly lifted her gaze, and it was then I saw the fear in her eyes. In the garden bed, near her feet, there was a coiled rattlesnake with its head up, preparing to strike. I stopped walking. I feared the vibration might set him off. I waved my arms in the air to attract the men's attention, and mouthed the word "snake". Domenic was beside me in an instant. Andrew picked up a long pole, a large pool skimmer with a net on the end. He cautiously moved closer and extended the net over the top of the bush until it was directly above the snake.

My heart was in my mouth. Andrew brought the net down swiftly, scooped up the snake and catapulted him over the wall surrounding the property. I moved forward, but Andrew was already there with his arms around Lisa, telling her everything was fine.

❧

Thank goodness everyone had calmed down and we were able to eat some of the lunch Andrew had prepared. Domenic and I cleared away the dishes, repacked remains of the luncheon into the cooler, and tidied up the kitchen, to allow Andrew and Lisa to have a quiet chat on the patio. There was no time like the present to let Domenic know what was happening to me. Actually, it had been happening so frequently it had begun to concern me.

"I wanted to discuss something with you."

"You look serious. What is it?"

"For as long as I can remember, I have had a sense of bad things coming, before they actually happen. Premonitions if you know what

I mean. They are usually limited to locations near and around me. I mean I'm not getting a flash of something in another part of the country, or in another city. Today I knew something was wrong before I saw the snake."

"Are these just feelings or do you get images?"

"No, just feelings. I don't see anything."

"Can you describe what you were feeling before?"

"A general sense of foreboding. The hairs on my arms and the back of my neck stood up, I had shivers down my spine. I sensed danger but put it down to being cold after my swim, instead of trusting these feelings and trying to work out what's going on."

"Has it happened often?"

"It has happened a lot lately. More often than it has for years."

"What other things were you aware of before they happened?"

"When we met at the club. Being uneasy was the reason I had to get out of there."

"The big guy who grabbed you, and wouldn't let you go?"

"Yes. I bumped into him on the way out."

"And the next time?"

"The little boy who collapsed in the hospital. Peter, I think."

"Yes, the boy I operated on."

"Then the robbery at the bar."

"I do remember now you said you were worried something bad was going to happen."

"And today. The strange thing was I was sitting beside the pool only a few feet from where that snake was, the first time I felt uneasy. I shrugged it off. I put my towel to dry over the other side of the bush where the snake was asleep in the sun. I didn't see him. Lisa must have disturbed him."

"It does seem to be happening often."

"When I think about it, it has been happening regularly since I met you in the hospital cafeteria. It hadn't happened for at least a year before we met."

"Strange."

"Very! Why do you think it's happening now?"

"And Maggie Mae has appeared to you."

"Yes!"

"Maybe she is the reason you are having more episodes?"

"I need to get to the bottom of it."

"I think I have someone who can help."

"Who?"

"My godfather. Luc Nightingale."

DOMENIC

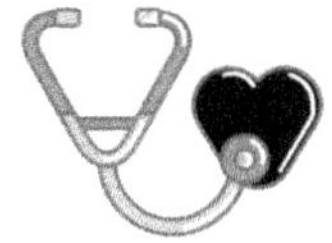

13th May 2017

There had to be a reason Sophie was experiencing these premonitions more regularly and that Maggie Mae had appeared to her. Sophie had intimated it was because I had entered her life, but I'm positive that there's more to it. I sent a telepathic message to Luc. He answered right away.

I need to discuss something with you. Sophie's been having premonitions and she's concerned they're happening more often now she's met me.

I think it's more likely to be connected to Maggie Mae.

I agree. It seems more logical that there's a connection between Sophie, me and Maggie Mae.

What would you like me to do?

Can you talk to Maggie Mae and ask her?

Bring Sophie to the house and we can try.

Thank you.

Don't thank me yet. She might not want to comply.

We packed up the car, tidied the kitchen and patio, and returned the pool equipment to the garage. The snake incident had made its mark on our day, and everyone was trying hard to return to the happy mood of the morning. Sophie had shared her concerns with Lisa and Andrew, and psychic phenomenon had been the topic of conversation on the trip back to the city.

"Do you mind if we stop off at my mother's house on the way home? I think my godfather might be able to answer some questions and put Sophie's mind at ease. He's very knowledgeable about psychic matters."

"I don't mind," Andrew replied.

"No problem," Lisa said. "I can visit with Max."

"Good I'll text and let them know."

"Do you really think Luc can help?" Sophie asked.

"Luc has amazing abilities. If anyone can help, he can."

I sent a message to Luc.

We're on the way to see Mom. Can you join us? I've persuaded Sophie to talk to you.

Yes, I think I can be there in about thirty minutes.

Perfect.

What did you tell her?

That you know a lot about psychic phenomenon.

Cameron had opened the gate in anticipation and was standing by the door of the Gatehouse. As we drove by, he saluted, and Sophie waved enthusiastically through the window. I noticed he smiled warmly at her. I think she's won his heart, as well as mine. Aimee showed us into the living room where my mother was waiting with coffee and cakes.

"It's lovely to see you again Sophie. And you brought new friends Domenic, how wonderful. And so fortunate that Aimee had made lemon tarts and almond slices today. She probably planned on delivering some to you, since she knows they're your favorite."

"Mom this is Andrew Campbell. Andrew's an audiologist at the hospital." Andrew shook her hand.

"My Goodness. Did you walk into something, or did someone give you that black eye?"

"No. Let's say I tried to help when I should've stayed out of it."

"Sounds mysterious."

And this is Lisa Russo, Sophie's housemate, and also a nurse at the hospital."

"So lovely to meet you Mrs Ericson. You have a beautiful house. It's so big," Lisa said.

"Thank you. Make yourselves comfortable. Who would like coffee?" Aimee appeared on cue, poured the coffee, and handed out coffee and cakes to everyone.

Lisa took a bite of the lemon tart and moaned in delight. "Oh, this is so delicious. My hips are saying back away from the plate, but my lips are saying give me more!"

"Aimee can pack up some lemon tarts to take home if you'd like some."

"That is so kind, thank you." Lisa cleared every little crumb from her plate.

Luc walked into the room with Max. Lisa bolted out of her chair, threw her arms around Max's neck and hugged him tight. Luc stopped and watched the exchange as Max gave Lisa a big slobbery lick up the side of her face. Luc arched one eyebrow and appeared surprised, but amused. It wasn't a look I had the pleasure of seeing on Luc's face very often. It made me smile.

"Andrew and Lisa, I'd like to introduce my godfather Luc Nightingale. Andrew, that besotted animal is Max."

"Hello," Lisa said, from her kneeling position on the floor with her arms around Max.

"You seem to have gained a faithful friend," Luc said.

Andrew stepped forward and shook Luc's hand. "It's a pleasure to meet you. I hear you know a lot about psychic abilities. I've attended a few séances myself, and the subject fascinates me."

"How do you feel about séances Sophie? Have you attended one?" Luc asked.

"Actually, I have, in college. But it seemed like a bit of a joke. No one took it seriously."

"Perhaps we could have a séance tonight. Try to find out why

Sophie is getting these unusual premonitions," Andrew said. "What do you say Sophie. It's worth a try."

"I'm willing. Do you think it would work, Luc?" Sophie asked.

"There's no harm in trying," Luc said.

⹂

Aimee turned off the overhead light. The tall candelabra she placed on the table was the only illumination in the dining room. Max sat guarding the entrance to the room, keenly aware of every sound, every movement. As we took our places around the table, shadows danced on the walls. Andrew attempted to sit at the head of the table, but Sophie guided him into the next chair down, Lisa sat beside him on his right. He raised his eyebrows but didn't question it. Sophie sat beside Lisa, and I took the next chair. My mother and Luc sat opposite to Sophie and asked everyone to place their hands on the table, palms down, and close their eyes.

"Try to clear your mind of anything other than the reason we are here. Which is to find out who is coming through from the other side, warning Sophie of dangers in this world," Luc said.

"Don't you think we should cleanse the space first?" Andrew said.

"Shhhh. Close your eyes. Concentrate," Lisa said.

"Does anyone else feel a cold draught?" Sophie asked.

Max stood up, his ears pointing skywards, his head cocked. He began to growl, low and constant.

"Show yourself. We have questions for you." Luc spoke to the darkened room.

A throaty laugh echoed in the air. The hairs on my neck stood up. Everyone's eyes flew open. There were audible gasps. A ghostly figure of a woman stood at the head of the table, hands on hips, enjoying the show.

"Oh my god. Do you all see her?" Sophie asked. "That's Maggie Mae, she was the one I saw in your apartment Domenic."

"It's amazing," Andrew said. He reached out, but his hand passed right through her ghostly figure.

"Keep your hands on the table," Luc commanded.

"I don't believe what I'm seeing," Lisa said. "This must be a trick, she's not real."

"She's real alright. What I want to know is why she's doing this to me?" Sophie said.

"Maggie Mae tell Sophie what's going on," Luc said.

Maggie Mae faded a bit, then became more solid in appearance. When she spoke, her Irish accent was noticeable.

"Well, this is a fine kettle of fish. I'm getting a bad reputation when all I wanted to do was help you. Warn you. Tis the least I can do, as you're a relative of mine, and I don't want anything bad to happen to you."

"Does this mean you're watching me?" Sophie asked.

"I am watching over you, yes. I have no power to stop these things from happening, but I want you to be alert. And to start using the powers you have deep inside. The powers you've been denying since you were a child."

"What powers?"

"The power of clairvoyance. If you trust your instincts, you can help people. You have a precious gift and you're not using it. You had it when you were a lass, but you've locked it away since then. Your parents took you to live in another country because when you had visions and tried to forecast the future, the villagers were scared. They taunted you and called you a witch because of me. But you can't keep denying your heritage Sophie."

"Why now. Why are you appearing to me now?"

"Because you're going to have a child who will make a difference in this world. But you need to be ready to guide her. To help her to realize all her powers. I can only do so much. You need to accept what you are and practice your gifts and be the one to support her in a practical way."

"I'm going to have a child!" Sophie squealed. "When?"

"Soon."

"With whom."

"Domenic of course. He is the only one who can help you bring this special child into the world."

"I don't believe this," Andrew said.

"Believe it young man. And if I can give you a bit of advice, I think you should buy that house your parents will offer to you when they return from their trip. They're going to want to travel the world and they don't need a big house to worry about. You need to stop living in the past, put down roots, get married. There's happiness for you ahead if you open yourself up to it," Maggie Mae said.

A cool draft swept through the room, and the candles flickered and went out. I jumped up to turn on the light. Maggie Mae had gone.

Back in my apartment I poured a glass of wine for myself, and one for Sophie who was curled up on the sofa. She hadn't said much after the séance, or in Andrew's car on the way here. Andrew had dropped us off before taking Lisa home. My guess was that they wanted some more time alone.

"Can we talk about what happened tonight." I handed her a glass.

"I'm still trying to come to terms with the fact that someone, or some ghostly entity, is watching me twenty-four-seven."

"I believe we all have someone watching us twenty-four-seven. At least yours is trying to help you and keep you safe."

"She told me to trust my instincts. Well, I'm sure there's more to it than trying to keep me safe. She wasn't telling us everything."

"How do you feel about her prediction that we're going to have a child?"

"I've always wanted to be a mother. It's just that I hadn't imagined having a child who is . . . to quote Maggie Mae . . . going to make a difference in the world. What does that even mean?"

"If my abilities were passed on and your abilities were passed on, I think our child would be very special."

"Your abilities as a doctor?"

"I think there are some things I need to discuss with you."

"You sound so serious. Why do I have the feeling I'm not going to like what you say?"

"You know that I love you and I want us to have a future together. It's only fair that I tell you about my family so you can make a decision about your future with all the facts. You've been able to accept you have ghostly apparitions appearing before you, so I'm banking on you not freaking out and being able to accept what I'm about to share with you."

"You're scaring me now."

"Okay, look at me. When I place my hand on a patient's skin, I have the ability to download their medical history directly into my brain in seconds. Either by shaking hands or touching them to examine them. I also have the ability to read their character and sometimes I have visions of things that have either happened in their lives or are going to happen. Although this part is new to me, and I haven't quite got the hang of that yet."

"Really? Wow! It's amazing! Is that why you're able to operate with such success on your cardiac patients?"

"As far as I can determine, having a full roadmap of a patient's body and history of all illnesses and medical interventions, has been the key to saving them."

"How long have you had this ability?"

"What, the data download? Since birth, or as long as I can remember. That's why I avoid touching anyone if I can avoid it. The visions though are recent, since my 25th Birthday. It was a gift from my godfather, Luc. You see Sophie, Luc is the Devil, and he's responsible for me being born in the first place."

"The Devil. Stop it Domenic, I've always found him charming."

"No. I mean he is *the Devil*. Satan. From Hell. I know he's not quite what you expected, but I can assure you the stories about him are not accurate. He has a good side that people don't see. And as far as my family are concerned, we only know the positive side of his nature."

"You're trying to tell me that the Devil is your Godfather, and he lives with your family? I must be dreaming. This is insane."

"You're not dreaming. The reality is that the Devil is real, but not the monster everyone assumes he is twenty-four-seven. Yes, he can punish people, but these people have done atrocious things. It's a long story, but the short version is that I have some of the Devil's DNA in me, as does my mother, and I am able to telepathically connect to Luc."

"So Luc is your father?"

"No, Richard is my father. He died when I was a child."

"I don't believe you. Why are you saying all this? Did Maggie Mae's comment about having a child scare you? Are you trying to break up with me and you think by telling me a ridiculous story I'll leave and never look back?" Sophie stood up. She placed the glass on the table with a shaking hand.

"No, I'm telling you the truth. Let me prove it to you. I'll send a message to Luc. Hold on."

Luc can you please come to the apartment. I've told Sophie a little about you, about us, and she doesn't believe me that you are the Devil.

You're taking a big risk. What if she cannot accept the family situation.

Then I'll ask you to wipe her memory. Please come. I think she can handle it if she can see you as the Devil. I want to spend the rest of my life with this woman and she deserves the truth about us.

"Please sit down. Luc will be here in a minute."

"Hello Sophie." Luc appeared behind Sophie. She jumped and spun around.

"How did you get here so fast?" Sophie asked.

"Domenic has shared a bit about our bond. We have a telepathic connection. He asked me to come."

"You drove here?"

"I popped in. Unconventional I know, but it is useful on so many occasions. Let me demonstrate."

Luc disappeared in front of us. He reappeared on the balcony. Sophie sat down hard and stared, open mouthed. Luc disappeared once more and returned to stand before her.

"Okay you can do magic tricks. It does not mean you are the Devil."

"What would you like me to do to prove it to you?"

"A little fire and brimstone would be good for a start," Sophie said.

"As you wish." Luc turned toward the balcony and raised his hand, palm up.

The balcony turned into an inferno, the metal chairs melted, the concrete split and plumes of steam gushed from them. The heat radiated into the room.

Sophie squealed. "Stop it, stop it! I believe you."

Luc lowered his hand. The balcony and temperature returned back to normal.

"It's true?" Sophie turned to me with tears in her eyes.

"Yes, it's true. But you don't have to be afraid. Luc is not the ghastly creature he has been made out to be." I took her hand in mine.

"Sophie, I can assure you that Harper, Domenic and Lucia are the people who mean the most to me in the world. Good people need not fear me. The scum of the earth however should be worried." Luc said. "And on that note, I have business to attend to."

Luc disappeared and I waited for Sophie to talk.

"Let me get this straight. Luc is the Devil. And you and your mother have Luc's DNA."

"And Lucia."

"But he's not your father."

"No. Richard Ericson was my father."

"You have special powers. Does Lucia have special powers?"

"Yes. She speaks several languages fluently, is very intelligent, has a photographic memory and gets every test 100% correct. But she usually fudges some of the answers, so her teachers don't ask too many questions. She has the ability to change her appearance, to look older or younger than she really is. And she also has a telepathic bond with Luc and with me. If she has any other abilities, she hasn't shared or discovered them yet."

"What about your mother?"

"No, she doesn't have any unusual abilities. Other than being fearless, and a bit of a daredevil when she was younger. She doesn't have the ability to communicate telepathically to anyone."

"It's a lot to take in."

"I know. But you've met my mother. And Lucia. You've been to my family home. Do you think my mother would entertain Luc or allow him anywhere near her children if he was a monster? Everyone deserves a chance to show they have good in them. You have been brought up as a catholic. You know the story. Luc was an angel once."

"I can't think straight. If we are going to be together, he would be in my life too. Our children would have his DNA. What if they took on the bad side of his character?"

"*If* we are to be together? You have doubts now?"

"Yes, I have doubts! Do you blame me? It's not some little insignificant fact I can push to one side. It will be with me always. I have to work out if I can live with it. Or not."

"I know. But you haven't run from the building so that's a good start."

"I'm not going anywhere. Yet!"

"You look exhausted, I'll take you home if you like."

"Are you serious? I don't want to leave you. I want to be held, to sleep with you beside me, so if I wake up afraid you can tell me everything's going to be alright."

"I can do that."

"On Monday I have to go back to work. Back to the real world, whatever that is, and business as usual. I need time to process all this and believe it or not I feel safe here. Domenic *you* are my happy place."

"And you are *my* happy place. Come on, let's go to bed."

I switched off the lights and took Sophie's hand. She leant into me wearily. I scooped her up in my arms and carried her to my bed. I held her till she fell asleep.

Thank you, Luc.

You're welcome. Sophie will be fine. Believe me.

I hope so.

She needs time to get used to this situation.

I'm going to ask her to marry me.

Take my advice. Give her a few days first. She may have more questions.

Advice taken.

25

SOPHIE

15th May 2017

*M*y shift started early on Monday morning. I dragged myself out of bed and into the shower, still trying to come to terms with the fact that the Devil appears to be the head of Domenic's family. I have lots of questions. For a start how did Harper, Domenic and Lucia acquire the Devil's DNA. But I need to push these questions aside for now and get back into my professional headspace. I owe it to my patients to be present and focused.

When I arrived at the hospital the emergency department was full to bursting, due to a motor vehicle pile-up, including a tourist bus, on the highway. Patients were being treated and assigned to units or floors. The ambulances kept coming, the police and emergency services filled the corridors. I was run off my feet, but that was probably a good thing.

Then a message came through from my mom that overtook all my other concerns. I paged Domenic to call me.

"My dad has been admitted here, to the hospital."

"What happened?" Domenic asked.

"He collapsed at home. They think it's a heart attack. Can you . . . "

"I'll go check on him now."

"Thank you." I hung up and prayed that whatever was wrong with my dad, Domenic could fix it.

It was an anxious time sitting in the waiting room with my mum, holding her hand, bringing her cups of weak vending machine coffee, trying to reassure her that she needn't worry, when all the time I was sick to my stomach. My two older brothers Declan and Calum arrived, and we paced the corridor together. When Domenic walked through the swing doors, I searched his face for clues as to how it all went, and if his words matched his expression. The operation went well. I let out the breath I'd been holding. I wanted to throw my arms around Domenic, but I managed to maintain my composure. I stood back to let my mother talk to him. No one at the hospital knew we were dating except Lisa and Andrew, and I didn't want to compromise Domenic's position as Resident physician.

I thanked him, along with the rest of my family, but kept my distance and hoped he could see the love and gratitude in my eyes, before he turned away and returned to the OR.

"I'm impressed with that doctor. He didn't hold back. He gave me all the information, the good and the bad. I don't want to be kept in the dark, and he sensed that. Your father will have to change a few things when he gets home. But I think this heart attack gave him a fright," Mum said.

"It certainly gave me a fright." I hugged my mum.

"You don't have to wait here with me. The nurse will let me know when he's out of recovery. Go home and get some rest. You can all see him tomorrow. He'll probably not even be awake when they let me check on him."

"Are you sure Mum?" Calum asked.

"Yes, go home to your families. I'll call you in the morning, and you can come back."

"Give Dad our love," Declan said.

"I'll stay with you Mum," I offered.

"No need. You've worked all day, and then stayed with me for hours. I'm fine. That nice doctor said they would come and get me. Go."

"Okay if you're sure. I'll be back in the morning before my shift."

I messaged Domenic from the car to let him know I was going home. I yawned and dropped the phone on the seat beside me. The events of the last few days came crashing down on me. *Should I be considering driving home when I am so exhausted?* I crossed my arms on the steering wheel, put my head down and closed my eyes. A fifteen-minute power nap should do it.

The repetitive tapping on the driver's window woke me up. I had been asleep for an hour. Domenic's concerned face peered at me through the glass. I opened the door, stepped out and was enclosed in Domenic's embrace. I breathed in the smell of his aftershave, and absorbed the comforting warmth of his chest.

"How did you know I was here?"

"You didn't answer my texts. I guessed."

"How did you find me?"

"I drove around until I saw your car."

"I thought I'd have a few minutes to get myself together before I drove home."

"Come home with me, we'll be there in under ten minutes. Leave your car here. I'll bring you back in the morning."

"I have no clothes."

Domenic raised one eyebrow at me. "You don't need clothes where we're going."

"Did I mention I'm exhausted?"

"Did I mention I give a fabulous full body massage?"

"What the hell are we waiting for?"

I locked my car and jumped into the passenger seat of the Porsche.

Domenic handed me a robe, threw my work uniform and all my clothes into the washer, then the drier, poured me a glass of wine and gave me the best massage of my life. After a few hours of solid sleep, I awoke to the sun peeping over the tops of the buildings, and the sound of a shower running in the master bath.

Domenic didn't look surprised when I opened the door and joined him under the warm spray. I needed to show my appreciation in a mutually beneficial way. Needless to say, breakfast that morning was coffee in a travel cup and an apple. But I wasn't complaining.

After spending the night in a chair, sleeping fitfully, mum had dark shadows under her eyes and her face appeared drawn. She assured me she was fine. I can imagine how she must feel, with her husband of forty-one years going through life-saving surgery and seeing him hooked up to all these machines. I left the cardiac ward happy that I had at least been able to check up on my dad before my shift and had given my mum a hug.

I stashed my belongings in my locker and sat down to change my shoes. Lisa rushed in, plonked herself down on the bench, threw her arms around me, and hugged me tight.

"Are you alright? You poor thing. How's your papa this morning?" Lisa asked.

"I'm okay, and he's recovering well. They're happy with his progress. My mum stayed with him, and she looks like she's been through the wringer."

"I'm glad you stayed with Domenic last night."

"How did you know?"

"He messaged me to let me know not to worry. You were asleep."

"I should've guessed. He's thoughtful like that."

"Maybe you should stay with him tonight."

"No. I'll go see Dad, then I'm coming home."

"I'll cook something nice for dinner."

"Good I've missed your cooking."

"I must run, I'm on a coffee break. Ciao Bella." Lisa disappeared as quickly as she had arrived.

Why is it that when you're tired or stressed the day drags! It didn't matter how many times I checked the clock on the wall, the morning seemed as if it was never going to end. The only bright spot in my working day was when Domenic joined me for lunch in the cafeteria.

"I've done the rounds and your father is doing remarkably well. How are you?"

"I'm better now I've heard that news."

"His prognosis is good. You can relax a bit."

"Thanks, I'm trying. I'm going home tonight. Lisa's cooking me something delicious."

"With all that's happened the last few days, I guess you have a lot to talk about."

"There are some things I can discuss. But there are other things even I haven't been able to get my head around. I won't be discussing those with her."

"I was going to mention to you that it's best you keep what I told you close to your chest. I wouldn't share if I were you."

"Don't worry, I had no intention. Who'd believe me anyway."

"I know you probably have more questions, but you seem to be handling it."

"Did you think I would run away?"

"I banked on the indisputable fact that I love you, and you love me."

"Risky."

"No. Not from where I stand. There's a reason, Maggie Mae has made that clear. Fate and other powerful sources have conspired to bring us together. How could you run away from that? If you can accept Maggie Mae in your life, you can accept Luc as well."

"You've got it all figured out, haven't you?"

"I've had a lot of time to think about it."

Domenic received a message from his paging service. Thankfully it wasn't the cardiac ward, but his office calling him. We cleared the trays from the table, dumped the sandwich wrappers in the trash, and went our separate ways.

26

LUC

15th May 2017

I thought I would drop in on Harper and let her know what had transpired the other night with Domenic and Sophie. I checked the house, but to no avail. I was surprised to see Harper sitting in the garden in the late afternoon sun, in the shade of a tree, reading a script.

"You look relaxed. Interesting script?"

"I am. It's been a lovely afternoon. I've been trialing a new scriptwriter, and he's rather good."

"You have some color in your cheeks. You need to spend more time outdoors."

"It's hard when you're busy. It's lovely to see you, can you stay for dinner? Lucia will be home soon, and Domenic is calling in. I'm sure he'd love to see you too."

"Perhaps. If I don't get called away. I wanted to let you know what happened the other night. Domenic has opened up to Sophie. He called on me to demonstrate my devilish abilities to her."

"Why on earth would he do that and put our family at risk?" Harper sat up straighter and closed the script on her lap.

"You know he intends to marry this girl. His rationale is that he feels Sophie needs to know what she's marrying into."

"How did she handle it?"

"All things considered she handled it well. Don't worry I've been keeping a close eye on her. If she'd shown signs of weakness, and told anyone I would've stepped in."

"How much did he tell her?"

"You'll have to ask him. Only the basics I think and that I'm the Devil."

"Knowing this makes me uneasy."

"I believe that Domenic thought if she could handle the séance and seeing a ghostly figure appear before her, she could handle knowing that the Devil is not such a bad guy."

"No, the Devil is definitely not such a bad guy." Harper smiled and I noticed she automatically reached up to clasp the gold heart-shaped locket on the chain around her neck. "Ah here's Lucia."

Lucia appeared through the patio door, bringing a bubble of happiness with her.

"Good rehearsal?" I asked.

"A great rehearsal. I can't wait for opening night. You're coming right?"

"I wouldn't miss it for the world," I replied.

"I'm trying to persuade Luc to stay for dinner. Domenic should be here soon," Harper said.

Domenic walked onto the patio. He carried a bouquet of flowers.

"Did I hear my name mentioned?"

"Hi big brother," Lucia said.

"You look pleased with yourself," Domenic said.

"I am. Rehearsal went well, and tickets are on sale tomorrow. First in line gets the best seats." Lucia picked up her backpack. "I'm going to get changed before dinner."

I turned to watch Lucia enter the house.

"I've told your mother about the fire and brimstone."

"Ah. That was why I'm here." Domenic handed the flowers to Harper. "And I wanted to thank you for the other night, hosting my friends and being involved in the séance."

"Thank you they're beautiful, and you're very welcome. Now tell me how much Sophie knows. I'm not going to lie and say I feel comfortable about the fact that someone outside the family has information that could harm us."

"She deserved to know. If I'm going to be married to this woman, she will see everything eventually. We shouldn't have to hide Luc popping in and out, or the fact that he can communicate with Lucia and with me. Or the fact that I have abilities that make it very difficult to shake hands or have normal social interactions without getting information overload. I haven't shared the fact that Max is a Hellhound, who can travel back and forth to Hell, or that Aimee and Cameron are now working for us on an ongoing "good behavior" pass from Hell, and that they never age."

"Luc says she's managing all this so far."

"She's doing well considering her father had a major heart attack, and I operated on him the other day. He's recovering, but the family are going to have to make some changes. I think what happened on the weekend was pushed aside to concentrate her mental energy on her father's recovery."

"That's terrible. Poor girl she's had a lot thrown at her lately, hasn't she?" Harper said.

"I'm giving her some time on her own. I don't want to pressure her. I'm sure she's going to come back with more questions," Domenic said.

"Do you want me to talk to her?" Harper asked.

"At some stage I think that would be good. But not now."

"Please keep me updated on her father's progress. I'll send some flowers, or a fruit basket to the hospital."

"I think Sophie would appreciate that gesture. Thank you."

"Let's go inside. I'm sure dinner will be ready soon." Harper stood and I held out my arm for her. Her perfume was light and floral, and it floated up to my nostrils when she tucked her arm in mine. It was times like these that I wished I could bend my head and kiss her. Not on the cheek as I often do as a friend, but on the lips to show her how much I miss her.

But that is not my right. I cannot lay claim to her lips as I once did. I forfeited that right when I chose to protect my family and return to Hell to focus on my responsibilities to the underworld.

I did not know how hard it would be to live that lie.

27

SOPHIE

15th May 2017

I used a piece of crusty bread to scrape up every last morsel of pasta and deliciously creamy carbonara sauce from the bottom of the bowl. Lisa knew my weakness, and had outdone herself tonight, with both the pasta and the bottle of Pinot Gris.

"I'm a very happy girl right now." I sat back and looked down at my ever-increasing waistline. "You'll make someone a fabulous wife one day." I patted my full stomach.

"Thanks. In my family, pasta is King, and it was my duty to my Italian nonna to learn how to cook well."

"You're going to have to teach me. Cooking is not my strong point, and Domenic is used to good food."

"Have you made it official then?"

"No, he hasn't asked me to marry him. It's just been a sort of understanding we have that this is going somewhere. Do you know what I mean?"

"It sounds pretty serious to me. I've seen the way he looks at you. I'd like someone to look at me like that."

"I think you're on your way. Andrew seems really keen to me. He can't keep his hands off you when you're together."

"It means nothing until you get that ring on your finger, as mamma keeps telling me." Lisa picked up the pasta bowls and began to load the dishwasher. "Let's take our wine and get comfortable on the sofa. We can clean up later."

"You cooked and I'll clean up. That was the deal."

"Whatever. Let's take a break now. I want to talk about the séance. You haven't said much about it," Lisa said.

"Dad's heart attack overtook everything else."

"How do you feel about this Maggie Mae person appearing and predicting you're going to have a child?"

"You know how much I want kids. It seems strange to think that this decision was made for me. Although don't get me wrong I think Domenic will make a great dad. It's just that things are moving quickly and I'm struggling to keep up. I thought I would be nursing for a few more years, then get married and then have kids down the track. I had the feeling that it's actually going to happen much sooner than I expected, by the way she spoke."

"Andrew and I talked about the séance. It freaked me out. He coped better with seeing a ghost. I haven't even talked about it with my family."

"I think it's best to keep it to yourself. People will think we're crazy. Or on drugs."

"Let's make a pact. This can be our secret. We won't talk about it with anyone else. But you will tell me if you get another visit from Maggie Mae? Won't you?"

"I promise I will tell you."

"I like Domenic's family. I felt like I'd walked onto a movie set though. That house is huge. And servants! Come on. They must have serious money."

"Yes, they're great. You didn't meet Lucia, Domenic's younger sister. She is a bright young thing, full of energy. I think you two would get along."

"Where's their papa?"

"He died before Lucia was born. I don't know the details."

"Domenic's mamma still looks beautiful. I saw pictures of her on the wall, taken when she was younger. Doing stunt work for Mindy Michaels. There were pictures of them together."

"Domenic is very protective of her. As is Luc."

"What's the story with Luc. Does he live there?"

"I don't think so. All good questions. I think I need to ask Domenic more about the family."

"What does Luc do?"

I remembered the last time I saw Luc. The inferno on the balcony, the heat radiating through the door, the disbelief that this was actually happening to me. Where did I fit into all this? Was I just there to provide a child for Domenic to fulfill his destiny? Did I have any choice in this decision? Did I really want to marry into a family with the Devil as their advisor?

"Hello? Anyone home?" Lisa waved her hand in front of my face.

"Sorry."

"Where did you go?"

"I was thinking about the future. Do you mind if I go and clean up now? I feel exhausted all of a sudden."

"Come on, I'll help you. We'll get it done in half the time." Lisa stood up, took my hand and pulled me to my feet.

"I really am glad we're such close friends you know." I reached out and hugged Lisa. Tears sprung to my eyes. "After all that has happened, I know I can count on you."

"You sure can. Stop with the water works. You'll have me crying next."

"Your mum's right you know. Nothing is final until there's a ring on your finger! I should stop worrying about everything."

"I'm sure Domenic knows what he's doing. He's not going to ask you to marry him right after your papa has a heart attack. Give him some credit."

"That's true."

"And you *are* going to say yes. Aren't you?"

"I'm not sure."

"Girlfriend, you would be crazy to pass up an opportunity to never have to work and live a life of luxury with a handsome doctor, in a penthouse apartment. Your kids would be gorgeous. There are some great genes in that family."

I heard Domenic's voice in my head. *I have some of the Devil's DNA in me.* That would mean that our child would also have some of the Devil's DNA. When you think of the Devil, you think of a monster. But when I think of Domenic, Lucia, Harper and especially Luc, it is to the contrary.

Lisa snapped her fingers in front of my face.

"You've disappeared again. You should go to bed and get some rest. I'll finish cleaning up. I think the events in the last couple of weeks plus your papa's heart attack is stressing you out." Lisa pushed me toward the stairs.

"Okay, I'm going."

"Goodnight."

"Make sure you lock up."

"Sure boss."

"Goodnight."

I got changed for bed and went into the bathroom. I removed my makeup and ran the hot water to wash my face. I bent down to brush my teeth and rinse and spit in the basin. When I straightened up again, words appeared on the fogged-up mirror.

Good girl. Some things we need to keep to ourselves.

Luc

I dropped the toothbrush and it clattered in the basin. The reality hit me hard. I'm being watched by an unseen powerful entity. I really have moved into the twilight zone!

As soon as I got to the hospital, I called Domenic from the car.

"Where are you? I've got half an hour before my shift, and I need to talk to you."

"I'm driving into the parking lot."

"Come up to level three near the ramp. I'll wait here."

I saw the Porsche drive around the corner. He parked a few cars away. I got out, walked to the car, and climbed into the passenger seat. I leant across and kissed Domenic and was rewarded with a mild zap of electricity.

"This was an unexpected bonus." Domenic looked at my solemn expression and his smile disappeared. "What's wrong?"

"I'm being watched, and to tell you the truth I don't like it."

"By whom?"

"By Luc."

"How do know?"

"He left me a signed note on the bathroom mirror last night."

"I see."

"That's all you're going to say?"

"You do understand the concept of omnipresence?"

"Yes. But I never really thought about the fact that he could be everywhere, and I would have no privacy."

"Luc is making sure that you keep our family safe. He's also making sure *you* are safe. You have no idea how many lunatics are out there, who would take advantage, if they had any idea . . . "

"You needn't worry. I'm not planning on talking to anyone. As a matter of fact, Lisa and I had that conversation last night. We're not going to discuss the séance with anyone else, not even our family. They will think we're crazy. Heavens knows I don't want to discuss your family situation with anyone either."

"I know this is hard for you, but I think you just need time to get used to it. Maggie Mae is going to be popping in and out of your life, and Luc is going to be around. I'd rather live in a world where Luc transports the ever-increasing numbers of crazy people to Hell. I think what you need to do is see Luc from the other side. He's not a monster. Not where our family is concerned. He takes care of us, provides us with a house, money, and Cameron and Aimee to look after the house and grounds. He gives advice when asked, he guides us constantly toward what makes us happy. He gives large cash donations anonymously to the hospital where you and I work, and other charities. He prevents anything or anyone attempting to harm our family."

"I hadn't thought about it that way. I'm tired and I'm still worried about my dad."

"Your father will be fine. I made sure of that. He's recovering well. I'm not convinced you should be going to work though."

"I'm okay. Honestly."

"Can I take you to dinner tonight?"

"I'd really prefer to be home."

"I've bought tickets for Lucia's play next Saturday night. We promised to attend."

"And I will. Just give me a couple of days on my own. Okay?"

"As you wish."

"Don't be hurt Domenic. You've had a lifetime to adjust, I need a little more time to work out if I can be with someone and yet keep secrets from my large Irish Catholic family, who want to know *everything*."

"Take all the time you need. I do understand this is hard for you."

"I'll see you on Saturday. I'm looking forward to Lucia's play."

HARPER

20th May 2017

I've seen Domenic twice this week, and each time he visited the house he seemed sadder. I've gone through a lot with Domenic over the years, but he's never been a child to complain or bemoan his situation. As a young boy he was often left out of play with children his own age, considered a misfit, other than at school with gifted children like him. As a teenager he was in university, and again dismissed as too young to be taken seriously around his peers. But despite all that, he triumphed and became the doctor he always wanted to be. It has surprised me that now, a woman has brought him to a state of anxiety.

I want to help. Not just Domenic, but Sophie too. I'm not a fan of the fact that Sophie knows so much, but there are elements that neither Domenic nor Luc can explain. Regardless of the end result, she deserved to know how I became involved with Luc and why our family is tight, fiercely private, and could be seen as insular from an outside perspective.

Cameron buzzed me to let me know he was planning to leave to pick up Sophie in ten minutes. I picked up my bag and the gift I had bought for Sophie and walked to the front door.

"Aimee I'm off. Make sure to put the champagne on ice. Some canapes would be lovely for supper. We won't be late. I'll bring Domenic and Sophie back with me hopefully straight after the performance, and Cameron can return for Lucia. Luc will come when Luc is ready."

"Leave everything to me. Go and enjoy the performance. I'm sure Lucia will be wonderful," Aimee said. "Give her my love."

❧

We pulled up at Sophie's house and I noticed a group of young men congregating around their cars on the other side of the street.

"I'm not enamored of this neighborhood Cameron. Those young men look like they are itching for trouble."

"Don't worry. I'm keeping my eye on them. Will you be long inside?"

"About twenty minutes should do it."

"I'll come back in twenty minutes." Cameron got out and opened the rear door.

While walking up the path, I heard the low wolf whistles and vulgar comments and chose to ignore them. I rang the bell. I heard someone call out. *"Coming"*. The door opened and Sophie stopped suddenly, her mouth a perfect O.

"I thought we could drive to the theatre together. But first I have a little gift for you." I handed over the large flat box.

"Come in." Sophie held open the door and pointed to the living room.

"Is Lisa home?"

"No, we're alone. She's gone to see Andrew."

"Open it, please." I nodded to the box.

Sophie opened the box, peeled back the white tissue paper and carefully lifted out the summer dress. The soft yellow fabric floated out and wafted around her as she held the dress to her bosom with one hand and felt the hem of the fabric with the other. The tiny blue flowers and green foliage printed on the chiffon overlay were subtle but complimented her coloring so well.

"It's so pretty. But I can't accept this?"

"Why not?"

"It's too generous. It's a designer label." Sophie held the label in her hand.

"I want you to have it. I was shopping today and saw this and immediately thought of you. It's made for your coloring. At least try it on."

"Okay. I'll be back in a minute." She ran upstairs with the dress.

While I waited, I looked around at the art on the walls and the decorations. There was a large display of fresh flowers on the table. I knew they had come from Domenic, because I recognized the arrangement our family florist used. I could see it was a comfortable home, neat and tidy, with a few pieces of good quality unmatched furniture scattered around the room, probably passed down from family members. I remembered living like this when I was young, when I first got married. That all seemed like an eternity ago.

Sophie came back down wearing the dress and pair of nude heels and clutching a nude purse. She had tied back her hair with a pale green ribbon.

"You look stunning. You must accept the dress. It was made for you."

"I love it. Thank you. You are too generous."

"I was young once too. I didn't have much money, and I wanted to feel pretty and wear beautiful clothes. Actually, that was how I met Luc. I borrowed a dress Mindy Michael's had been sent by a designer. One of many I might add. They meant nothing to her. People sent her things all the time. Designers, clothing labels, accessory companies, cosmetics companies. They all hoped she would endorse their products. Anyway, I wore the dress to a nightclub, I felt a million dollars, and I met Luc. Of course, I didn't know who he was, just that he was handsome, and I was drawn to him."

"Domenic told you I'm having difficulty with all this."

"Yes, he did. And I know my son. He's hurting right now, and I thought I could help you understand."

"When did you find out who Luc was?"

"It was shortly after that, in Hawaii. He offered to fix something for me, and without really knowing what I was doing I shook hands and made a deal with the Devil. But I need you to understand that at no time did I feel afraid of Luc, and at no time did I feel he would harm me. Luc was given a job to do. It wasn't his choice to be considered in such a bad light. But the job is not the man. There's more to Luc that being the Devil."

"I don't feel afraid of Luc. It's just a lot to take in."

"He's my son's godfather, and he takes that role very seriously. If you love my son, as much as he loves you, you will know that Domenic would do anything for those he loves. And he loves and respects Luc."

"Domenic is a good man, with a big heart."

"Yes. I trust you won't break it."

My phone rang. Cameron had returned.

"Are you ready? We can continue our talk in the car. I think we're going to enjoy the play tonight."

"I'm excited to see what Lucia can do."

"She's been so wound up all week, I expect tonight will be a relief."

As I got up, Sophie put her hand on my arm. "I want to thank you not only for the dress but coming to talk to me. I hope we can do it again. I do have a lot of questions."

"I'm happy to. But I think you should start with Domenic, and if he cannot answer them, then come to me. He would be hurt if he thought you couldn't talk to him."

"I understand. Let's go."

2 9

DOMENIC

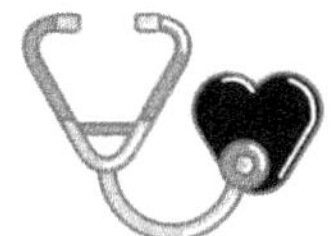

My apartment feels lonely without Sophie. Which is crazy, because I've lived happily in this space until a few months ago. I haven't even seen a glimpse of her at the hospital for days due to our different schedules. I think she's been deliberately avoiding the cafeteria. My mother and Luc want me to wait, to get to know Sophie, but the longer I'm away from her the more I'm certain she's the one for me.

I sent flowers earlier today to Sophie's house, with a note explaining Cameron would pick her up for Lucia's play and I would meet them at the theatre, which is walking distance from my apartment. Selecting something appropriate to wear had never been difficult before. But tonight, I changed shirts and jackets a few times before admitting that I was nervous. I pocketed my keys, wallet and phone and headed for the elevator.

Sophie has had time to think about things, to consider if a life with me was possible. What if she's decided that she can't do it? What then? How will I persuade her to give me a chance to show her it will work? That we could have a fabulous life together. Although I haven't officially asked her yet, I have no idea what I'm going to do if she says she cannot marry me.

167

The night air was fresh after a short rain shower. I took a step off the sidewalk to cross the street and a silver car came careering down the street, travelling way too fast, flew past me and ran the red light. The collision in the middle of the intersection between the two vehicles, appeared to happen in slow motion. The silver car flipped over, rolled a couple of times, and ended up on its roof, fifty yards down the road. The red car had only just taken off and was going slowly, so was pushed to the sidewalk. People were running from all directions to the damaged vehicles. I headed for the car on its roof. I could see the man behind the wheel, the seatbelt still attached, and blood running from a head wound splattered on the door. Broken glass from the headlights and windshield littered the road. I took a hold of the crumpled door and yanked it hard. My hands slipped in the blood. It moved fractionally but did not open. I reached in through the open side window and checked his neck for a heartbeat.

The vision pulsed through me and shocked me to my core. This man was a monster. I saw the money he had stolen, the child he had abused, the woman he had murdered, as if through his eyes. The emotions and visions flashed through my mind and almost brought me to my knees. He enjoyed hurting people, he enjoyed inflicting pain. His life was flashing before him and I was witness to it. Fetid, black smoke billowed out from below his feet. The engine had caught fire. I let go of him and staggered back still reeling from the shock of what I saw, what I had experienced. I called Luc who appeared almost immediately.

"Take him. He's done terrible unspeakable things."

"Not worth saving?" Luc asked.

"His pulse is weak, and he has a head wound. But it's what I see inside his mind that causes concern."

"I trust your judgement." Luc took me by my elbow, and we stepped a few paces back. He blew out a breath and the flames grew.

The fire in the car became more ferocious by the minute. Several bystanders had tried to get near to pull him free but were forced back with the heat and the smoke. The sirens rang in the air. Luc snapped his fingers, and we were back in my apartment.

"Get out of those smoke infused clothes and have a quick shower, or we'll be late."

"Luc . . . what I saw. What I felt. I don't think I can go tonight . . . "

Luc touched my temple with his fingertips. My eyes closed. The last thing I saw clearly was when I was running toward the man in the car.

"What happened. Is he alright? Did you get the man out of the car?"

"No, we were too late. The car caught fire and exploded."

"That's terrible. Why can't I remember it? Why are we back here?"

"We were going to be late. Go shower and change. We don't want to upset your mother," Luc said sternly.

I knew there was more to it. But I've learned to not question Luc, when he clearly does not want to talk about it. I showered, changed, and returned in fifteen minutes. Luc snapped us into the Theatre parking lot moments before Cameron arrived.

Sophie stepped out of the car, and I swear my heart felt lighter. She looked amazing. Her hair was an abundance of curls held back from her face with a green ribbon. As she walked toward me, her pretty floral dress floated out behind her. She was a summers day, a picnic in the park, a magical celebration all tied up in one beautiful package. I longed to touch her, which spoke volumes to me. Her soft lips pressed against mine and my happiness bubbled to the surface in my smile.

"I'm so happy to see you. You look beautiful, and dare I say, happy to see me too?"

Sophie reached up, laid her palm against my cheek and looked into my eyes. "I *am* happy to see you. I've missed you like crazy."

"That's good to hear. Maybe we should go back to my apartment . . ."

"No. We can't disappoint Lucia. Besides I have been looking forward to this play."

"Can I at least look forward to *after* the play?"

"Yes, I'll let you have that." Sophie laughed. "Eager?"

"Where you're concerned? Always!"

I turned and noticed Luc talking to Cameron, who was opening the back door of the car. My mother got out. Luc kissed her on both cheeks, and she took Luc's arm.

"Did my mom drive here with you?" I asked Sophie

"Yes, she did. She bought me this dress, which was very kind of her. And she's helped me to see things a bit clearer."

"What did she tell you?"

"She shared a little of what it was like for her when she first met Luc. And what it has meant to be a part of Luc's life."

"I see."

"It wasn't easy for her either. She understands what I was struggling with. We have a lot in common actually. She was also told she was going to have a child, a long time before she did. The difference is that she didn't think she could be a mother because of her job. I would be happy to give up my job to be a full-time mother."

"Let's go inside. I'm just pleased you're here with me tonight. I'll thank her later."

The curtain rose and the play began. I watched my little sister outshine anything she had ever done before. She was magnificent. I believed every word she uttered. She had the audience under her spell. When she came forward to take a bow at curtain call, they rose to their feet and clapped long and hard.

DOMENIC

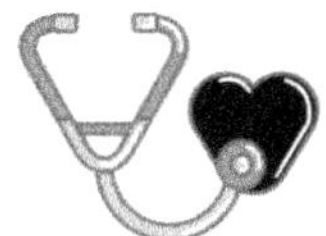

lthough I wanted to go straight back to my apartment after the theatre and unwrap the beautiful package that was Sophie, my mother had other ideas. She had arranged a small supper party for the family to celebrate Lucia's special night. We drove back to the house with mom and Cameron dropped us off and returned soon after with a triumphant Lucia. I have never seen my little sister looking so confident and proud of herself. She exuded a glow, an almost tangible field of energy around her, and we were all drawn to it.

My mother stood beside Luc and lifted her glass to make a toast. They beamed at her.

"To Lucia, a wonderful Lady McBeth if ever I saw one. You were magnificent my darling. You had everyone in the theatre enthralled."

"To Lucia," we all chorused.

"Thank you. What can I say? I loved every moment of it." Lucia took a sip of her soda.

"You're a natural on stage," Sophie said.

"I hope so. I've decided I want to be an actress!" Lucia announced.

Luc and my mother said in unison. "No, you won't."

"Why not?" Lucia asked.

"With your brains, you could be anything you want to be."

"I *want* to be an actress!"

"Not happening. I know all about that career choice, and I'm sure it's worse now with the myriad of drugs available."

"That's hypocritical. You were in the movie business," Lucia said.

"I had little choice back then. Plus. I was a stunt double. I didn't lead the self-centered life of a movie star I can assure you. I earned every dollar I made and took many falls for that spoiled brat Mindy Michaels."

"Mindy Michaels is still famous. She's gorgeous and she's about fifty."

"Try sixty. She's had so much work done on her I'm surprised she can smile."

"Jealous?"

"Lucia! Remember where you are and to whom you are talking!" Luc's raised voice stopped everyone dead. "Apologize. Now!"

"I'm sorry Mom. I didn't mean to . . . ". Lucia turned and ran from the room.

Luc took hold of my mother's arm. "Let her go. I think the excitement got the better of her tonight. Let her calm down. I'll go talk to her in a while."

❧

Lucia was understandably upset. Luc never raised his voice to her unless he was extremely angry. She knew she had stepped over the line. This was a side of Lucia I had not seen. But then again, I hadn't been home a lot lately. I walked out onto the patio and sent a message to her. She didn't reply. I sent another message.

Lucia, are you okay?

No. Not really. They never take me seriously.

You must admit telling them you're going to be an actress was a bit out of left field.

But I'm good at it.

You're good at a lot of things. You just never apply yourself to them.

Who sounds like a parent now?

You speak several languages, you ace all your exams, you're a whiz in math, in English literature, in science. In pretty much all the subjects you take. You could do much more with your life than being an actress.

But when I'm up on stage and I feel the admiration from the audience it's like . . .

A drug.

Yes.

You can get that same feeling from many other occupations.

Do you feel like that?

Actually, I do. When I save someone's life on the operating table, I receive admiration from the other surgeons, from the theatre staff, and of course from their family.

You knew what you wanted to be from as long as you can remember.

There never seemed to be a choice for me. Medicine was chosen for me, it was a part of who I was. I cannot imagine being anything other than a cardiac surgeon.

Acting is the first thing that I've ever felt a connection with. I took command of that audience. I looked down on them and saw they were in the palm of my hand.

Maybe we have to find another career for you. Maybe a teacher if you like an audience?

You're kidding, right? Me. A teacher. Bor-ing.

Let's put our heads together and think about it.

Goodnight big brother.

Goodnight little sister.

I returned to the living room, to where my mother was talking to Sophie, and Aimee was offering canapes to Luc.

"How is she?" Luc asked.

"She's okay. She's sorry."

"I won't have anyone disrespect you mother. She doesn't deserve Lucia's angry words."

"She's seventeen. It's a confusing time in her life."

"I was hoping she had chosen a worthwhile career by now."

"She has the brains, we know that. But Lucia is exceptionally beautiful, and so many young women think that beauty is their key to a wonderful life. She can see herself up on the big screen, or even on the internet, being adored by millions. It's the technical age we live in."

"We've never had to worry about you Domenic. You've had your head screwed on from the time you were a child. I'm very proud of you. Your mother is too, naturally. But as your godfather, and not your natural father, the pride I have for you is different. I see the whole person that makes up the man. Your intelligence, your compassion, your dedication to what you believe in, and your big heart. Yes, you have a tiny part of me in you, I'm proud to say. And it came from the best part of me." Luc placed his hand on my shoulder, and I felt the love conveyed in those words, and in that touch.

Cameron drove us back to my apartment. I pressed the elevator button and stood back for Sophie to enter.

"Cameron is a good sport. He's been driving back and forth all night."

"That is his job."

"Yes, but I feel sorry for him. He's probably tired."

"He's happy to do it. Talking about being tired. I think I'll forgo the night-cap and go straight to bed. What do you say?"

"Subtle."

I opened the apartment door. "After you."

Once inside Sophie grabbed my lapels, pulled my head down and planted a very demanding kiss on my lips. Her tongue danced along mine, and tiny electrical charges zapped between us.

"I've wanted to do that all night," she said, touching her lips with her fingertips.

"I'm glad I wasn't the only one," I said, unzipping the back of her dress. Sophie stepped back, and the dress slid to the floor. She was back in my arms within seconds. I found her bra fastening, and flicked it open with one hand.

"Impressive."

"I'm getting the hang of this stuff." Her warm breasts were pliant in my hands, her nipples had contracted, and the tiny peaks pushed between my fingers for attention. I bent my head and licked one, and then the other, teasing the tip with my tongue. I enjoyed the soft moans from Sophie's lips. I sucked a nipple into my mouth, and her moans became louder. She threw back her head and I plundered her neck, nipping gently upwards to her ear. Her sharp intake of breath when I took her earlobe into my mouth, was the only signal I needed. I swept her up into my arms, and marched down the hall to the living room, where I laid her gently on the silk carpet. Tonight, I wanted to live the fantasy that had been my constant companion for months. Here on the floor of my apartment, on a silk carpet which had come from a land far away, meticulously hand woven, and intricately designed, I would make love to a beautiful woman. I discarded my jacket, pulled my shirt over my head, unzipped, slid my pants and underwear off, and kicked them to the side along with my shoes and socks, in my haste to undress and lay beside her.

"You're breaking the land speed record." Sophie giggled, slipped off her remaining underwear and rolled on top of me.

"This is a fantasy of mine."

"What? Making out on the floor?"

"No. Making *love* on this magic silken carpet." I pushed back her curls, cupped her face in my hands and kissed her. Her hair hung down around my head like a curtain. We were in our own world. Her warm tongue danced around mine, her hands gripped my shoulders, fingernails digging into my flesh. Sophie sat up, straddling me, holding her hair on the top of her head with both hands, rocking back and forth and guiding me inside her. Her small pert breasts swayed in time, almost hypnotic in movement. Very soon we were caught up in a well-known rhythm, with whispered words of encouragement and pleasure building, notching higher and higher. I could hear my heart pumping so hard, as it pumped all the blood in my body south to my very impressive erection.

"Damn. Condom!" I croaked.

"Too late. Too late," Sophie said breathlessly.

Sophie's body closed around me, making it impossible to deny the release I knew was coming. Pleasure soared. It was so exquisite it was almost painful. Sophie rode on, determined to extract every last vestige of ecstasy from this moment.

We'd showered, dressed in toweling robes, and were sitting on the sofa drinking coffee.

"I've missed you," Sophie said. She took another sip of her hot coffee.

"I think I got that memo." I laughed.

"I was a little too eager."

"I'm *never* going to think you're too eager."

"It was really good for me. I mean *really* good."

"Should we discuss the condom situation. Or lack thereof?"

"I'll go see the doctor tomorrow. The morning after pill, you know."

"I'm sorry."

"I'm just as much to blame. I wasn't thinking."

"Can we discuss our future now? What have you decided?"

"I've thought about pretty much nothing else all week."

"And?"

"I'm not going anywhere. I'm yours if you want me."

"Oh, I definitely want you. Come on." I took her by the hand and pulled her to her feet. I put our coffee cups on the table, opened the door to the balcony, and pulled her over to the railing. The city lights twinkled below us. In the midnight sky, the stars twinkled above.

"This wasn't quite how I imagined it, dressed in bathrobes, but I've learned since meeting you to go with my feelings." I dropped down to one knee and took her hands in mine. "Sophie O'Connor, will you do me the great honor of becoming my wife. I promise to love you, to treat you with respect, to value your opinions, to allow you to grow and most important of all, to protect you from harm with my life. I have no ring, because I'm being spontaneous for once in my life. But I want you to choose something that has special meaning to both of us."

Sophie was wide eyed, with tears running down her face and dripping on our joined hands. I waited for what seemed like an eternity, before she spoke.

"This wasn't quite how I had imagined it either. Neither the setting of the proposal, or the events leading up to it. But after this very long and lonely week, I cannot imagine my life without you Domenic Ericson. I promise to love you, to treat you with respect, to always remember there is more than one side to any story, to remember that some families are made up of very diverse individuals and most importantly, I will stand by your side through thick and thin."

"So, it's a yes?" I asked.

"Yes, I'll marry you."

"I needed to hear the words."

"I'll say it again then. Yes, I'll marry you." Sophie wrapped her arms around my neck and kissed me. I could taste her salty tears.

"Well, this night ended better than I thought it would."

"Come on. Let's go inside," Sophie said. I got up, swept her off her feet and carried her through the doorway. She pulled the door closed behind us.

I looked down at the silk carpet and saw my beautiful Sophie laying there, in my mind's eye, with her red hair flowing around her. I sighed. Sophie followed my gaze.

"It was a magic carpet after all," Sophie said.

"It was indeed." I kissed my future wife, long and hard. "Let's celebrate."

I knelt once more on the magic carpet.

31

LUC

I'm convinced there's a shift in vibration around the world. The calls to collect souls are coming fast and furious, the numbers in Hell are climbing, and I have a feeling that things are going to get worse. Everyone seems to be on edge, from the barista at the café to the local car wash, to the CEO of that high-flying company. People are short tempered, abusive, turning on each other and ready to blame everyone else for any little mistake.

I was relieved to go to Hell for once, where the surrounds are predicable. Rourke had gathered some information about the O'Connor family in Ireland, and I was interested in what he'd found out. He was already standing to attention by my office door when I arrived in Hell.

"At ease Rourke."

"Good morning. Here's my report. There wasn't a great deal of information recorded. I gathered most of my information from the locals."

I scanned the paperwork and stopped when I read the part about the villagers setting fire to Maggie Mae's house and burning her alive. The house had been repaired and rebuilt. Rooms had been added to the damaged dwelling over time, and the property had been handed down through the family for many generations.

"Did you find out what happened to Maggie Mae's body?"

"From what I gather, after villagers who supported her put out the fire, they never found her body."

"Strange."

"But rumor has it that the family left the village when Sophie was a small child, because she kept having visions. One of the visions told her to look between the walls of the house. That was where they found human bones. The villagers called Sophie a witch and there was talk of Maggie Mae then. The family sold up and left pretty quickly after that and moved to America."

"I think Maggie Mae has attached herself to Sophie since that time. She has only recently been showing herself."

"I wonder why she's been appearing now?"

"I think it's because Sophie met Domenic."

"Do you think she had anything to do with that?"

"I am becoming more convinced of it."

"What do you think she wants?"

"That's the burning question . . . pardon the pun."

Still in the shadowland I popped in to check on Domenic. I watched briefly as he proposed on the balcony. Well, he's finally done it. I'd hoped he would wait a bit longer, but I sense this is the real thing for Domenic. Sophie is a charming young woman, with a good heart and she'll be a valuable addition to the family. I do hope that whatever Maggie Mae is planning, I don't have to get involved.

32

SOPHIE

23rd May 2017

I hadn't seen Lisa for days. I caught up with her in the hospital cafeteria.

"Hello stranger. Do I need to advertise for a new housemate?" I said, tapping her on the shoulder. I took a seat beside her at the small table.

"I'm sorry. I haven't been around much lately. I know."

"Is there something you want to tell me?"

"I've been spending a bit of time at Andrew's place."

"No kidding. I guessed that. Anything else you want to tell me? Like how wonderful I am and how you owe me big time for introducing you to Andrew in the first place."

"Yeah, I guess I owe you one."

"Good. Cos you can be my Maid of Honor."

Lisa squealed! "What! You're getting married. O.M.G. I must've been away longer than I thought. When did this happen?"

"After the play the other night."

180

"Show me your ring!"

"He didn't have one. It was a bit of a spontaneous proposal. We're going to pick one together."

"Congratulations! I'm very happy for you." Lisa turned, threw her arms around me and hugged me tight.

"Does that mean you'll be my Maid of Honor?"

"Try and stop me. But can you promise you won't dress me in a hideous gown in a horrible shade of orange. Just so you can look gorgeous."

"Oh you spoiled my surprise. I've ordered the horrible orange dress already."

"Bitch!" Lisa pulled back.

"Hey, watch your language, or I'll make you pay for that dress. And the matching orange shoes."

"You'd better be kidding." Lisa laughed at my sober expression and hugged me again. When she pulled away, there were tears in her eyes. "Oh no! This means *I'm* going to have to advertise for a new housemate!"

"We haven't set a date yet. But I guess it would be a good idea to start looking."

"Andrew and I have talked about the neighborhood. He's already mentioned he wasn't keen on you and I living there."

"Maybe it's time to look for something nearer the hospital?"

"Let's not worry about it now. We still have about 3 months left on this year's lease."

"I don't know if we're going to wait that long to get married!"

"What's the hurry? Hey . . . you're not . . ."

"No, I'm not."

"Everyone's going to think you are."

"Have I ever worried about what people think?"

"What did your folks say when you told them you're getting married?"

"I'm going to tell them tonight after work. I imagine there will be a lot of yelling."

"They'll settle down when they know his family's loaded."

"Lisa, it's not all about money."

"Maybe not. But I bet when your folks find out who he is, it will make a difference. I would start with "You know that rich doctor who repaired your heart? Well, we're getting hitched." You might not hear as much yelling."

"You're right. They liked him. And I'm sure that getting married to a doctor would be a plus in their eyes."

"At least you won't have to work."

"Don't be silly. Of course, I'll work. I wouldn't know what to do with myself all day if I wasn't at the hospital."

"Until you start popping out all those kids. And that's another reason to be annoyed at you. We were going to have kids together, years from now, when we had partied hard, but right before our eggs had shriveled up! You're not making this easy for me, are you? Where am I going to find another housemate, slash best friends, slash neat freak who loves my cooking and lets me borrow their shoes?"

"You're crazy, you know that don't you?" My turn to throw my arms around her and hug her tight. "I'm going to miss you."

"Good. I want you to suffer." Lisa sniffed back tears.

"Don't! Or I'll cry too. Let's have a night out next weekend, before I become an old married woman."

"Will you let me borrow those rose gold shoes you bought to wear to the art auction?"

"They are very high. Your feet will be killing you by the end of the night."

"But they will make me taller, and they will make my ass look better. Especially if you let me borrow that tight black bodycon dress you bought on sale last year."

"Its two sizes too small for you!"

"No. It fits me like a very tight glove. There is a difference."

"Andrew won't be happy that you are shakin' your booty around on the dancefloor."

"Well, we won't tell him, will we?"

"I don't think my fiancé will be happy either. I'm amazed every time I say 'fiancé.'"

"You're lucky. Domenic is a great guy. Anybody can see how much he loves you."

"I want this for you too Lisa. This special feeling knowing someone wants to spend the rest of their life with you. Knowing you're the chosen one."

"Wasn't there a horror movie with that title?"

"Stop it! You know what I mean!"

"I'm just jealous as Hell. Hey, I get to pick the theme of the Hen's party."

"I'm not sure I want a party."

"Oh, come on. It's your last opportunity to dance the night away as a single woman."

"I think you see it as an opportunity to hire a male stripper."

"Well, yes, there's that benefit too."

"You are incorrigible."

"But you love me anyway."

"I'd better get back to work. See you later at home."

"Good luck with your folks."

"Thanks. I'll take your advice and lead with the doctor scenario."

"Rich-handsome-life-saving-doctor scenario."

"Got it."

I was still smiling when I got back to the floor. I was really going to miss living with Lisa. But I was entering a new phase of my life, with a man I loved. With a man who loved me in return.

33

DOMENIC

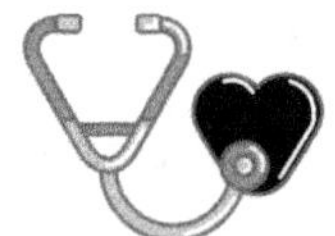

*W*hen I arrived at the house my mother was sitting out by the pool, while Lucia was doing laps. It had been a beautiful day, and the evening air was still warm and perfumed by the profusion of flowers in this part of the garden. I was amazed by Cameron's green thumb. He managed to plant almost anything, and have it flourish. He had recently set up some beehives at the far end of the estate near the garden wall, and the garden was thriving. The added bonus of fresh honey outweighed the concern of being stung. At least that was what he told me.

"Hello family," I called out. "How are you Mom?" I bent and kissed her cheek.

"I'm wonderful darling. Sit. I'll get Aimee to bring some iced tea." She pulled her phone out of her pocket and sent a text message to Aimee.

"Thanks. I came to tell you all my news. I proposed to Sophie."

"Wow. You didn't waste any time!" Lucia said. She swam up to the steps and climbed out. She picked up a towel, dried off, and wrapped it around her hips.

"When you know, you know," I answered.

"Congratulations are in order then. Where's Sophie tonight?" my mother said.

"She's gone to tell her family. She thought it was better to tell them first, on her own."

"Haven't you met them?"

"No. Not officially."

"Is there a reason you haven't met them yet?"

"I operated on her father. I've met them all. But in a medical capacity. Sophie didn't want to say anything because it might've been a problem at the hospital."

"I see. Don't you think they'll approve?"

"Sophie thinks they'll be surprised, because she hasn't mentioned she's been dating. But she's hoping they'll be accepting. Her family is pretty tight."

"I can appreciate that. Our family is pretty tight too. Ah here comes Aimee with the tea. Tell her your news."

"Aimee, Sophie and I are getting married."

"I had a good feeling about that young lady. Come here and let me give you a hug." Aimee wrapped her arms around me and squeezed me tight. She was as close to a grandmother as I was ever going to get. Her hugs were always appreciated.

'Mom I was thinking that we could have a small reception here, after the wedding. For immediate family and a couple of friends. And I would love it if Aimee could make the wedding breakfast? We'd hire some help. What do you say Aimee?"

"I would be honored." Aimee had tears in her eyes.

"Domenic I would be very happy to host a small reception. Have you thought about having a garden wedding here? Cameron has worked so hard on the grounds, and we have the ideal setting for a marquee."

"Mom, are you sure? Lots of strangers in your house?"

"They wouldn't be in the house. They would be in the grounds. The wedding guests can use the pool-house bathroom facilities."

"I'll discuss it with Sophie. But that's a very generous offer, thank you."

"Have you set a date?" Lucia asked.

"Not yet. But I'd like it to be soon. I'm sure her catholic family won't want her to move in with me before we're married. And I want her with me now. I'm not really keen on the neighborhood she lives in."

"Let me know when you talk to Sophie. This calls for a celebration," my mother said.

"Let's hold off on that celebration until we pick a ring."

"I'm surprised you didn't have a ring."

"You advised me to wait if I remember correctly. The proposal was a spontaneous thing the other night. We're going to choose something together."

"I'm excited to plan a wedding cake! Oh, I do hope Sophie agrees. I'm going to tell Cameron now. I can't believe our young Domenic is going to be married." Aimee pulled a handkerchief from her apron pocket, dabbed at her eyes, and rushed off in the direction of the Gatehouse.

"You've made Aimee very happy."

"It feels right Mom. I know getting married is a big step, but I'm more myself with Sophie that at any other time. She brings out the best in me. I was so focused on my studies and my patients and being a better doctor. Now I want to be a better man, have a family eventually, bring some laughter and joy into all our lives. Are you looking forward to being a grandmother one day?"

"Could we just take it one step at a time. I'm only getting used to the idea I will be someone's mother-in-law. Never mind someone's grandmother. I'm not old enough to be someone's grandmother."

"Technically, you are," Lucia said.

"Don't remind me how old I am. In my head I'm still young."

"Mom you will always be young, no matter how many birthdays you have."

"Oh, someone's sucking up," Lucia said, with a grin.

"Don't knock it. Have you thought about the fact that if our mother looks so stunning, there's a fair chance you will also look as good when you're older?"

"You do have a point," Lucia agreed.

"Thank you for the compliment Domenic. Let's go inside. Can you stay for dinner?"

"No, thank you, I'd better get moving. I've got a full day of surgery tomorrow."

"But you have to eat. It's salad and it's all prepared. Stay."

"Okay. But I have to make a quick call to Sophie."

I walked to the patio and called her number.

"Hello handsome."

"How did it go with your parents?"

"There were a lot of questions, and I think they're in shock, but all in all they handled it better than I thought they would."

"I was concerned about your father. I hope he's not stressed."

"Actually, when I told him who I was engaged to, he was the one calming my mother down. Hang on I've just pulled up at home, I'm getting out of the car."

"Take your time."

"Are you still there? I'm changing hands to get my keys out of my bag. Hang on. The door is open. I keep telling Lisa to lock the doors . . . but she . . . Oh!"

"Oh what? Sophie. What's wrong?"

"I have to go Andrew. Nice to talk to you."

"Andrew? . . . Sophie? Sophie?" The line was dead. She'd hung up. I tried to call back, but the phone was off. I messaged Luc.

Luc, there's something wrong with Sophie. We were on a call, she just arrived home, and she ended it abruptly. She called me Andrew and hung up.

A slip of the tongue? Maybe she was thinking about Andrew.

No there's something wrong.

Leave it to me.

3 4

L U C

I appraised the situation from the shadowland. Sophie was standing at the kitchen door. Opposite to her, a man had his arm around Lisa's chest and was holding a hunting knife near her neck. I could have stopped everything, removed the man and their memories, but this was an ideal situation to show Sophie that it wasn't a bad thing to have a Devil in your corner.

I walked up behind Sophie, and to her credit she did not jump when I put my hand on her shoulder. I had assumed the appearance of Domenic, so Lisa wouldn't be surprised.

"So now you have three hostages. How are you going to manage to overpower us all?"

"Shut up. Don't you see this knife? I'll cut her," he snarled.

"I don't think so. The arm you're holding the knife with is cramping up. You're going to drop the knife in a second. Let her go."

"You don't know what you are talking about. My arm is arrrgggh-hh." He dropped the knife. He stared incredulously at the useless limb, hanging by his side.

Lisa twisted out of his grasp and kneed him viciously in the balls. "Take that you bastard." Lisa yelled. He dropped to his knees. She kicked him hard in the thigh a couple of times. I picked up the hunting knife and pulled her away before she broke her foot kicking him. Sophie put her arms around Lisa.

"Take her into the living room," I asked Sophie. She dragged Lisa, who looked like she wanted to have another shot at revenge, out of the kitchen.

"Get up. We're going for a little walk," I said to the kneeling man, who was bent over and holding onto his scrotum.

"Fuck off." He tried to rise. He got to his feet a little unsteady. Lisa had done a real good job with her knee. I looked at him and removed my disguise to show him my real Devil appearance for a few seconds. I returned back to Domenic. He backed away to the sink with a terrified look on his face. "What the fuck?"

I took him by the arm and marched him through the living room to the front door. He had no choice because I had removed his will to fight me. I noticed the girl's possessions stuffed into a pillowcase, and a laptop and keyboard sticking out of a backpack beside the sofa. He was obviously robbing the place, when the girls disturbed him.

"Are you going to be alright girls?" I asked.

"We'll be fine. Where are you going?" Sophie said.

"I'm taking him to the authorities. Lock the door behind me."

As soon as we were outside, I discarded Domenic's appearance and took on my own.

I zapped this degenerate to the local prison, into the cell of the worst sexual offender. I knew exactly where to go because I had earmarked this sexual predator, nicknamed "Dog" by his fellow inmates, for future collection. At the same time, removing his clothes along with his identification, and his memory of the last twenty-four hours. It would be some time before the authorities worked out that he didn't belong there. He didn't actually hurt anyone tonight, but a stint in jail would be a good lesson to show him where he will eventually end up if he doesn't mend his ways. And as far as the real prisoner was concerned, when an attractive young man appeared at the bottom of his bed, naked as the day he was born, he thought that all his Christmas wishes had come at once.

All good Domenic. Call Sophie. She'll tell you what happened. She's fine.

Thank God.
By the way, I took on your appearance. You're a hero.
Thank you. I think.
You're welcome.

3 5

DOMENIC

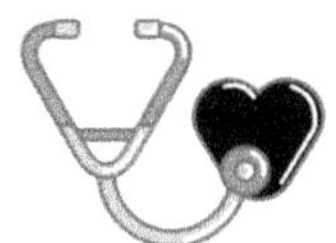

I called Sophie's mobile phone. She answered after the fourth ring.

"Are you alright?"

"A bit shaken up, but we're fine."

"What happened?"

"Lisa got home just before me. She noticed things had been moved, piled up in the living room. She was on her phone trying to call the cops, checking rooms, and walked into the kitchen. A guy grabbed her from behind. He had a knife. Then I arrived home."

"Lucky you were on the phone to me."

"Where are you?"

"I'm driving to your house. I called Luc."

"Yes, I guessed as much."

"He was the only one who could get to you quickly. He told me Lisa thinks it was me."

"I'll have to thank him. He did it without raising a finger. In fact, Lisa was the one who got stuck into the guy."

"You have to appreciate Luc has his good side."

"Lisa will want to know where Luc . . . where *you* took him."

"To the local authorities. Where's Lisa now?"

191

"On the phone to Andrew. He wants us to move out."

"He's not alone there. Are you sure your parents would object if you moved in with me?"

"Are *you* sure you don't want my father to have another heart attack? He thinks his little girl is a virgin."

"I'm going to have an alarm system installed if you stay there. At least that way I will know the house is secure."

"We'll talk about it later. How long till you arrive."

"I'm pulling up now. Pack a bag. You're both coming home with me tonight."

Andrew put his arms around Lisa and pulled her over to his side of the sofa. Sophie was sitting on the floor with her back against my legs, nursing a cup of peppermint tea.

"I can't believe how lucky you both were that Domenic decided to visit. That bastard could have hurt you," Andrew said.

"He was the one hurt in the end. You should have seen Lisa laying into him," Sophie said.

"He deserved it," Lisa said.

"You fight dirty," Sophie said.

"I have two brothers. I learned to defend myself," Lisa said.

"What's the plan now?" Andrew asked. "You can't stay with Domenic forever and I'm not happy for you to return to that neighborhood."

"I'm going to arrange for an alarm system tomorrow, with cameras you can operate from your phones." I squeezed Sophie's shoulder. "If you're going to stay there till the wedding, I need to make sure you're safe."

"Wedding? What wedding?" Andrew asked.

"Sophie and I are getting married. We haven't set a date yet, but I'm hoping it's soon."

"Congratulations. Why didn't you tell me?" Andrew said.

"I was planning on it. I was also going to ask if you would be my

Best Man?"

"It would be my pleasure. This will be my first time as anyone's Best Man."

"And I'm Maid of Honor. I'm really looking forward to this."

"I get to plan the bachelor party, don't I?" Andrew asked.

"I don't want a bachelor party," I said.

"And I get to plan the bachelorette party." Lisa laughed.

"I don't want one of those either," Sophie said.

"Oh, come on, you two party poopers! It'll be fun," Lisa said.

"Could the four of us just do something together. Maybe go out for a nice dinner?" Sophie said.

"Or to an expensive Health Spa and have pamper sessions. Get facials, and massages," Lisa said.

"I'll never live it down if the guys at the hospital hear I've had a facial," Andrew said.

"What's wrong with getting in touch with your feminine side?" Lisa laughed.

"Come on guys, it could be fun," Sophie said.

"Let's cross that bridge when we discuss a date for the wedding." I said. "I'm ready to retire for the night. Andrew, you are welcome to stay." I stood and took Sophie's hand.

"Thank you. I will. Goodnight." Andrew hugged Lisa tighter.

We left them sitting on the sofa, wrapped in each other's arms. I knew what Andrew was feeling because I was also remembering the gut churning anxiety earlier when I instinctively knew something was wrong.

Now it was my turn to show Sophie how precious she is to me.

"I can see the benefit of living here," Sophie said. She popped another piece of bacon into her mouth and grinned at me.

"I don't have a big repertoire, but I do make a mean breakfast."

"Did someone say breakfast? Yes, I'd love some of those scrambled eggs. Light on the bacon though. I'm watching my figure."

Lisa appeared from the bedroom and slid onto a barstool beside Sophie.

"How did you sleep?" Sophie asked.

"Pretty well, when we eventually did get to sleep."

"I can imagine!" Sophie smiled and took a sip of her coffee.

"Get your mind out of the gutter! We were talking about living arrangements," Lisa said.

The bedroom door opened. Andrew joined them in the kitchen. "And I want Lisa to come live with me till she finds a place closer to the hospital. Especially if you two are getting married."

"It would make sense. But I'm not planning on moving in with Domenic until after we're married. My folks would have a fit. We have three months left on the lease," Sophie said.

"There has to be a way around this," I said. "Let me think about it."

"Let me know what you come up with. I've got to run," Andrew said.

"No breakfast?" I asked.

"No, I want to go home and change before I have to be at my office. Lisa, are you coming with me?"

"No, I'm not missing out on a cooked breakfast. I'll catch a ride with Sophie, if that's alright?"

"Thanks Domenic. Bye Sophie. I'll call *you* later." Andrew kissed Lisa and left the apartment.

"Ohhh I saw tongue then. It must be serious," Sophie teased.

"Shut up." Lisa tried to hide a grin and punched Sophie in the arm.

"I'm happy you two are getting along so well," I offered.

"It will make the wedding arrangements much easier." Sophie gave Lisa a hug.

"Eat up ladies. I've got a busy day. We're leaving in fifteen minutes."

"Arrrggghhh. I'll load the dishwasher while you finish getting ready." Sophie shoved the last forkful of the scrambled egg into her mouth, slid off the stool and pointed her finger toward the bathroom. "Lisa, go!"

"He's not serious. Fifteen minutes! How am I going to get ready in fifteen minutes?"

"Stop talking and start walking!"

"Yes, sergeant major. You're both as bad as each other."

"Get your Italian bottom moving and go brush your teeth. Now."

I headed for the master suite. As I walked down the hall, I could hear them rushing around behind me. I smiled.

I shut the bedroom door. It was going to be fun living with Sophie.

I called my mother when I got to the office.

"Mom I have a proposition for you. Could Sophie theoretically move in with you till the wedding? There was a break-in at her house, and I'm not happy for her to stay there."

"What do you mean 'theoretically'?"

"Her parents wouldn't approve of her staying with me before the wedding. I was thinking, if she said she was staying with you, then . . . "

"I'm not happy with lying to her parents. If you want her to move in with me officially, then that would be fine. We have spare rooms, and I presume it's only for a short time."

"Thanks. I'll let her know. I'm looking at all possibilities."

I'm not about to add any more complications to my mother's life, by having Sophie live there. It's time to talk with someone I presume has better advice to give me.

Luc, I'm worried about Sophie and Lisa staying in that house. Sophie doesn't want to move in with me because her parents wouldn't approve. My mother has offered a spare room for Sophie to stay with her, but I don't want to cause her extra work. Then there's still the issue of Lisa. They have three months left on the lease and I'm hoping to convince Sophie to marry me by then.

I might have a solution for you.

I was counting on it.

I could have a Demon move into the house. I can assure you the girls will be safer.

It won't be hard to explain that to Sophie, but what will I tell Lisa?

He's a friend of the family and needs temporary accommodation. Maybe he's a web designer, so he'll be working from home twenty-four-seven.

You think that would work?

You can try.

The Demon I'm thinking of would pass for one of those degenerates who seem to always be hanging out on their street. He's young, he's fit, he's extremely strong and he has shown he wants to move up in my organization. This would be an ideal assignment for him.

I'll let you know.

❧

I called Sophie and left a message. She called back on her break.

"Luc has a solution to the living scenario for the next couple of months."

"He has?"

"He suggested placing one of his trusted men in your house to keep an eye on the place, and make sure you're both safe."

"A trusted man? And you're okay with this? Do you know him?"

"No, I don't, but does that matter? Do you honestly think that Luc would ask someone to do this if he doubted him?"

"I imagine not. I guess it's worth a try. I'll check with Lisa. I suppose we could clear out the room downstairs we use for storage. It's very small."

"He won't need a lot of space."

"Is he going to pay for food etc."

"He won't need food."

"Why?"

"He won't be eating."

"Is he from Hell too?"

"Yes."

"I wish I hadn't asked that question."

"Tell Lisa that I have a family friend who needs a roof over his head for a couple of months, and in turn he will be all the security you need."

§

Lisa was easier to convince than Sophie thought. She told me they moved the boxes into the garage storeroom to clear a space in the bedroom. They made up the double bed and pushed it against the wall and set up a makeshift desk out of a camping table, ready for their house guest.

Luc asked me to meet them at my apartment at seven o'clock, and I agreed to take Drake to his new assignment.

They appeared in my living room at seven precisely. I was surprised to note how healthy and alive the man accompanying Luc appeared. I would have taken him for human in any circumstance. A very well-built specimen in my opinion, and although I don't lean that way, I found him to be extremely attractive. His face was reminiscent of a Greek God, but with the body of the Terminator.

"Domenic this is Drake. I'm sorry to do this but I have to leave you to it. Keep me informed if there's any trouble."

"Yes sir." Drake saluted.

Luc disappeared. There was an awkward silence for a few seconds.

Drake was a little taller than me. I estimated him to be about six feet six inches tall. He had black hair pulled back in a short ponytail that curled into the nape of his thick neck and dark eyes. He was clean shaven, with not even a hint of stubble and was built like a linebacker. The black tee shirt he wore could barely contain the muscles underneath. Tattoos of snakes and skulls and blood red roses made their way up from the leather wrist bands he wore, wound around both his arms and disappeared under the sleeves of his tee shirt. The head of one snake reappeared on his neck, fangs showing. Anyone crazy enough to take him on deserved a medal.

"I expect Luc has filled you in on all the details?"

"Yes sir."

"Please drop the sir. Domenic's fine. Is this all you have?" I pointed to a backpack and laptop bag.

"I travel light."

"Let's go. Sophie and Lisa are expecting you."

The usual suspects were out by their cars in the street. I got out and walked around my car to the sidewalk. I could hear the comments but chose to ignore them. Drake took his time climbing out of the passenger's side and turned toward the men in the street. He scanned them all and the murmuring died down.

"Everything okay?" I asked as we walked up the path to the house.

"I have a photographic memory. They're all logged in now."

"Good to know."

Sophie opened the front door. Her eyes widened. Yes, I knew what she was thinking. She stood back and allowed us to enter the living room. Lisa called out to Sophie then appeared from the kitchen. She stopped talking mid-sentence and blinked a couple of times. Drake was having a profound effect on everyone it seems.

"Drake, this is Sophie. And this is Lisa."

Drake nodded to both of them. The room suddenly seemed smaller, with the four of us standing in the middle of the living room. Drake took up more than his fair share of the space.

Finally, Sophie spoke. "I'll show you the room. Sorry it's so small, but it's at the front of the house and has a big window you can open for fresh air, and you don't have to do anything but sleep in there." She swallowed and cleared her throat. "Unless you want to." She pushed open the door. Drake squeezed past her and put his backpack and laptop on the bed. I imagined his feet would be hanging off the end if he tried to sleep there.

"It's fine," Drake said. He glanced around taking inventory.

"Let us know if you need anything else. We put this together in a hurry."

"I'm going to check the perimeter." Drake disappeared out the front door. We returned to the living room.

I could tell both girls were dying to say something.

"Oh My God he's gorgeous!" Lisa said.

"He's huge. He won't fit in that bed!" Sophie said.

"I'm sure he'll manage. It's only for a short while," I said.

"Sophie said he works from home?"

"He's a web designer."

"He doesn't look like any nerdy tech guy I know. If you said he was a bodybuilder or a strong man in a circus troupe, I'd believe you more," Lisa said.

"What do you mean?"

"Come on! I'm not stupid. You hired a professional bodyguard to take care of us, didn't you?" Lisa said

"You're too smart for me Lisa."

"I knew it."

"But it's our little secret, okay. At least this way I'll be sure you're safe."

"My lips are sealed. Except for Andrew."

"Of course."

"He's not going to be too crazy about Adonis sharing the house. But a little jealousy isn't a bad thing." Lisa had a big smile on her face.

In truth, I wasn't too keen on Adonis sharing their house either. But I kept my opinions to myself. Luc had come up with the goods and I was more than grateful.

"All good?" I asked Drake when he returned.

"As good as it's going to get. I moved the ladder into the storeroom at the back of the garage. We'll need a key for that door," Drake said.

"Oh, we have one," Lisa said.

"Then let's use it." He held out his hand for the key.

Lisa disappeared and came back with a key ring, and a loose key.

"These are your house keys. And the garage key."

"Does anyone else have a key to this house?"

"Only the landlord. As far as I know. Apart from the three of us now."

"How did the burglary happen?"

"He broke the glass in the back door. There was a key inside, in the door. Those keys you have in your hand actually."

"No more keys left in door, okay?"

"Okay," both girls said in unison, scolded like naughty little children.

Drake went into his bedroom and closed the door.

"Does he ever smile?" Lisa asked.

"He doesn't get paid to smile," Sophie said. "Thank you." She stood on tiptoe and kissed my cheek. "How about a glass of wine?"

"Good idea."

Sophie went into the kitchen and returned with three glasses of red wine balanced very precariously in her hands. Lisa and I took one.

"Cheers. Can we arrange a time to go and pick out a ring? I feel as if everything has been put on hold because of the last few days," I said.

"I'm not scheduled on call, until the afternoon tomorrow. Does that suit?"

"Perfect. I have no surgery scheduled. Can you meet me? I'll text you the time and the address. It's not a big store. We have to make an appointment for a private showing."

"Intriguing."

"I want you to have something special. I operated on the jeweler's wife. He's an outstanding craftsman, with a great reputation. He'll have a collection of rings for you to try. If you don't find anything you like, he'll make one for you."

"I feel very special."

"I want you to be happy with your choice. You're going to be looking at it every day."

"I'm very lucky."

"No. I'm the lucky one!"

Lisa got up off the sofa, pretending to vomit.

"Get a room, you two! I'm going to make dinner."

Sophie laughed. "You wait till it's your turn."

"I'll go so you can have dinner." I headed for the front door and knocked on Drake's bedroom door. He opened it a couple of inches. I handed him my business card.

"Here's my number. Leave a message if you can't reach me, and I'll call back."

"Yes sir . . . sorry. Domenic." He closed the door.

On the doorstep, I pulled Sophie into my arms, enjoying her perfume and the warmth of her body against mine. "I'll see you tomorrow." I kissed her lips lightly.

"I can't wait. I'm very excited to try on some rings."

"Lock the door behind me."

"Yes sir."

"I'm warming to 'sir'."

"Don't get any ideas. I was being facetious."

36

SOPHIE

End of May 2017

"*I* can't stop looking at it."

"I'm pleased you like it." Domenic squeezed my right hand.

"Like it? I love it. Look at it sparkle."

"I'm glad we also picked out the wedding rings today. I'll collect them next week. He'll give me a call when they're engraved."

"I can't wait to show your mum."

"She sounded excited when I called to say we were coming over."

"I'd like to visit my parents tonight. Are you up for it?"

"Of course."

"Can you pick me up from the hospital after my shift. I know it will be late, but I want you to meet them properly, now that it's official. And to show them my ring."

We pulled up at the gate. It slid open. Cameron walked forward to my side of the car. I lowered the window.

"Congratulations. Aimee said you have the ring?"

"Yes. Isn't it stunning?" I held up my hand.

"It certainly is." He stepped back and we drove on.

Aimee was waiting on the front step. She hugged me, and then Domenic, and wanted to see my ring.

"It is wonderful. And so pretty on your slim fingers," Aimee said.

"Thank you."

"Go on down to the sunroom. I've laid out some sandwiches and cold drinks."

The table in the sunroom was set up for a small buffet lunch. A large vase of colorful blooms sat in the center of the table, with a vintage tea set spread out on an embroidered tablecloth. It was so sweet of Aimee to want to do something special. We couldn't have alcohol because both Domenic and I were going to be working later in the afternoon.

"Hello Sophie, hello darling. Congratulations. Let me see this wonderful ring." Harper called out, as she walked into the room. She examined my outstretched hand.

"Isn't it stunning?" I said.

"It's magnificent. Well done on selecting a beautifully designed engagement ring."

"Thanks Mom," Domenic said.

"Aimee has put on a lovely quick lunch. I know you have to get back to the hospital."

"We wanted to show you the ring right away. We're going to see my parents tonight."

"What do you think about having the garden wedding here Sophie? Domenic never got back to me about it."

"I haven't had a chance to talk about it yet," Domenic said.

"Let's talk about it now. I suggested to Domenic that we hold an intimate garden wedding for you in the grounds. We could put up a marquee. There's ample space, and Cameron has done a wonderful job with the garden. What do you think Sophie?"

"Mom, we really need time to talk about it and give Sophie a chance to consider it and make up her mind. She might've dreamt of a big church wedding, and a huge reception." Domenic looked concerned. He was glancing between me and his mother.

"I don't have to think about it. I would love a garden wedding. But isn't it going to be a lot of work for you, and Aimee and Cameron?"

"I have offered to pay for help. Aimee wants to make the wedding breakfast," Domenic said. He picked up a sandwich and started to eat. He looked relieved.

"That's settled then. We're having our first wedding on the property. Oh, it will be wonderful. We'll have such fun Sophie, choosing all the decorations, planning the menu."

"What am I going to contribute?" Domenic asked.

"You can pay for it," Harper said.

We all laughed.

"Dad, Mum, I think you know Domenic Ericson. My fiancé." I couldn't hold back the smile every time I said that F word.

Domenic approached my dad and shook his hand. He didn't have a problem touching him, because he already knew all there was to know about his medical history. He kissed my mother's cheek. My mother on the other hand, was new to Domenic and I imagine the contact would have been enlightening for him.

"We were wondering when we'd get to meet you. As Sophie's young man, and not as the doctor who saved my husband's life," Mum said.

"Our lass kept you quiet. We only just found out that you two had been seeing each other. It was a real surprise," Dad said.

"A pleasant surprise I hope," Domenic said.

"Well, I was thrilled when she told me she was seeing a doctor. Of course, we'd always hoped she would wait till she was a little older to get married and settle down. But if my daughter has chosen you, we're sure you must be a kind and thoughtful man. Our Sophie does not suffer fools gladly," Mum said.

"I can assure you I will take very good care of your daughter," Domenic said

"Let me see the ring darlin'. Come on." My mother took my hand in hers. "Aye it's beautiful."

"It must have cost a pretty penny!" Dad said.

"Dad! You're not supposed to talk about money. It's the mark of commitment."

"Commitment comes at a fair price now. I remember when your mother and I were about to be engaged. I couldn't afford a ring, and I worked two jobs to get the money before I proposed."

"I thought he was never going to propose, and that he had his eye on another lass in the village!"

"No other lass was as beautiful or as talented in the kitchen as you. And didn't I know it. I was the lucky one," Dad said. My mum and dad exchanged a knowing smile.

I breathed a sigh of relief as the conversation moved from discussing the ring and the engagement, to talk of my father's health. I hadn't been looking forward to this evening and introduction, but it hadn't been as stressful as I'd thought. Domenic was charming them, and that was no easy feat, as my father was super critical of every boyfriend that I had ever brought home to meet him.

When it was time to leave, I hugged my dad and he whispered in my ear. "You've got a good one there. I can feel it in my waters."

"Thanks Dad. I really believe I do."

"Now don't be strangers. We should have a party and invite all the family over. When your father is fully recovered of course," Mum said.

"We'll see them all at the wedding soon. You don't need to bother with a party."

"What do you mean *soon*? Why the rush?" Dad asked.

"Oh. Does this mean what I think it means?" My mum clutched her pearls.

"Have you taken advantage of my daughter?" Dad's smile had disappeared.

"No Mum. No Dad. I'm not pregnant. Keep your hat on." I took Domenic's arm. "We're just excited to start our life together."

"What do *your* folks think about this?" Dad asked Domenic.

"My mother is happy for us. She's offered to have the wedding in her garden on the estate."

"An estate. Oh Sophie, how posh." Mum was beaming at me.

"We're going to have a small wedding. We're not inviting half of Ireland Mum. Just immediate family, okay."

"Okay dear, whatever you say."

"A posh wedding. That's going to cost a pretty penny," Dad said.

"Don't worry Mr O'Connor. I'm paying for this wedding. And the one job I have will suffice." Domenic smiled at my dad, and he smiled back. Relieved I imagined.

37

HARPER

Middle of July 2017

There were men coming out of the Gatehouse. Lots of men. More men than I imagined could fit into the Gatehouse at any one time. They were tall, dark-haired, well-built men dressed in black pants, white business shirts, and wearing fitted gold brocade vests, all marching in time to a silent beat. They stopped and stood to attention, lined up by the wall, while Drake marched up and down presumably giving them a list of their duties for the day.

I witnessed all this from the front steps where I waited for the florist and her assistants to arrive with the table arrangements for the bridal marquee.

"Why are you down here, wearing a silk robe and not getting dressed?" Luc appeared beside me.

"I offered to wait for the florist. I needed some fresh air. Aimee's busy in the kitchen."

"I'll get someone else to help. They should be going around the back."

A man broke free of the line beside the wall and came marching up to the house. It dawned on me then that Luc could communicate with them, as he does with all Demons.

"Are all these men from . . . ?" I let the last word hang in the air.

"Yes."

"I was concerned when they were all coming out of the Gatehouse. I hadn't noticed them going in."

"There's a gateway to the underworld in the Gatehouse."

"How did I not know this?"

"It isn't open all the time. Only when necessary. Cameron and Aimee have to be able to return from time to time. They don't have wings. Only a winged being can take them otherwise."

"Ah. It makes sense now."

"You didn't think I would allow strangers on the property, did you? I can trust these men. Drake selected them."

"Then I'll leave you to it."

The man had reached the front steps. He looked to be mid to late twenties in appearance, about six feet tall, and although he was handsome by anyone's standards, he wore a guarded expression. Little wonder. He probably thought he had done something wrong to be called away from the group.

"Cole, this is Mrs Ericson. It's her son who's being married today."

"Ma'am." Cole gave a slight bow of his head.

"Good afternoon Cole."

"You will be assigned to the front door, to accept deliveries and greet guests when they arrive, and direct them around the side of the house, to the rear. The guests do not enter the house. Understood." Luc said. "Drake will send someone to valet the cars."

"Yes sir." Cole stood to attention by the door.

"Also, I would like you to be specifically attentive to any needs Mrs Ericson may have. She will call on you for help if required."

"Yes sir. You can count on me." Cole turned to me and gave another slight bow of his head. "Ma'am."

Luc closed the front door. "You can leave it to him now. No one will enter."

"Let me just say how handsome you look today." I touched Luc's cheek with the palm of my hand. He tried to stay solemn, but his eyes twinkled and accepted the compliment.

"Same black suit."

"No. There's something different today. Black suit yes. Same suit no. This fabric is stunning, the cut is beautiful. Don't pretend to me that you haven't gone to any trouble. Even your beard looks trimmed to perfection. And not a hair out of place." I could see that Luc was clenching his jaw and trying not to smile. I noticed, and he appreciated that I noticed every little detail. How many years had we been friends, had we been close? He can't fool me. He loves Domenic as much as I do, and he's as proud as any father would be on this day, I'm sure of that.

Luc kissed my cheek and disappeared before my eyes. I made my way upstairs to the master suite where Amber, the hairdresser who was also the beautician, was making final adjustments to Sophie's make-up. The door was open, and I could see Sophie's reflection in the dresser mirror opposite to where she was seated. Her red hair was swept up on top of her head, clasped with an assortment of pearls and ribbons, with a few soft tendrils curling down the back of her neck. The small glittering tiara which would hold the short veil had been pinned in place. Sophie's maid of honor came forward to help. Lisa was already made up, with her long black hair fashioned in an elegant bun on top of her head, and dressed in layers of soft pink chiffon, which floated around her and fell to just above her matching satin heels. The sleeveless empire line bodice crossed at the front and gave a lovely vee neckline to enhance her décolletage. A short single strand of pearls and matching stud earrings completed the ensemble.

Sophie stood and removed the white cotton robe she had worn whilst having her makeup applied. Lisa and Amber helped Sophie step into her dress and attached the veil, flipping it back exposing her face and being careful to avoid smudging her make-up or spoiling her carefully styled hair. Lisa fastened the many covered buttons up the back of her wedding dress and adjusted the train. They each took a step to the sides to allow her to view the dress in the full length, over-sized silver framed mirror leaning against the bedroom wall.

Sophie looked stunningly beautiful, fragile, almost translucent, with her fine bone structure, fair skin and bright red hair, indicative of her Irish ancestors. The strapless fitted long white dress, with an overlay of delicate lace was one of a kind. The short train of single layer lace fanned out behind her. Sophie's overseas family members had sent her a bolt of Irish lace, and we had a dressmaker in Beverly Hills create something very special, which incorporated her rich heritage. We all had tears in our eyes. It was time to give Sophie my gift.

"You look absolutely stunning my dear. I know you selected some costume jewelry to match your dress, but I want you to consider something borrowed to wear today. My contribution to the tradition. These diamond earrings were given to me by Domenic's father. If you wear them today, I'll feel he's with us in some way. Yes, I would like them back." I laughed and Sophie grinned back at me. "I also want to give you something new. A diamond necklace from Luc. This is his gift to you, and it will be the perfect accompaniment to your dress, and of course the earrings. Yes, we conspired together for just the right piece to wear. Now, you just need something old and something blue." I opened up the black velvet box to display the diamonds nestled in the cream satin lining.

"My goodness, I'm going to cry." Sophie fanned the air in front of her face to ward off the tears. "Of course I'll wear the earrings. That's a lovely gesture. Thank you. And the necklace is divine. I'll be sure to thank Luc later." Sophie gently lifted the delicate gold necklace studded with five diamonds out of the box. I fastened it onto her neck, while she attached the earrings.

"I have something blue for you." Lisa held up a white garter with tiny bluebirds embroidered on it.

"Oh, that's darling. Thank you, Lisa." Sophie held out a bare foot and Lisa slipped the garter up her leg to her thigh. She stepped into her white satin heels. Lisa straightened the hem of the dress.

"You need something old," I said, searching for something on the dressing table.

There was a blast of cool air in the room. The curtains fluttered but the window was not open. The ghostly figure of Maggie Mae appeared in the corner. She was smiling but had tears in her eyes, which she dabbed with a scrap of white fabric. Everyone stood transfixed by the appearance of this apparition. Amber clasped her hand over her mouth to stifle a squeal. The door flew open, and Maggie Mae disappeared. A piece of cloth fluttered to the floor. I picked it up. It was a monogrammed handkerchief with the letters M.M.O. embroidered on the edge.

"I think you have your something old." I handed the scrap of fabric to Sophie, who lifted the hem of her skirt once more and tucked the thin handkerchief into the elastic of the garter.

"I'm all set now. Something from every era of my family. The lace from my O'Connor Aunts, the handkerchief from my ancestor, and the diamonds from my new family," Sophie said.

"Hang on. No one seems surprised by what just happened?" Amber exclaimed.

"Maggie Mae is an ancestor of Sophie's. She's appeared before!" Lisa replied.

"This is a first for me. I've never seen a ghost. Wait till I tell my husband, he loves this stuff." Amber still looked shocked. "But I bet he won't believe me."

My phone bleeped in my pocket. I'd received a text to say the photographer had arrived downstairs to take some shots of the girls before the wedding. Aimee brought him up, I left them to it and moved to the guest bedroom with Amber to finish getting ready.

Amber's hands shook a little and it took her a while to get settled again. Seeing a ghost will do that to you. My hair and makeup had been done, but we refreshed the lipstick, and Amber pinned some fresh flowers in my hair. I slipped off my robe and stepped into the sleeveless fitted knee length dress, with a lace bodice, in a dusty rose color. Amber zipped me up. As I stepped into nude heels, she held open the matching cropped jacket. I was checking my earrings in the mirror when Lucia entered the room.

Lucia was a vision in peach chiffon. Her long dark chestnut hair had also been styled in a bun on top of her head, she wore a dress similar in style to Lisa's, but it was her sparkling eyes and pink cheeks which drew my attention. She was flushed and smiling like I'd never seen her smiling before.

"Mom, have you *seen* all the gorgeous men in the garden? Luscious does not adequately describe them!" she gushed.

"Yes, I *have* seen them. Luc brought them to help with the wedding guests."

"They can help me any time."

"Please remember this is your brother's wedding and behave like a lady."

"As if I'm going to forget. I'd better go, I'm supposed to be with Lisa helping Sophie." Lucia rushed off, leaving a light trail of fragrant perfume in her wake.

"I think she's running a little late on that part," Amber said. "Lisa has it covered."

"Teenagers!" I laughed.

I checked my image in the mirror. Gold studs in my ears, my gold heart locket nestled in the vee neckline of my dress, my watch on my wrist in the event I had to time anything. I looked around, grabbed my purse, and stuffed it with a stack of tissues I knew I was going to need. I touched the locket, rubbing the warm gold between my thumb and forefinger, closed my eyes and sent up a silent prayer to Richard, wishing he was here to see his firstborn get married.

"Okay, let's go downstairs Amber."

"I'll get going and leave you to it," Amber said.

"Nonsense. There's a glass of champagne with your name on it."

"I shouldn't stay."

"Why not? Don't you want to watch the wedding? Or do you have another function today?"

"No. I'm done for the day. Okay, I would love to watch the happy couple getting married."

"And you shall. I want to thank you for all your hard work today. I've paid your invoice. But here's a little something extra you and your husband might enjoy." I handed her an envelope containing a gift certificate for a hotel in town. "Remember what goes on in the Ericson household, stays here."

She pulled out the voucher and gasped. "You're buying my silence with an all-expenses-paid night at this hotel?"

"Sure am."

"My lips are well and truly sealed."

"Good. Then we will use you again. When required."

Downstairs, I directed Amber toward the garden, where an usher stood holding a tray of champagne. In the kitchen Aimee was rushing about like a mad woman, issuing orders to a half a dozen catering staff in smart white uniforms and a couple of men in Chef's hats. She looked to be in her element.

"Aimee, it's time to get dressed. You don't want to miss the bride walking down the aisle."

"I'll get right on it. By the way, I put Mr O'Connor in the sunroom, ready for his daughter. One of the young ushers took Mrs O'Connor into the garden to be seated," Aimee said. I sent a text with these details to Lisa upstairs.

Although I'd met Sophie's parents, Shamus and Kate, at a dinner Domenic had arranged, I didn't know them well enough to want to go into the sunroom alone to make small talk to her father. Nerves were getting the better of me, and I imagined he would feel the same. On cue, Domenic arrived, with Andrew his best man. They entered the sunroom which took the pressure off, and I held back for a few minutes considering my options.

Luc appeared beside me and gave a low whistle.

"Wow. You're taking my breath away. You look gorgeous," Luc

said.

"Thank you. I hope I look good enough for the mother of the groom."

"You look better than any mother of the groom I've *ever* encountered."

"And you would have encountered how many?"

"Just let's say enough to know the difference, and to put you at the top of the list."

I knew it was cheesy, but I was thrilled with Luc's flattering compliments. He hardly ever failed to make me feel better, make me laugh, and turn a special day into a more memorable one. I wish I could make him smile when he was feeling sad. He didn't think I noticed, but I did. Acutely. There were days where his sorrow was a tangible thing in the house between us. On those days I wanted to reach out to him, but on the occasions when I had tried this tactic, he looked even more upset. I learned to just be there, or nearby, and hope my presence helped in some way.

"Shall we?" Luc offered his arm to me and we exited through the patio doors, around to the right side of the walled garden, to where rows and rows of white collapsible chairs had been set up on a large wooden floor to be used for dancing at the reception later. A string quartet, playing classical background music, had been set up off to the left near the marquee. As we strolled down the aisle festooned with flowers, I recognized a few people and said hello. There would be more time for a chat later. At the bottom of the aisle, dark green vines lush with perfumed blooms were woven through an arbor constructed for the ceremony. Luc escorted me to the front row and took his leave. I was a little surprised as I'd hoped he would sit with me to watch the wedding. But then all became clear when Domenic and Andrew walked to the front of the guests and Luc joined them. He was to be part of the wedding ceremony! They had kept that a secret from me.

My heart expanded and my eyes filled with tears, and I watched him stand tall and proud with my son and his best man, waiting for the bride to appear. I turned to see Cameron and Aimee sitting at the back of the guests and motioned for them to come and join me in the front row. They were like members of the family, had helped to bring my children up and loved them as if they were their own. They deserved to be by my side. I squeezed Aimee's hand as she took the seat next to mine. She looked lovely in a navy coat dress and white pillbox hat. Cameron, superbly dressed in a morning suit, was attempting to keep a British "stiff upper lip", but he was losing the battle. I caught a smile tugging at his mouth.

The music changed, became louder and everyone turned and watched Lucia walking down the carpeted walkway, which was running from the house, down the aisle to the floral arbor. She held a small posy of white flowers tied with ribbons a shade deeper than her peach dress, and stared straight ahead, stepping slowly in time to the classical music, obviously taking her bridesmaid roll seriously. My little girl had grown up. More tears sprung to my eyes, and I dabbed them away. She was a beautiful young woman now and she carried herself with poise and grace.

Lisa appeared behind her, holding a similar posy of white flowers, the ribbons a shade deeper than her pink dress. Her dress fluttered as she walked, the soft chiffon floating out around her. She looked beautiful and I could tell she was emotional but holding it together very well.

Then all the guests craned their necks to see Sophie appear on her father's arm, cradling a profusion of white flowers in her bouquet, with her veil covering her face. They walked through the garden, then stepped carefully up onto the wooden floor to take that long walk down the aisle. I chanced a glance at Domenic watching his wife-to-be approaching. I had never seen my son's face so full of wonder. If I had any doubts at all this blew them all away. He loved her, it was written all over his face, and in the moisture in his eyes, which he dashed away quickly. I hadn't noticed Fiona, the celebrant, until she stepped forward to officiate. Fiona was stylishly dressed in a sky-blue suit of Thai silk and had her platinum hair fashioned in a French roll. Her glasses were hanging on a silver chain around her neck.

Fiona smiled warmly at Domenic and Sophie, who were now

standing side by side. She placed the glasses on the bridge of her nose and addressed the guests, welcoming them to the marriage of Domenic Ericson and Sophie O'Connor. She then asked who would give away the bride. Sophie's father answered, lifted back her veil, kissed her cheek and held her in his arms a few seconds longer. I don't know what he whispered to her, but I noticed she nodded, before she turned to Domenic. When Sophie's father gave away his daughter, by passing over her hand to her future husband, I noticed Domenic stood tall and proud.

The ceremony went quite quickly. I was thankful the event was being filmed, because I was lost in thoughts and memories of Domenic growing up, of my own wedding to Richard, and of all the events in the future and the celebrations I would be attending on my own. Of course, I could count on Luc. If he was available. But it's not the same as having my husband here with me. I tugged on my heart necklace, and it fell into my hands. The clasp on the chain was loose with the constant wear. I really needed to get it fixed. I quickly fastened it once more around my neck.

I heard the words "You may kiss your bride." And I came back to earth to see Domenic press his lips to Sophie's, their first kiss as man and wife. They turned to the guests and held their joined hands in the air triumphantly.

My son was now a husband, and I had a new daughter. Life was richer by the minute.

LUC

How I've kept my hands to myself today I do not know. Harper looked so beautiful and elegant, yet so emotional. I wanted to sweep her off her feet, take her to the bedroom we had shared, make passionate love to her and bring back the happiness to her eyes. If only.

But no, I had to be strong, to do the right thing, provide a strong arm for support, and in no uncertain terms, keep a friendly distance. I couldn't slip from this platonic guise although I desperately wanted to. By the look on her face, she'd been surprised and delighted to see me stand with Domenic. I was honored when he'd asked me, and we agreed to keep it between ourselves until the ceremony. I watched Harper when they said their vows, and I knew by that far-away-look in her eyes that she was thinking of her own wedding. She held the necklace tightly and it comforted her, yet I knew she had no idea why. My heart thudded faster, knowing that the tiny piece of metal contained the best years of our lives together as a couple.

If only things could've been different. I've often wished that I'd held Harper's hand and offered words of love back in the time when it was possible, in front of witnesses . . . not God . . . he cares nothing for my current state of mind. Harper is my love, Domenic, my stepson,

Lucia, my daughter. *My family.* Yet I have been denied that pleasure for so many years. And to what end. Is it working? Am I holding the demons of Hell at bay? For it's my belief that each day, each year there seems to be more chaos on Earth that I alone can control.

For now, I need to push my concerns to the side, and concentrate on making this day memorable for Domenic and Sophie.

39

DOMENIC

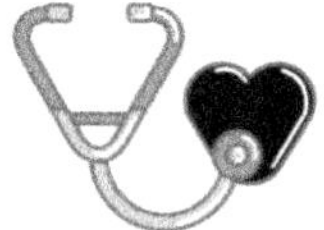

The day has come. The day I was both longing for it and dreading at the same time. Lots of friends, members of Sophie's family I have never met and a few work colleagues from the hospital, all would be expecting me to shake their hands today and I don't think I can go through with absorbing all that information into my brain.

I nod my head at those I pass on the way to the arbor and catch the eye of Fiona McGill the celebrant standing discretely off to one side.

Fiona whispered, "It's okay. You look a little like a deer caught in the headlights. Take a deep breath."

As instructed, I inhaled deeply and tried to calm my mind from racing. I watched Luc escorting my beautiful mother to her seat in the front row. Her puzzled expression when Luc left her, gave way to joy when she realized he was standing with me for the ceremony. Luc has been my constant support from the time I was born, he knows me better than anyone else and I wanted to acknowledge it.

The change in music jolted me out of my reminiscing. I turned with everyone else to watch Lucia walking down the aisle. My baby sister has grown up. She's an elegant young lady today, no mischief in her eyes, totally concentrating on the job at hand.

219

You look beautiful Lucia. I'm so proud of you.
Don't distract me. I don't want to fall over.
You won't fall over. I can see the determination on your face.
I'm so happy for you, big brother.
Thank you, that means a lot.
I'm going to miss you.
I'm not going anywhere.
You're gaining a wife today. You won't have time for me.
I'll always have time for my little sister. Never fear.
Promise?
I promise.

Lisa stepped into the aisle, also looking beautiful, and I glanced at Andrew to see him beaming. She was looking straight ahead, trying not to be distracted, but the pink flush of her cheeks indicated to me that she was aware of Andrew's admiration.

Then I caught my first glimpse of Sophie, approaching on her father's arm, and I couldn't breathe. Stunning did not adequately describe how beautiful she looked to me. A short veil covered her face, but I could see her eyes searching for me. As soon as we locked eyes my heart felt as if it would leap from my chest with love for her. We were both nervous, but we had each other now.

When her father lifted her veil, kissed her cheek and placed her hand in mine, I became calm, overriding all my concerns.

I answered when spoken to and followed instructions and then it was time to say my vows. I pulled a few notecards from my jacket pocket, took a deep breath, and faced Sophie. I tried to imagine we were the only ones in the world, no one else existed, and these words were for her ears only.

"Today I'm marrying my best friend. I consider myself lucky to have found someone who knows me intimately, accepts me with all my flaws and yet loves me anyway. Being there for you in sickness and in health goes without saying. Sophie, I promise to be there for every joyful moment, to allow you to grow to be the wonderful wife and mother you are destined to be, to celebrate your success and cheer you on in all you do. I promise to also be there for any heartache, to soothe when I can, to be supportive and to try to make you laugh. You are my one and only. The one I had hoped to find. I love you more than words can say."

Sophie looked at me with love and I knew beyond any shadow of a doubt she could see into my heart. I wanted to give her the world. When she spoke, I tried very hard to concentrate and not miss one single word.

"My life changed the day I met you. I thought nursing was my chosen path and my life would be dedicated to caring for others. But you've shown me that it's just as important to allow someone to care for me. You've opened my eyes to an unseen world of possibilities, you've taught me that there are two sides to every story, and then there's the truth. You've shown me the kind of love found in fairy tales, when the handsome prince comes and sweeps the heroine off her feet to live happily ever after. Domenic, I promise to support you through thick and thin, and on whatever path you take. To cherish you. I promise to laugh with you, to remember to dance under the stars, and never forget that we are stronger together than apart. I didn't know how much space there was in my heart to love someone. It turns out that my heart is full to bursting with love for you."

Fiona was talking and I dragged my gaze away from Sophie to finish the ceremony. And then she announced the words I had been longing to hear. "You may kiss your bride." I bent my head and kissed my wife, and due to the many onlookers, it was the sweetest, chaste kiss we had exchanged. We raised our joined hands triumphantly and walked down the aisle.

Well-wishers came forward holding out their hands and I gritted my teeth. Sophie held my hand in hers. People touched me, slapped me on the shoulder or patted me on the back, and that wasn't an issue on top of my jacket. But I noticed when women kissed or patted my cheek, I wasn't getting the download of information that usually occurred. Sophie broke away to hug her mother and the next person who shook my hand, passed over their medical history. I grabbed Sophie's hand once more. She gave me a curious look.

"Please keep holding my hand. Otherwise, I'm going to have to refuse to shake hands with this crowd of people." I whispered in her ear. "I'm not getting the downloads with your hand in mine."

"How is that possible?" she whispered. She looked shocked.

"I don't know, but I'm not looking a gift horse in the mouth. You are my saving grace. In more ways than one, it seems."

Sophie did not leave my side or let go of my left hand. When we had reached the end of the aisle of guests, we broke away to have professional photographs taken in the front garden, in the sunroom and by the wedding car Cameron had arranged for us. In the meantime, our guests were being offered glasses of champagne and escorted to the marquee so that the chairs could be folded up and decorations could be set up around the dancefloor.

40

SOPHIE

We did it. We got married. After all the rushing and preparing and lists made and invitations sent and accepted, we finally tied the knot. I'll admit I was nervous and scared and had panic attacks before the ceremony. But once I arrived at Domenic's side and he looked into my eyes, calm descended, and I knew beyond a shadow of a doubt that we were doing the right thing.

Now I'm a married woman with a husband who has just found out I have a physiological effect on his body! Why is it happening? How is that even possible? For now, I need to park my questions and concentrate on the professional photographs and the reception.

Domenic put his arm around my waist and led me through the house to the front garden, where the bridal party was waiting. On the front porch Lisa produced a make-up bag with a mirror and I refreshed my lipstick. Cameron was by the limousine to lend a hand, dressed as the chauffeur, and we got some wonderful shots outside by the car, in the garden, and then inside the sunroom, before it was time to return to our guests.

Lisa and Lucia followed me upstairs to freshen up before the reception, and of course to compare notes. We unfastened and removed my train, because it was going to be an issue on the dance-floor later.

"Okay girls how did I do? I managed to give the whole speech without stumbling over my words. Did it sound alright?"

"It was more than alright. It was beautiful," Lisa said, hanging the lace train over the back of a chair.

"I watched Dom. He was really emotional. I could tell," Lucia said.

"I loved Domenic's vows. It was so sweet when he said, 'Today I'm marrying my best friend.' Tears filled my eyes then." Lisa said, reapplying a layer of lipstick. "And your Godfather taking his place standing by Domenic's side. That was so special Lucia."

"Mom was so happy Luc was standing with Dom. We didn't tell her. It was supposed to be a surprise."

"And talk about surprises. Did you notice all the gorgeous men down there? Did someone hire them from a local strip joint? They are all built like . . . wow!" Lisa giggled.

"Lisa! Don't let Andrew hear you. Aren't you spoken for?" I asked.

"I can look. I'm not married."

"Yet!"

"Right! I'm not married *yet*. So therefore, I can look," Lisa said.

"You're not the only one looking, I can assure you," Lucia said.

We all laughed.

"Thank you so much for being here for me. It means a lot." I hugged them both.

"Are you kidding? I wouldn't have missed this wedding for the world." Lisa laughed. "The champagne alone would have cost a fortune!"

"And I'm so happy for you and my brother. He's changed since he met you. He doesn't have time to pick on me as much. And for that I'm grateful."

"Come on then ladies. Let's hustle. We'd better get back downstairs, before they send out a search party." I picked up my bridal bouquet and ushered them out of the room.

❧

Aimee had orchestrated a spectacular wedding feast. Each course was delicious and beautifully presented. After the speeches, as the sun was going down, the ushers opened up the entire side of the marquee to allow easy transition from the tables to the dancefloor. They had set up potted trees around the perimeter, decorated with tiny lights, and a small stage for the band. A singer had joined the string quartet, and she sang the introduction of the song we had chosen for our first dance. Domenic took my hand and we walked to the center of the dancefloor and had our first dance as man and wife. Then couples joined us on the dancefloor, and I looked around at our family and friends, all happily smiling and enjoying our wedding, and felt very blessed.

When it was time to throw the bouquet all the female guests lined up on the edge of the dancefloor. I stood near the orchestra, turned my back and threw it high into the air. I turned to see it land easily in Lisa's hands. She looked delighted by this turn of events, especially when Andrew came over and planted a big kiss on her lips. Maybe there will be another wedding in the coming year. I looked around for Lucia, but she wasn't in the crowd of women who had scrambled for the bouquet. She'd been paying attention to one of the ushers in particular. I couldn't see him either.

"Honey, I think you should go and find your sister. I have a feeling she's snuck off with one of the ushers, and she might get into trouble if your Mum finds out."

"I'll go and find her," Domenic said.

They returned a few minutes later, and I was glad to note Lucia was smiling, had her arm through Domenic's and didn't have a hair out of place.

"All good," I asked Domenic after he dropped off Lucia to sit beside his mother.

"They were only talking in the kitchen."

"I didn't want her to get into trouble tonight."

"Thank you. She's perfectly capable of doing that any day of the week. But it was a good idea to bring her back to join the party."

Luc approached and asked me to dance. Domenic went in search of his mother.

"You look stunning." Luc led me onto the dance floor.

"Thank you. It has been a wonderful day. I know I should be tired, but I feel full of excited energy."

"It's been an eventful day for all of us."

"Harper looks so happy dancing with Domenic."

"Arranging this wedding has been good for Harper, I think. It has certainly brought a lot of life back to the house."

"You've all welcomed me into this family, and I can't thank you enough. I'm excited for the future."

"The welfare and happiness of this family is paramount to me. I will go to the ends of the Earth to insure they are all protected."

I knew this to be true. I had only scratched the surface of what was possible in this family.

"I want to thank you for my beautiful diamond necklace. It's exquisite."

"My pleasure. I wanted you to have something meaningful on this day. I selected each and every one of the five diamonds myself. Plucked from deep in the center of the Earth. Each one represents a member of the family. When you have a child, I will add another stone."

"That's very generous of you."

"I had a craftsman with magical powers make this necklace. He has woven a spell over it. The necklace connects you to all of us."

"Does this necklace have anything to do with Domenic being able to touch others without sensory overload when he holds my hand."

"I imagine it does."

"Then I shall wear it when I want to harness and magnify that connection."

"You gave him a gift today. I've never seen him smile when he's had to touch someone before. I'm sure it was an experience he won't forget in a hurry." Luc glanced over at Domenic who was dancing with Harper. They both looked happy.

"What is it about a wedding that brings families closer together?"

"I'm not an expert on weddings, or families. But I do know that there's a lot of joy in the air tonight."

"Yes. You're right. And hope for the future."

"That one gets my vote," Luc said.

41

HARPER

The bride and groom and all their guests had finally gone, and I was so ready for bed I could hardly keep my eyes open. I was halfway up the stairs when a noise from the front of the house had me turning around and heading back down again. I pulled open the front door and noticed the ushers lined up near the Gatehouse and Drake marching up and down. The ushers with Drake at the helm, had done a fabulous job today, looking after the guests, serving, waiting on tables, clearing everything into the kitchen. Then packing up and dismantling the marquee and dance floor ready for the contractors to collect in the morning. But for some reason Drake didn't look happy.

Luc appeared at my side.

"What's going on?"

"We're looking for a missing usher."

"But I thought you and Drake were connected to them all."

"We are. But he's blocking our request to return to the Gatehouse."

"How is that possible?"

"I'm not sure. Don't worry. Go to bed. Drake will handle it." Luc walked off toward Drake and the ushers.

I climbed the stairs once more and noticed an eerie flickering light showing under Lucia's door. I knocked and tried to open the door, but it wouldn't budge.

"Lucia. Lucia. Are you okay? Open the door." Goosebumps had appeared on my arms. I placed my hand on the wood which vibrated against my palm. My heart began to beat faster. There was something wrong with my daughter and she was inside a locked room. I leant over the balustrade and yelled into the void.

"Luc, can you hear me? There's something wrong up here!" Luc appeared beside me, and the door burst open. We looked on in awe at Lucia, standing in the center of the room with her arms around the neck of the usher she had been flirting with all night, their eyes closed, their lips and bodies pressed tightly together, encased in what appeared to be a sheer purple bubble.

"Lucia!" Luc called out angrily, and the room shook. The bubble disappeared. The usher appeared stunned as if awakening from a dream. Lucia looked annoyed.

"Are you trying to give me a heart attack Lucia? What was that?" I asked.

"She set up a force field around them. No wonder he couldn't hear Drake," Luc said.

"You shouldn't have brought him up here, young lady, and you know it," I said.

"Go!" Luc yelled at the usher, who sprinted past me. "As for you, Lucia, did you think we wouldn't notice he was missing."

"I just wanted some time with Ryan before he went back. I knew they wouldn't be able to find him if I created a force field around us. We were only making out. It was harmless."

"Do you realize what you've done? He'll be punished. Severely," Luc said.

"But why? It was all me. Ryan didn't know I was going to do that."

"Regardless of who's fault it was, he should never have agreed to come up here with you. Now he has to pay that price," Luc said.

"Can you talk to Drake? Tell him I created the bubble, and locked Ryan inside."

"I wasn't aware your skills had progressed to this level. We need to have a talk in the morning," Luc announced.

"I'm sorry."

"Lucia, you're turning eighteen in a week. I thought you were in trouble when I couldn't open the door. You have to start thinking more responsibly." I said. "I'm exhausted. Luc's right, we'll talk tomorrow. It's time for all of us to get some sleep."

"Goodnight Mom. Goodnight Luc."

I closed her bedroom door and stepped back quickly, caught my high heel on the carpet, and lost my footing. Luc caught me before I landed on the floor and swept me up into his arms. I had a strange sense of Déjà vu. He strode down the hall and I could feel his heart thudding again my chest, it even sounded loud in my ears. He placed me on the end of my bed. The look on his face told me he appeared to be struggling with an emotion. I reached up to clasp my necklace and realized it was gone.

"My necklace!" I felt around in the bodice of my dress. I stood up and checked the bed. "It's not here." Panic rose in my chest. "Luc, it's not here."

"Calm down. We'll find it. When did you last remember having it around your neck?"

"When I was dancing."

Luc held up his hand to stop me from talking. He was obviously communicating with the men downstairs. "They will find it. Sit down. Be calm."

"The clasp has been loose for a while. I kept meaning to get it fixed." I couldn't sit still. I began pacing the room. "I'll never forgive myself if it's gone."

I tried to remember where I'd been, and if I had noticed it after we had danced. I couldn't remember if I had it when Domenic and Sophie left the reception.

After a few minutes Luc held up his hand again. "They found it on the patio. Actually, Ryan found it. So maybe he will get a reprieve from Drake. I'll be back in a moment." Luc disappeared.

I should've done something about the faulty clasp the first time it happened, but I don't like to be without the necklace. Luc reappeared.

"Here you go." He handed the heart locket to me. He held up the faulty chain. "Tomorrow I'll take the chain to my jeweler friend who will fix it on the spot, and I will return it to you."

"Thank you." It felt good having my locket back. I reached up and laid my palm against his cheek. "What would I do without you?"

"Don't worry, you'll never have to find out. I think it's time you turned in. It's been a long day."

"A long day but a wonderful one. I have a new daughter-in-law. Didn't they make a beautiful couple?"

"They did. I was very proud of your son today. He did a wonderful job. Did he tell you that when Sophie holds his hand, and someone shakes his, he doesn't get sensory overload?"

"No. That's amazing."

"I think it has something to do with the five diamonds in the necklace. One diamond for each of us. A craftsman with special powers made the necklace for me and cast a spell over them to link us all together."

"I imagine he is feeling happy that he has a work around. Domenic has struggled with this all his life."

"I'm convinced Sophie will be a benefit to this family."

"If Maggie Mae's prediction comes true, they will have a child soon. Won't it be wonderful to have a baby in the family again?"

"Yes, it will be wonderful. You will make a beautiful grandmother."

"Well, I do have the grey hair now to fit the part."

"I don't see gray. I see strands of silver and gold."

"You never fail to make me feel better. Thank you for returning my locket."

"I'd better let you get your rest. Goodnight." Luc leant down and kissed my cheek.

I reached out and hugged him. I held on to him for a minute. He always had a calming effect on me.

"Goodnight," I whispered.

"Goodnight." Luc gave me a hug and disappeared.

I placed my heart locket on the nightstand, undressed and removed my makeup, and climbed into bed beneath the cool cotton sheets. I reached over and turned off the bedside lamp. My necklace seemed to be glowing in the subdued light. I picked it up and turned it over. There appeared to be a crack in the metal, at the clasp. It must have happened when it fell on the patio. I poked it with the tip of my nail, and it moved slightly. I would have to get Luc to take the locket to his friend tomorrow to repair it too. It would be hard to be without it.

I lay back on the pillow clasping the locket where it normally lay nestled between my breasts. I wished Richard had been here today to see his son married. I was drifting off to sleep when I realized the necklace was heating up. I lifted it to look at it once more. A fine red mist was leaking from the crack. A sharp pain pierced my temple, and I closed my eyes. My world was tilting, and I felt dizzy and disorientated. Surely the few glasses of champagne I had drunk were not having this effect. I tried to recall how much I had drunk.

A memory of feeling unwell once before came to mind, when I was pregnant with Lucia, and was dizzy like this and thought I was going to pass out. Then another memory when I was holding the pregnancy kits and talking to Luc in my head. Wait what? Talking to Luc? Being able to communicate with Luc because the baby inside me was making this possible. Luc's baby? No. Lucia is Richards's child! What's the matter with me? Another memory flashed into my brain of making love to Luc in this very bed. Lust pure and hot suddenly shot up through my body, arching my hips off the bed and taking my breath away. I had finally made love to him after Richard's death, after months of wanting him, years of wanting him if the truth be told. The heat from our joined bodies had nearly consumed me. Memories of his lips on mine, his mouth on my breasts and between my legs, his tongue sweeping over my most sensitive parts. I remember he told me he loved me.

I remember.

4 2

L U C

I had just escorted an unsavory individual to Hell and was considering whether to check the paperwork in my office, when my heart contracted painfully in my chest. There was only one reason that occurred.

Something was wrong with Harper.

I returned to the bedroom. Harper was sitting on the side of the bed with her hands covering her face. I knelt down and peeled away her hands. Her face was wet with tears. I held her shaking hands in mine.

"What's wrong?"

"I remember."

"You remember what?"

"I remember everything."

"Just to be clear we're talking about . . . "

"I remember you making love to me in this bed."

"You do?"

"I remember giving birth to Lucia. You were with me."

"Yes, I was there."

233

"Because she is *your* daughter. Lucia is *your* daughter. *Not* Richards."

"Harper."

"I remember Luc. Don't try to tell me otherwise."

What could I say? She's somehow remembered and unlocked the past after seventeen years.

"What happened?"

"What do you mean?"

"To make you remember."

"I was going to sleep, and holding the locket, then I noticed it was heating up. It has a crack in it, see, right here. After I touched it, I had a searing pain in my forehead. And I remembered you told me you loved me. Is that true?"

"Yes."

"That you had loved me for years."

"Yes."

"I know now that we had a child together. Not Richard's, your child."

"Yes."

"Now tell me what happened. How did I lose my memory? How is it possible that I thought all these years that Lucia was Richard's?"

"I took your memories of the time we were together and placed them in the locket. I encouraged you to believe Richard was the father to protect you and Lucia. There had been an attempt to kidnap both of you. I did this to protect my family, and to save you more pain when I had to return to Hell."

Harper stares at me but doesn't say a word. My heart is still aching in my chest, so hers must be too. I long to touch her, to comfort her. But I'd made a promise all those years ago. To protect her I had to walk away from that physical relationship, pretend we were just friends. If people wanted to destroy me, I could not risk her being in harm's way. Her beautiful tearstained face only inches away from mine, studies me and my heart is aching to connect with her.

Fuck it. I want her. I need her. There has never been another living soul who has affected me the way Harper does. I'm tired of playing the martyr. When I pull her hands toward me and place them on my chest, there's no doubt she can feel my heart pounding, almost bursting through the skin.

"Harper, I never wanted to hurt you. It was the hardest thing for me to return to Hell to look after those demons imprisoned there, but that was what I had to do. An uprising had occurred with threats of more. I had to take command once again after being absent for years. Leaving you, leaving my family and all that we had built here on Earth was the hardest thing I've had to do. Not being there for you, to hold you when you were going through depression was physically painful. When your heart hurts, mine does too. But the emotional pain was more excruciating. I wanted to be there to help Lucia and Domenic, not just pop in now and again on special occasions. Forgive me. I can't bare it if you . . . "

Her lips were on mine, her hands coming up to touch my face. She knelt on the carpet with me and pressed her body firmly against my own, and I lost any self-control I had managed to hang on to. I wanted to make love to her and have her all to myself with no possible interruptions. I swept her into my arms, unfurled my wings and took her to a house I owned nearby in Hollywood where I liked to stay when I wanted to be close to the family.

I set her down on the king-sized bed, snapped my fingers and the room filled with flickering candles. Music played softly in the background. I removed my jacket and unbuttoned my shirt. Her hands came up to stroke my chest. I unbuttoned her cotton pajama top, but she pulled the top closed with one hand.

"I don't have the body I once had," she said softly.

"Harper. I know every inch of your skin. I have seen your body, although you haven't seen me. I am with you often, but I couldn't let you know. Please do not cover up your beautiful self. I want to make love to you. I want to love every tiny inch of you. If you'll let me."

She answered by slipping off her pajamas.

"I want you to make love to me. I want to feel the weight of you on my body, and the pressure of your arms around me. I want to leave this place with you and soar to the heavens as we once did."

"Your wish is my command." I snapped my fingers and my clothes disappeared. Her eyes grew wide when she saw how much I wanted her. It wasn't about impressing her. She knew what was coming and she welcomed it. In all the time we had been intimate together she had never said no, had never turned me away, had opened her arms to me at any time of the day or night. She wanted me just as much as I wanted her. That was all I cared about.

I began at her ankles, placing tiny kisses up her legs, spending a great deal of time from her knees to her thigh. Soft moans encouraged me. When I'd almost reached the apex of her thighs, she gripped the sheets. I moved her over to her stomach in order to worship her back. Her groan of protest made me smile. I wanted this night to be something she remembered for a long time, and that wasn't going to happen if it was all over in two minutes. Which by the way, was how long it would take me, I was wound tighter than a clock spring.

I massaged her spine and left kisses all the way up to her shoulders. Her neck was my next port of call, and I happened to know that Harper's neck was a prime erogenous zone. She squirmed and moaned when my hot tongue lathed her neck. I turned her onto her back once more and she sighed and opened her eyes, watching me take first one nipple, and then the other into my mouth, and sucking hard. She bucked off the bed and pulled my mouth to hers. Her tongue danced with mine, then her lips moved on along my jaw, leaving kisses in their wake. I palmed her breast teasing the nipple between my fingers, and her soft moans encouraged my growing erection, which now desperately wanted to be deep inside her. She spread her legs welcoming me in. I rested on my forearms and slowly lowered my body down onto her just as she had asked me to. Her beaming smile was confirmation that she enjoyed my weight on her once more. Our eyes locked the moment I entered her and the surge of joy I experienced at being with my love once more was an experience I shall remember till the day I am no longer a part of this universe.

I was home, at last, and I could not have been happier.

43

SOPHIE

*W*aking up in Paris felt like a dream. I slid quietly out of bed, crept to the bathroom, brushed my teeth and pulled a comb through my hair. I wanted to look as attractive as I could to my new husband when he woke up. The light was filtering through the frosted glass of the bathroom window, but it was early. I walked back into the bedroom, pulled back the heavy drapes and looked out of the window at the iconic structure of the Eiffel Tower in the distance, to make sure I hadn't imagined it. Domenic yawned, stretched his arms above his chest and beckoned me back to bed. I slipped beneath the covers and attached myself to his warm naked body. He greeted me with a soft press of his lips on mine.

"What time is it?" he asked.

"Early. Close your eyes for a little while, we don't need to be downstairs for breakfast for an hour or so."

"Maybe we should skip breakfast and stay in bed. I can order room service."

"But we're in Paris. The most magical city in the world. Don't you want to explore, see the sights, take the tours?"

"There is only one thing I want to explore, see and tour. And she is in bed with me now."

"There will be plenty of time for that later. How many times will we get to visit Paris? Not many I bet. Especially when we have a family. We need to make the most of it."

"Okay, you win. But there is one thing I want to do before we get up and storm Paris."

"What's that?"

"Work on starting that family." Domenic rolled on top of me. His morning glory was wedged between us.

"In that case what can I say? I've never turned down a hard days' work in my life." I smiled at my husband, enjoying the banter, which I knew was going to turn very serious any minute.

"I love you Mrs Ericson."

"I love you too, Mr Ericson." I kissed his chin.

"Hang on!" Domenic rolled over to the other side of the bed and sat up. He held up his hand to ask me to wait a moment.

4 4

DOMENIC

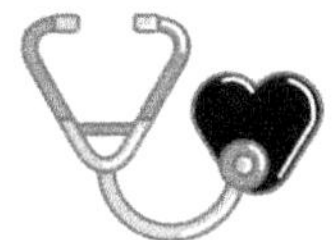

*D*omenic! *Are you awake?*

Yes, I'm awake. You do remember I'm on my honeymoon.

Mom has disappeared.

What do you mean disappeared?

I went to bed last night, and she went to bed. I haven't seen her since. She's nowhere in the house or grounds. Her room is empty, her purse, phone and keys are there. She is not.

Have you asked Luc?

He's upset with me. I didn't want to contact him.

What did you do?

That's right. Presume I did something wrong.

Like I asked, what did you do?

I was caught kissing one of the ushers in my bedroom.

The ushers were demons Lucia!

Duh, I know that. They were spectacular though, didn't you notice, they had muscles   on muscles, and they all looked like they could . . .

Lucia!

Okay. I'm worried. It's not like her to disappear. Aimee doesn't know where she is, and Cameron doesn't know where she is.

Give me a minute. I will contact Luc.

239

Luc? Can you hear me.

Yes.

Lucia contacted me. Mom has disappeared.

She contacted you on your honeymoon?

I've already gone through that with her. She felt she had no choice. Can you track down mom and get back to me?

Your mother is with me.

Oh.

She has her memory back Domenic. She knows everything.

Everything?

Yes. Tell Lucia not to worry. Harper is staying with me for a day or two. We have a bit of catching up to do.

I will.

Thank you.

Luc, is she alright?

Yes, she's fine. Trust me, I'm taking good care of her.

Lucia?

Yes?

Luc is with mom. She has her memory back. He said for you not to worry about her, and that she's fine. I think you should let them have some time alone.

That's a relief. Thanks Dom. I'll tell Aimee and Cameron not to worry.

Oh, and Lucia.

Yes?

Stay home and do NOT get into any trouble. Please. Just for a couple of days. They deserve some time alone and not being worried about you.

I'll stay home. Now get back to your honeymoon. Enjoy.

Merci. Au revoir.

I turned back to face Sophie who was looking anxious.

"Sorry. I got a call."

"We have to have some sort of signal when that's happening. Not just "talk to the hand". I didn't know what was going on, you looked worried."

"I was asking you to wait one minute. Not "talk to the hand".

"Maybe tap your forehead or something? Or a time-out sign? Maybe we need to workshop this. Who called?"

"Lucia called me. Mom had disappeared and she didn't want to call Luc. I called Luc and found out that Mom is with him. There's more to the story but to be honest I don't want to go into it now. Suffice to say Mom is fine and Luc is taking good care of her. I'll explain more later. Trust me, you are going to want a glass of wine when I explain."

"Now I'm even more curious. Come back to bed."

"I'll be back in a moment."

I took my leave to visit the bathroom. I thought about my mother and what she must be going through now that she knows Lucia is Luc's child. I wondered how she was coping with the fact that she has missed out on years with the man she loved. For I have no doubt she loves Luc with all her heart. I know Luc loves my mother and has sacrificed a lot for us.

I returned to the bedroom, climbed into bed once more and wrapped my arms around Sophie. The warmth of her body, her breasts and pebbled nipples pressed against my chest, and her lips on my neck had begun to work on my libido. I stroked my hands down her back and heard her purring in my ear like a cat.

"Oh, that feels nice," she whispered.

"You never fail to help me rise to the occasion," I murmured.

"Glad to be of service."

"All jokes aside. You've made me a very happy man."

"That makes two of us. Happy I mean. Now kiss me. Please."

"With pleasure."

No more talking. Only hands and fingers and mouths were on the agenda in the next hour, and the pleasure given and taken. Paris, the city of love, continued to work its magic.

Needless to say, we missed breakfast in the hotel. But we made up for it in our consumption of cheese and wine later in the day.

During the days that followed we found out-of-the-way bars and interesting buildings off the beaten track. We wanted to know the real Paris, not only the tourist haunts. Of course, we visited the Eiffel Tower, enjoyed a show at the Moulin Rouge and strolled along the famous Parisian streets. But we had the most fun when we visited local markets, bought croissants, baguettes, wine and cheese, sat by the river and tried to blend in as if we had lived in Paris for years.

SOPHIE

While exploring the city we came across a tiny boutique owned by Jean Michel Dupuis, an up-and-coming new French designer I had read about co-incidentally, while researching modern day Paris. The boutique was a wonderful accidental find, tucked away in a side street. There is something about a well-designed, beautifully tailored item of clothing that enhances the figure and makes a woman feel like a million dollars. I'd tried on a few dresses and couldn't make up my mind, they all looked good to me. Domenic bought them all, even though I exclaimed he was spending too much. He laughed at me and told me I didn't have to worry about money. I didn't know what I did to deserve such a generous husband, or the treat, but I wasn't going to complain.

Since then, dressing for dinner in Paris had become one of the highlights of my day. Tonight, I'd chosen a navy off the shoulder dress, which hugged my body, but surprisingly didn't show the extra pounds gained from all the wonderful cheese we had sampled in France. I was going through my small collection of jewelry for something appropriate, when Domenic came up behind me and fastened a necklace around my neck. A large amethyst, suspended on a silver chain, nestled against my skin. The deep purple hue of the expertly cut crystal was exquisite.

"It's stunning. What's this for?"

"It's our first week anniversary. I wanted to give you something to mark the day."

"It's beautiful. But I haven't got anything for you."

"My gift will be delivered later."

"Later?"

"Amethysts look their best when worn naked."

"I'm not taking this dress off now, we have dinner reservations."

"Later, after dinner, I plan to make love to you wearing only the Amethyst. These crystals are known for their healing abilities. It's also a powerful protection stone. Luc gave it to me a long time ago, and I had it made into a necklace for you. I do believe it will connect us in ways we can only imagine. Maybe the child we're going to bring into the world will be conceived in Paris, with the help of this powerful gem."

"Well in that case I'm looking forward to testing out your theory."

❧

The maître d'hôtel showed us to our table. I noticed a few eyes following us through the room.

"What are they looking at?" I whispered to my husband.

"You, my darling."

"Why?"

"You are glowing."

"Glowing?"

"Your luscious red curls, alabaster skin, and slim figure in that wonderful dress. You are giving all the men in the room ideas. Not to mention some of the women. French women are very sexually uninhibited I've been told."

"Stop it," I pleaded.

The waiter pulled out the chair for me, unfolded a linen napkin from the table with a flourish, and placed it on my lap. Domenic sat opposite. The waiter handed him a wine list and left.

"Why are you grinning like a Cheshire cat?"

"Because I get to take you back to the hotel tonight, and I get to receive my gift. Unwrapped. Remember?" Domenic winked at me. "How adorable, you're bushing."

"Because it was as if you announced to the restaurant that you want to . . . you know." My cheeks were heating up. I glanced around, but no one was paying us any attention.

"Relax. I'm teasing you. But anyone in this restaurant with any sense at all, will know exactly what I want to do to my beautiful wife tonight." Domenic smiled at me, looked down and perused the wine list.

The waiter arrived at our table and Domenic ordered a bottle of wine and carried on a conversation in fluent French.

"Before we came to Paris, I never knew you spoke French."

"I speak a couple of languages. Not as many as Lucia though."

"I must admit to being a little jealous. Lucia is gifted."

"In more ways than one."

"I hope we can spend more time together, now that I officially have a little sister. Lucia is fun."

"Lucia is growing up fast. Too fast in some ways. She is a lot to handle for my mother."

"Seventeen is a difficult age. You must remember being seventeen yourself, getting into trouble?"

"Actually no. My life was about study. I was always focused on becoming a heart surgeon. Nothing else really mattered to me. Other than my family."

"What does Lucia plan to do when she's older? Does she have a career in mind?"

"Unfortunately, no. She's still trying to make up her mind. If you could make a career out of being in trouble, she would be perfect for that role."

"Come on, surely she hasn't been that bad."

"Believe me if it had not been for Luc coming to the rescue on several occasions, I don't think she would be the sweet and funny Lucia you want to get to know better."

The waiter returned and poured our wine. Domenic discussed the menu with the waiter, in French. Then with me, in English. He ordered our food in French.

"I think you should continue to speak to me in French after our honeymoon is over. It gives me tingles the way you can swap so easily from French to English and back again without even pausing."

"I would be happy to. Especially if it has that effect on you. Like Tish and Gomez Adams, in the Adams Family."

"I loved that show."

"I enjoyed it because their family was strange. And somehow, I felt connected to them, because my family was equally as strange."

"You were going to tell me about your mother. You said I needed a glass of wine. Cheers." I lifted my glass and took a sip of the ruby red liquid.

"I'm not sure that this is the best place for that conversation."

"Surely it can't be that bad."

Domenic took a sip of his red wine and stared at me, gathering his thoughts. When he spoke, he spoke quietly.

"When my father died, my mother was heartbroken. She loved my father deeply. I have no doubt about this. I mention it because I believe she has loved Luc since they met years before. They never acted on it, but I believe the attraction was always there. Some months after my father died, Luc and my mother finally got together. Lucia was the consequence of that."

"Lucia is Luc's daughter? I don't understand. Harper talks about Richard as being Lucia's father. She told me she wished he'd been able to walk his daughter down the aisle when her time comes."

"She believed that was the truth. Until now."

"Is that why she disappeared?"

"I'm not sure of the details. But Luc said she knows the truth now."

"Why did she believe it before?"

"After my father died, when Luc and Mom were finally together, we moved into the estate, and Aimee and Cameron came to look after the house. Then Lucia was born, and we were like a normal happy 'all American' family. Mom worked from home. Luc traveled for work. But Luc was spending too much time here with us and there was an uprising in the underworld, with dire consequences. There was an attempt to abduct my mother and my baby sister. Luc had to go back, to protect us, and he knew how much losing the two loves of her life would destroy my mother. He removed her memories of the time they spent together to make it easier for her. He replaced those memories with memories of Richard being responsible for Lucia."

"I don't believe this. Lucia is the daughter of the . . . "

"Yes. And now you know why it is so hard for her to be an average teenager."

Our entree arrived and the conversation halted. Many questions were chasing each other in my head. I looked over at my husband who was now lost in his own thoughts. I realized suddenly that this conversation would have had a different effect on my mental health only a few short months ago. I had become used to discussing the Devil in conversation as if the inclusion was about a normal family member. The fact that Lucia was the daughter of the Devil though, was mind blowing.

My thoughts turned to Harper. What was she going through now, realizing that the last seventeen years had been a lie?

HARPER

When I awoke Luc was sitting on a chair by the open French doors reading a book.

"Good morning." I stretched.

"Sleep well?"

"I did. It looks like a beautiful day out there." I could see the sun sparkling off the ocean. The sheer curtains were pulled back. The room was bathed in early morning light.

"Do you feel like a walk on the beach? Or breakfast first? I can call Ramon to set up on the patio."

"Let me get dressed and we can have a walk." I got up and went into the bathroom. The woman staring back at me, in the sexy black satin nightgown held up with with tiny spaghetti straps, looks calm and rested. Her face is younger than I remember her looking for a long time. Sure, there are wrinkles around the eyes, which I jokingly call laugh lines, and the lips are not as full, and the cheeks have filled out a little. But all in all, this woman looks refreshed and happy. This woman has a man who lusts after her and has told her she's beautiful. This woman knows she's sexy, even with bed hair.

I brushed my teeth, combed my hair and tied it back, slipped into my magenta swimsuit that had been hung over the handle in the shower, drip-drying from last night's swim in the pool. The black cotton kimono on the back of the door would be adequate for a walk along the beach. I slid my arms into it and returned to the bedroom. Luc hadn't moved and was still fully dressed.

"I'm ready," I said, tilting my head, with my hands on my hips.

He snapped his fingers, and his black trousers, dark red shirt, and expensive leather shoes disappeared and were replaced with a pair of black swim shorts. I cast an appreciative glance at his tight stomach and muscled chest and shoulders. His long bare feet with perfectly straight toes. He put down his book and stood up next to me. He looked like a very handsome young man.

"Could you please fix this." I tapped his temple.

His hair turned salt and pepper at the temple immediately, similar laugh lines to my own appeared on his face. He aged appropriately before my eyes.

"I am constantly amazed at both the big things and the small things you can do to change your appearance at will."

"I want you to be comfortable," Luc said, kissing my cheek.

"You know me so well."

I had received a few strange looks the first day we had arrived on the island, and Luc had picked up on it when I dropped his hand walking into a restaurant for lunch. I had realized that I felt more comfortable if we appeared to be the same age, walking hand in hand along the beach, or giving Luc an affectionate kiss in public in this holiday destination. I didn't want to be taken for an older woman, on the arm of a paid gigolo. He's inside my head and constantly working out what he can do to make this time away special for me. I can appreciate that he's trying to make up for the years apart.

I'm not going to pretend that I'm happy about missing out on all these years. But I do understand why he did what he did. Being angry or holding a grudge would just mean bitterness and more years apart and I'm not made of stone. I want him in my life and in my bed and I'm thankful we're together now.

Luc chose a small Island, and a luxurious house by the beach, complete with staff, for our time away from the family and distractions. Ramon was on hand to fill our every need but was also discrete and unobtrusive when we wanted time alone. We had our own private chef, cleaning staff and masseur. Everything had been perfect. Sunny days, blue skies, lush green foliage surrounding a lagoon of turquoise water right outside our window. It only rained during the night, and when I made a remark about it, Luc announced that he had arranged that too. I didn't doubt him.

❧

The beach is relatively empty on our walk, the waves gently lapping the shore, and swirling around our feet in the shallows. Luc is quiet and reflective today and I wonder what's on his mind. I'm fairly sure of the answer, but I ask him anyway.

"We have to go back, don't we?"

"Yes."

"Is that why you're so quiet today?"

"I wanted you to have more time. But I'm being called back."

"I understand. It's been wonderful. I would have loved to have had longer with you, but I'm grateful for the time we've spent here." I stopped walking and turned to Luc.

"You have that sparkle in your eye again," Luc said.

"And I have you to thank for that. The kids will be back from their honeymoon tomorrow."

"And we'll be there to meet them. Together."

"Together?"

"No more secrets."

"I like the sound of that." I took Luc's hand, and we continued our walk. "And it was supposed to be Lucia's birthday party."

"I think we should still have one. After all, she's celebrated that day since she was a child. She can have two eighteenth birthday celebrations this time. We will rectify it next year."

"I think she'll be very happy with that. I haven't bought her a gift yet."

"Leave that to me. I think I know what she would like," Luc said.

"Shall we walk back and have breakfast now. I'm hungry all of a sudden."

"Sure."

&

Luc was staring at me across the table. This was our last meal alone on the island, and the chef had prepared a seafood banquet for us.

"What is it? Do I have food on my chin?"

"You are beautiful."

I bent my head and cut my food. I was only just getting used to the special attention from Luc, after so many years of friendship and no boundaries crossed.

"For a mature woman," I added.

"No. You are beautiful. 'Mature woman' need not be added to that sentence."

"You flatter me."

"Harper, believe me when I tell you that you are beautiful, and it has nothing to do with your age. You were beautiful as a young woman. You were beautiful as a thirty-year-old woman when I approached you, and you were beautiful when you gave birth to your son, and then our daughter. And you are still beautiful. You will always be beautiful to me because I see all of you. I see inside your soul, as well as your physical self." Luc reached across the table and put his hand on mine. "You are kind, thoughtful and intelligent, and you put other's needs before your own."

"I have a feeling this is leading somewhere."

"I'm concerned that perhaps you haven't allowed yourself to be angry when you discovered what I did. And you said you were okay to save my feelings."

"Why do you think that?"

"There were no angry words, no yelling, no . . ."

"There was no need to be angry. Don't you understand. I love you, have loved you for as long as I can remember. Even in the last few years I have loved you as my best friend. There were times that I felt I was standing on the precipice of something between us, and I didn't understand why I felt conflicted. When I got my memory back it was as if I had been given a gift. I didn't want to dwell on having it taken away. I understood why you did what you did."

"It pained me every day not to be able to reach out and touch you."

"Since we've been here on the island, you've shown me so much love, I have no doubt about your feelings. Please be reassured about mine. I love you Luc. I want to spend the rest of my life showing you how much you mean to me. I will never take what we have for granted."

"We have one last night together. There is something special I want to give you."

"What?'

Luc pulled a small box from his pocket and pushed it across the table.

"We still have to be very careful when we go back. We won't keep secrets from the family, but to the outside world things must remain the same. For the sake of your safety."

"I understand."

"But between us I want there to be no doubt about our relationship. A traditional marriage ceremony is not an option, but I want us to have our own mark of commitment. Open the box, please."

Inside the box there were two rings nestled in the red velvet lining. They looked like they were made of ivory. One was bigger than the other. There was a pattern etched into each of the rings. I picked up the larger of the two and turned it around for a closer look at the hieroglyphics, but I could not decipher. I placed it back in the box.

"These rings are special. No one will see them once placed on our fingers, only we will be able to see them. They will meld into our skin, become part of us."

Luc stood, picked up the box, took my hand and led me through the French doors onto the patio. A full moon shone down upon us.

"There is something I need to ask you," Luc said, facing me.

"Ask me."

"If you could capture this moment in time and stay exactly as we are, the two of us, would you desire it?"

"In love and with each other?" I reached up, placed my hands on his cheeks, looked into his eyes.

"Yes."

"I would."

"Granted."

"Just like that."

"That was the easy part."

I have something else to ask."

"Ask me anything." I smiled up at him and spread my arms wide.

"Harper will you consent to wearing my ring and being my love throughout all time?"

"I will." My breath hitched in my chest. Tears formed at the corners of my eyes.

"I belong to you, heart and soul, until the end of time." Luc said. He took my hand and slipped the ring onto my wedding finger. He held the box open for me.

I selected the larger ring and slipped it onto his finger.

"I belong to you, heart and soul, until the end of time," I said, trying not to cry.

He took both my hands and clasped them between his as if in prayer. My finger warmed. I looked at his hand and noticed the ring becoming faint, until I could no longer see it on his finger. He opened his hand and my ring had disappeared too.

"Are they really in our skin?"

Luc hovered his hand over the back of mine and the inscription on the ring embedded in my finger was clearly visible. It glowed beneath the skin like phosphorous. He did the same with his hand and showed me his ring.

"You are mine and I am yours." Luc smiled at me, took me in his arms and kissed me long and deep. "I think there's something else that should happen now."

"What's that?"

"Massage your finger where the ring is. Try focusing on something you want to say to me, without talking to me. Concentrate on slowing down your heart rate, close your eyes and see the words in your head. Now send me a message."

I love you Luc. You have made me a very happy woman.

I love you too.

Oh wow. We're connected telepathically. I remember that happened when I was pregnant with Lucia.

I was hoping it would work immediately.

How is that possible?

You have more of my DNA. The rings are made of my bone, with a few embellishments and spells. It has embedded into your bone now. Become a part of you.

Your bone?

I used one of my ribs. Not an original idea, but it appears that it worked.

Was that necessary?

For it to graft to your finger, yes. Don't worry. My rib will grow back.

"To all intents and purposes, we are a married couple," Luc said.

"I like the sound of that."

"We can share this with the immediate family, but with no one else I'm afraid. Based on what happened last time, if they can get to me through you, they will. It's my job to protect you. To protect my family. Which has now become larger."

"Larger?"

"Domenic and Sophie. And the baby."

"The baby!!"

"Yes. Although they are not aware yet. Let them be the ones to tell you in a few weeks. Domenic gave the Amethyst to Sophie. The one I gave him when he was younger, which he carried with him, and connected him to me. Now I am acutely aware of Sophie and the new life within."

"I'm going to be a grandmother. Oh my!"

"You look a little shocked."

"I think I need another drink."

"Yes, we need to make a toast." Luc snapped his fingers and a table with a bottle of expensive champagne in an ice bucket appeared. He uncorked the bottle with a loud pop, poured the bubbly alcohol into two tall flutes and passed one to me. "To the future!"

"To our future." I took a sip, enjoying the cool liquid and the explosion of bubbles on my tongue.

Music began playing softly in the background. Luc took the glass from me, placed the drinks back on the table, and pulled me to him to dance. He was an accomplished dancer and led me in such a way that I also felt light on my feet. As we swayed to the music, his hard body pressed against mine and suddenly I wanted to make love. I took his hand encouraging him toward the house.

It was a short walk to the bedroom which also opened onto the patio. A few steps more to the bed. I lay back and he followed me down, into my embrace. His lips were on my neck, my shoulders, my earlobes and everywhere they moved heat followed. He held himself above me teasing my lips with short sharp kisses, until I pulled his head down and devoured his mouth. His tongue probed and danced over mine, I reveled in the taste of him. When he drew back to grin down at me, I gasped from his sudden absence. Lust flared in his eyes, and I knew mine reflected that need. I unbuttoned his shirt and ran my hands over the smooth, firm, tanned flesh of his chest. I placed my lips against his warm skin, against his heart. I could hear it thudding in my ears . . . or was that mine?

Luc slipped the straps off my shoulders and lowered my dress and bra to expose my breasts. The cool air and arousal had hardened my nipples. He lowered his head, rasped his beard over the tips which quivered in response, then placed his mouth over the entire left nipple and sucked hard. Pleasure shot straight to my core, and I bucked off the bed. I angled my body for the same treatment to the right breast. Luc obliged. I wriggled out of my dress and tried to remove my underwear, but Luc stopped me.

"This is my job." He leant down and placed hot kisses along my hip bone, heading south, then edged the underwear down so slowly I thought I would scream. I wriggled. He looked up and raised an arched eyebrow at me, and I stopped. When the underwear had finally been cast aside, he pulled me to the edge of the bed knelt on the floor between my legs, ran his tongue up the insides of my thighs, stopping short of the place I desperately wanted his tongue to be. I strained upward. He raised an eyebrow once again. I had to give in to the fact that Luc was in control, close my eyes, and give myself over to enjoying the experience.

With my eyes closed, every sensation became magnified. His searing hot tongue lathed me. I moaned aloud. His hands gripped my hips, and the tip of his tongue found the sensitive nub and proceeded to demonstrate how well he knew my body. Wave after wave of pleasure coursed through me, and my body willingly opened up to him. But I wanted more, and I knew he could give so much more.

When he entered me, he seemed far bigger than I remembered. He stretched me to my limits, and I reveled in the fact that I could turn him on so much. And to my amazement he seemed to be still growing inside me. I climaxed over and over again, my body appeared to soar, transported to another place, another time. At last, when I attempted to open my eyes, Luc was no longer wearing the beautiful human mask he wore day to day. His large and powerful naked body towered over me, muscles bulging, his chest glistening with sweat, and his wings fully extended as he came to his release. Our eyes met. He changed back to the beautiful man the world only wanted to see. Yet I loved him.

He was the Devil in all his glory. And he was mine.

4 7

DOMENIC

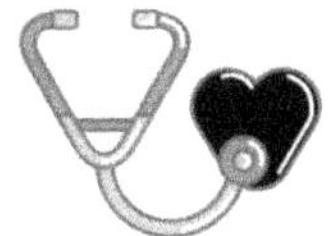

ameron met us at the airport, and for that I was grateful. Sophie wanted to call in to see her parents for a flying visit first, and then we were expected to be at my mother's house for an early dinner. We were trying to get back to our own time zone and staying up until our usual bedtime in California was the best way to do that. When we pulled up in front of the house Aimee came rushing out to greet us.

"It's lovely to see our newlyweds looking so happy. Did you have a good flight?"

"We did Aimee. We were so glad to see Cameron's smiling face at the airport too," Sophie said, saluting Cameron, who was standing by the driver's door.

"We're all looking forward to hearing about Paris. Your mother has asked Cameron and I to join you for dinner. I've made something special just for your return. Your mother and Luc are in the sunroom, and Lucia is somewhere in the house. I'm sure she'll join you soon."

We walked down to the far end of the house. My mother and Luc were standing by the sofa waiting on us, and I noticed Luc had his arm around my mother's shoulders. I walked forward and shook Luc's hand, and waited to kiss my mother's cheek until my wife and mother stepped apart. There was a glow about her that I hadn't seen for a long time.

"You look happy," I said.

"I am happy. Come sit, we have something to share with you both."

"I'll call Lucia," Luc said.

We sat on the sofa opposite. Sophie took my hand and squeezed. I had the feeling something big was going to be announced. Lucia appeared and rushed over to hug Sophie and then punched my arm.

"Hey newlyweds, how was Paris?" Lucia sat down beside Sophie.

"It was fabulous. We'll fill you in later. Mom has something to tell us it seems."

"Before I say anything, I want you to understand that what I am about to tell you is not to be discussed outside of this house. We are the only five people who will know about it, and that is how I want it to stay. I understand you may want to talk about it with each other, but not even your family can know Sophie. I need you to swear you will keep this between us."

"I will not discuss what goes on in this house with anyone. You can count on me." Sophie's hand gripped mine, tightly. She was trembling.

"Mom you're scaring Sophie, and if the truth be told I'm a little afraid of what comes next too."

"No, it's nothing to be afraid about. I got my memory back, and I know Luc is Lucia's father. I know why this has been kept a secret for so long. Now that I do know the truth, Luc and I want to be together, as much as possible. We can't have a wedding it would get out. I love Luc and we've made a commitment to each other. In essence we *are* a married couple." She turned to Luc and he held his hand over hers.

My mother stood and held out her hand to show us the markings, now glowing under her skin.

"This is my ring of commitment. Luc has one too. Because this ring was made from Luc's bone and DNA, it has fused with mine. It has also enabled me to talk to Luc telepathically, just as I did when I was pregnant with Lucia. Perhaps I can also talk to you Domenic? Let me try?"

It's so good to see you home again Domenic.

It's good to be back Mom.

"Wow it works."

Don't leave me out.

Lucia, I can hear you too. This is wonderful.

"I can talk to both of my children. That's amazing."

Luc stood up beside my mother and took her hand.

"We have much to be grateful for. But we must always be vigilant. Domenic remembers what happened the last time the Demons rose up against me and tried to kidnap Harper and Lucia. For their safety, and the safety of our entire family we must carry on as normal. Which means I have to spend quite a bit of time away from all of you for the time being."

"I understand. We'll make sure Mom and Lucia are okay," I said.

"That brings me to something else I wanted to discuss. I've bought the house adjacent to this estate. It's not as big, but it has potential, and a great view. We were hoping that you would accept this house as a wedding gift, from your mother and me. Until you can get on your feet and can afford to buy a house of your own."

"I have a house," I said.

"You have an apartment. You're planning on having a family and you'll need a yard and more bedrooms and somewhere for the nanny to live."

"I don't need or want a nanny," Sophie said. "But hang on we're getting a little ahead of ourselves. A house! As a wedding gift! Who gives a house as a wedding gift?"

"Well obviously my family does," I said. I was a little surprised by this generosity, if I had to tell the truth.

"Do you like the idea of a house next door? Or is that too close for comfort?" Luc asked? "I can buy another one nearby, if you don't want to be next door. I thought it would be handy. We could put a door in the wall, and the grandchildren could come and go . . ."

"I'm sure we could work something out if you don't like this house. There are a few on the market at the moment," my mother offered.

"Will everyone stop!" Sophie stood up and spread her arms, palms out. She sat down again quickly. "Can I have a glass of water? I think I'm feeling a bit woozy from the flight."

I walked over to the drink cart and poured some water from a cut crystal decanter. I scanned the other bottles on the tray.

"Maybe some brandy might help," I suggested.

"No," my mother said emphatically. Everyone turned to look at her. She came over and took the glass from me. "Best she has some water, and we go into the dining room shortly for an early dinner. You're probably just hungry Sophie."

"What's going on?"

"What do you mean?"

"You're not the only one with added powers Mom. Ever since we walked into this room, I felt it. There is something more you are not sharing. Come on, spit it out."

"I don't know what you mean."

"Look me in the eye and tell me that."

"This is my fault. I shared something with your mother that I should have kept to myself until you announced it." Luc said.

"Announced what?" Sophie asked, looking between my mother, Luc and me.

"You're pregnant," Luc said.

"What! How do you know that?" Sophie stood up, and then abruptly sat down again.

"Drink this, stay seated. You're looking pale." My mother handed Sophie the water and sat down beside her.

"You're sure about this?" I asked Luc.

"Devil," he said in a sarcastic tone.

Of course, he would know. I was still trying to get my head around the fact I was going to be someone's father.

"It's a bit of a shock. I wasn't expecting to get pregnant so quickly. I thought it might take months, years even," Sophie said

"It's not surprising. You're both healthy, in the prime of your lives. You've spent a couple of weeks on your honeymoon with little else to do than . . ."

"Let's get back to my question. How do you know this?" Sophie asked.

"Domenic gave you something that has connected me to you. The Amethyst necklace. I knew when the child was conceived, by the change in your body's chemistry."

"This is connecting me to you?" Sophie wrapped her hand around the stone of her necklace.

"Yes, it is. And I would ask that since you are in this delicate state, that you wear the necklace at all times, and I can come to your aid if you need me," Luc said.

There was no sound in the room for a few seconds. Everyone was taking it in. I'd forgotten Lucia was there, until she stood up and came bounding over to me.

"Hey, I'm going to be an aunt. How about that. You're going to be a father. Is this cool or what?" Lucia launched herself at me and threw her arms around my neck. "Congratulations." She went over and hugged Sophie too.

"Again. I'm going to ask that everyone keep this to themselves until we get through the first trimester."

"Of course," I said.

"Sure Mom," Lucia said, and winked at me.

Once dinner was brought from the kitchen and laid out, Aimee and Cameron joined us around the dining room table. Everyone wanted to hear about Paris, and it was good to be able to talk about our trip and relive the past couple of weeks in the telling.

By the time coffee . . . and herbal tea for Sophie . . . was served I was having trouble keeping my eyes open, and Sophie was yawning regularly. Cameron brought the car around to the door and took us home. Sophie fell asleep on my shoulder in the back seat of the car. I carried her up to the apartment, and Cameron brought up the luggage, over a couple of trips.

I removed her shoes, tucked Sophie fully dressed into bed so as not to wake her and climbed in beside her. I held her gently in my arms, overcome with love for her and in awe of this new life it appears we had created. I took her hand, felt for her pulse and allowed myself to go into doctor mode and absorb her medical data. The information quickly downloaded to me. All was in order, and Luc was right, we had a tiny being growing inside. For now, it was just a cluster of cells.

I placed my hand on Sophie's stomach and whispered. "I'm going to be the best father I can be. I promise." I closed my eyes, held my wife and went out like a light.

4 8

SOPHIE

December 2017

The house renovations have finally been completed and we're due to move into our new home on New Year's Eve. At this stage my pregnancy is beginning to show. I'm tired all the time and have been sorry to note my feet and ankles are swelling up a bit. Otherwise, I feel healthy, and thankfully all is well with "Peanut", she's thriving. Yes, we finally have confirmed that Peanut is a girl. Although truth be told I knew instinctively I would have a girl when Luc told me I was pregnant. I still cannot get over the fact that my father-in-law knew before I did - I think of Luc as father-in-law now, rather than the Devil, to keep the family situation as normal as it can be – and is now my personal bodyguard. I had a dizzy spell last week, and just as the room tilted, Luc appeared by my side with a glass of water, lifted me up and placed me on the sofa. When I asked him, he said he was "in the neighborhood, just passing by". I don't believe him.

After much persuasion by Domenic, Luc and Harper, I left nursing to concentrate on setting up the house and preparing for the new arrival. Having made that decision, I'm surprisingly eager to decorate our home and bring a bit of subtle color to my husband's monochromatic surroundings. When Peanut is growing up, Domenic will have to get used to all the brightly colored toys and books that will be scattered throughout the house. Colors are very important for brain and emotional development in babies, and this baby is going to get as much stimulation as I can give her.

Since we returned from our honeymoon, Aimee has been an angel, dropping off food and stocking our freezer at the apartment with delicious meals. I have been very lucky that cooking was not high on my list of things to do when I came home from a long day at the hospital. Now that I'm no longer working, I'm hoping that Aimee might teach me how to cook some of Domenic's favorite things. Especially if we're going to be living right next door.

Harper and Luc have been more than generous with their wedding gift. The four-bedroom dual level house has been modernized and the newly updated kitchen is spacious and bright. The master bedroom has had a connecting door added through to the nursery. A sunroom not unlike the one at Harper's house, has been built onto the rear of the house alongside the kitchen, and facing the garden and large lawn. An ideal setting for our future children to run around and explore.

Aimee and Cameron told me they're delighted to be able to re-establish the vegetable garden in this new house, which runs along the back wall separating the properties. It's in prime position with full sun running east to west, and the plants and seedlings are thriving with their tender care. There's enough space to provide fresh vegetables for both households. The gate that Luc wanted was cut into the stone wall and is hardly ever closed due to all the work going on. I noted that the tradesmen doing the renovations looked surprisingly like the ushers at our wedding, only now they're wearing overalls. Best not to ask questions. It's amazing what you get used to and accept as normal over time.

Luc pointed out that one of the reasons he had bought this house was that both properties share a high stone wall surrounding their perimeters, enabling the installation of several unobtrusive security cameras and an alarm system. Cameron informed me Max loves having the extra garden space to roam around. I'd better get used to seeing him popping in from time to time because Domenic says Max will be very protective once Peanut arrives.

I want for nothing it seems. I have merely to think of an item that would be useful in the house, and it appears in my new kitchen. I was beginning to think Luc could read my mind, until Domenic pointed out that he had discussed the items in question with Harper, who I discovered was my secret benefactor. As far as mothers-in-law go, I've struck gold with Harper. She's so kind and thoughtful, and I'm becoming more and more appreciative of her care of me. I understand now why Domenic is so close to his family.

Lisa is coming to have lunch today. I fluffed up the pillows on the sofa and rearranged the flowers on the dining room table. Although we often talk on the phone, I haven't seen Lisa outside of work since I returned from Paris a few months ago. She's been preoccupied moving out of the house we'd shared and settling into an apartment near to the hospital. When the buzzer announced her arrival downstairs, I was really excited about seeing her, and hearing more details about her new place.

"Come on up." I spoke into the intercom and pressed the button to allow her entry into the building. I checked my reflection in the full-length mirror by the door, placing my hand over my tiny bump protectively. "We're going to have lunch with Aunty Lisa, Peanut." I said aloud. I opened the door and waited for the elevator to arrive.

The elevator door opened, and a pink bakery box was thrust out into midair, ahead of the occupant.

"I've bought dessert," Lisa said loudly.

"Come on in and bring that sweet smelling gift with you." I leant over and kissed both her cheeks.

Lisa placed the bakery box on the kitchen counter.

"Something smells good. Did you cook?"

"No, Aimee brought over a quiche yesterday, and I thought it would be ideal for our lunch. It's heating in the oven. I did make a salad though."

"Sounds delicious. This angel food cake will top it off."

"My favorite cake. But you know that already."

"You look really well. Pregnancy obviously agrees with you."

"Thank you. I feel well, most of the time, but I'm craving weird things to eat, and I can't stand some smells, they make me want to vomit. That was one of the reasons I was happy to give up nursing."

"I'm sure things will get back to normal once the baby comes."

"Come sit down and tell me what's making you grin from ear to ear?" I patted the sofa beside me. Lisa perched on the edge.

"What grin?" Lisa said, lifting her left hand and tucking her hair behind her ear in slow motion.

"Oh My God! Is that a ring!!! Girl did you get engaged and did not tell me?" I threw my arms around her neck, tears welling up in my eyes. "Congratulations. Oh, this is the best news. When did this happen? Did you guess he was going to ask you?" I brushed away the tears and grabbed her hand to see the ring properly.

"Thank you. It was last night." Lisa pulled a tissue out of her purse to dab at her eyes. "I had no idea. It was a total shock. A fabulous shock, but completely out of left field. We've only been dating for a short while."

"You've been dating longer than we did. Tell me all about it. Hang on, do you want tea or coffee? A wine? Or something stronger? I can't have any, but you can."

"No. I don't want anything stronger if you can't have any. I'm good for now. Later coffee with the angel cake would be lovely."

"So! Tell me how he did it. I want all the juicy details."

"We were unpacking some boxes at the apartment. You know Andrew found that apartment for me, don't you? And it has a great view from the balcony, really big rooms and underground parking, and I can walk to work if I want to. I was worried it was too big for just me and thinking I needed a house-mate to help with the rent. . . ."

"Lisa!"

"Okay. I'm getting there. We were unpacking boxes and there were some champagne glasses in a box on the table, and I couldn't remember seeing them before, and Andrew said they were his and he brought them over to help me celebrate, and then he produced a bottle of champagne, so we opened it to have a toast to the apartment."

"And?"

"And we toasted the apartment and he said he'd found a house-mate for me, and I asked who, and he went down on one knee, held out a ring and said, "Me if you'll have me"."

"And of course, you said yes."

"Actually, I couldn't say anything, I was stunned. Yes, very unlike me I know!"

"But obviously you did say yes cos you're wearing the ring. It's beautiful."

"It's beautiful, I agree. And something I would've chosen, so he did well. It's me don't you think?" Lisa held her hand up alongside her face.

"It's definitely you."

"Have you picked a date for the wedding? What did your folks say?"

"No date yet. They're thrilled obviously. He's not a bum, he has a good job, he's intelligent, he dresses nicely, he can hold his alcohol with papa, he brings flowers to mama. Even both my brothers like him. And of course, the main thing is he loves me."

"You certainly struck gold there. Now all you have to do is produce many bambinos and your folks will be very happy."

"Tell me about it! Mama is already on my back about kids, espe-cially when she found out you were pregnant. Although not before the wedding, or papa will get out the shotgun."

"Maybe we'll get to have the next one together."

"You haven't even had this one yet. Maybe the whole childbirth thing will put you off."

"Domenic and I want more kids. And now we have a house with a big garden for them to run around."

"You are *so* lucky. A renovated house from Domenic's family. Now that is what I call a wedding gift. Is it nearly finished?"

"We're moving in on New Year's Eve. We want to have a few people over to celebrate and bring in the New Year. Will you and Andrew come?"

"Definitely. I can't wait to see it. Do you think it's going to be okay living next door to your mother-in-law?"

"I honestly think it will be fine. And I will have babysitters 'on call' when I want them. Harper says she cannot wait to look after the baby. Aimee and Cameron have said they want to help. Lucia is looking forward to being an aunt although I don't think she's the babysitting type."

"Have you picked out names for a boy and a girl?"

"It's a girl. There are a few names we like. But we're not sharing till she's born."

"I bet Domenic is thrilled."

"He's looking forward to being a father to a little girl. We want strong names. This baby will be something special, mark my words."

My stomach rumbled and the oven timer beeped. Perfect timing. I served up lunch and we spent a couple of hours talking about engagement parties and weddings and baby showers until it was time to say goodbye.

"Now that we don't live together or see each other at the hospital, and we have partners and busy lives, we have to make this a regular monthly thing. If we don't put on our calendars then time will get away from us, and I couldn't bear it if we lost touch with each other."

"That will never happen. I promise." Lisa gave me one last hug before she got into the elevator, with half the cake I made her take home in the bakery box. I didn't need the extra calories.

I returned to the apartment suddenly sad, yet excited for Lisa and all that was coming in the next few months and heard a message ping on my phone. It was a text from Lisa to add a lunch date at her new apartment, in exactly 4 weeks, into my calendar. And an invitation to be her Matron of Honor, with a picture of a pregnant woman in a horrible orange dress and shoes.

I snorted with laughter.

HARPER

December 30th 2017

Christmas was such a joyous occasion this year. I had my children at my table, my trusted friends and companions in Aimee and Cameron, and of course, my love. Luc has turned things around in this house in such a short space in time. He is attentive to all our needs, gracious to our guests and he is so generous to our children. I awake each day happy to be alive and with hope in my heart for the arrival of Domenic and Sophie's baby. For if I have to be very honest, I miss the time I spent with Lucia as a baby. Those cute, dimpled knees and fingers, the chubby cheeks, and that wonderful smell of a newborn. I am looking forward to an infant in the house again and will do everything in my power to make sure Sophie is supported during this pregnancy and birth.

I'm delighted that the renovation of their house is complete. They are moving in tomorrow, but apart from their clothes and personal items, everything has already been purchased to suit the decor and is in the new house. They decided to keep the apartment near to the hospital and rent it out, fully furnished.

I don't know if it is a good idea or a bad idea, but they want to have a New Year's Eve Party tomorrow night, for the immediate family and their close friends Lisa and Andrew who are newly engaged themselves. Aimee is helping with the catering, and I have arranged for a truckload of balloons and decorations to be delivered. I think it will be fitting to toast the New Year together and be grateful and celebrate all that we have accomplished this year. The wedding was a fabulous affair, and it would be hard to top that. However, the fact that Lucia is officially turning eighteen on New Year's Day, and we are expecting the arrival of a baby in the New Year, means we have a lot to look forward to.

NEW YEAR'S EVE - DECEMBER 31st 2017

It was nearly midnight. I asked Aimee to make sure that Shamus and Kate, Sophie's parents, had full glasses in hand. She wandered between the guests to top them up with Champagne. Andrew had his arm around Lisa's waist, and she had her head on his shoulder. It was lovely to witness such an affectionate couple. Everyone had dressed up for the occasion and had added some of the fun hats or accessories that were supplied with the decorations. Lucia looked very stylish on the eve of her eighteenth birthday, in a long, strapless silver dress, and long black evening gloves which came up above her elbows. She looked every inch a young Hollywood starlet with her hair swept up on top of her head, fastened under a small, glittering tiara. Of course, Luc was immaculately dressed in a black Armani suit, claret colored shirt and tie, and hand-made leather shoes, in which you could see your reflection. He told me he had selected a shirt in that color because it was the perfect match to my ankle length skirt and top in Thai silk.

We all made our way to stand by the floor to ceiling windows of the sunroom, waiting for the clock to strike the bewitching hour and the light display that Cameron had set up in the yard. As Max wasn't a fan of flashing lights, and anything could happen if he got too excited,

Domenic had brought him inside. He lay peacefully by the sofa, but his ears were twitching. He probably could hear Cameron in the garden and wondered why he wasn't allowed out there on his routine guard duty. None of us wanted Sophie's family to witness our family pet growing to the size of a pony before their eyes. Declan and Calum had brought their wives, but wisely had left their children at home with babysitters. It was nice to see our two families getting along so well.

"Ten, nine, eight, seven, six, five, four, three, two, one. Happy New Year!" Everyone chanted "Happy New Year". Glasses were clinked together, couples shared a kiss, or a hug. I noticed Domenic and Sophie shared a tender kiss. They looked so happy, it brought fresh tears to my eyes.

Luc put his arm around my shoulder and kissed me. It was a sweet kiss because we were in public, but it had promise of something far deeper when we were alone later. There was a twinkle in his eye. Then Domenic and Sophie made the rounds and wished everyone a Happy New Year and we turned our attention to the garden once more.

The switch was flipped and the whole yard was illuminated with brightly colored lights, which shone up into the branches of the trees, and a large movie screen flashed the words 'Happy New Year'. Pictures of fireworks, from other parts of the world, filled the screen. It was a very pretty sight, and it livened up the party once more.

The lights were turned off in the garden and the blinds were lowered on the sunroom windows. Everyone moved into the living room. Domenic turned up the music and Aimee passed around some nibbles for those who were hungry. Cameron refilled wine glasses and conversation started up again. Cameron took Max out for a stroll and to check the gardens surrounding the house.

I pulled Sophie to one side.

"How are you doing?"

"I'm starting to fade a bit. But it has been such a wonderful evening."

"You've been busy all day. It's no wonder you're tired. Perhaps you could retire early? I'll let Domenic know and I'll stay to make sure everyone is looked after. I'm sure people will be going home soon."

"I think that's a good idea. I'll say goodnight to my folks. Where is Domenic? And Luc? They're both missing."

Sophie and I walked out to the patio door. Caught in the moonlight, in the semi-darkened garden Domenic and Luc appeared to be arguing. We stopped when we heard their raised voices and caught the end of the conversation.

"It has always been the plan for you to take over one day, Domenic. Your mother agreed to it before you were even born."

"My mother might have agreed to it, but I didn't. What on earth made you think that I would want to be King of Hell. Look what it has cost you. I have a wife now, a child on the way. I have a full life here, which I am very happy to pursue. No amount of riches would get me to give that up."

"I didn't offer a choice, Domenic. I have lived this life for long enough. I want to spend time with Harper, and I cannot be in two places at once. You have to spend some time in my place now to learn the ropes. You are my natural successor."

"Forget it. It's not happening!"

"After all I have done you dare to oppose me!" Luc's voice rose.

Sophie began to move forward, out of the shadows, but I grabbed her arm to stop her.

Suddenly Lucia appeared out of nowhere, in the garden.

"Domenic does not want to do this. Allow him to be with his family. I will step up and be your successor."

"That isn't possible."

"Why?"

"Because you're a woman. This is a man's job!"

"Who determined that? You? God? I bet God didn't factor in that you would have a child with a human, did he? I bet he didn't think that I would be a 'chip off the old block'. That I'd not only be daddy's girl, but also daddy's very powerful and talented girl." Lucia lifted her arms and the flower garden over by the wall changed to rocks and lava. She lowered her arms, and everything returned to normal. She pointed at a large established tree, and it tore from the earth, raised up in the air a few feet, hovered for a second and disappeared into the heavens.

"You've been developing these talents from me in secret. Why?"

"Because you have always treated me like a child. I am a woman."

"You *are* a child. *My* child."

"I am no longer a child. I am eighteen, born on this very day, at this moment. I feel a change in my body already. I deserve a chance to prove that I can do this." Suddenly Lucia bent over clutching her chest. She fell down on one knee.

I wanted to move out of the shadows, to go to my daughter, and it was Sophie who grabbed my arm this time, to stop me. I thought Luc had brought her to her knees, but he looked as confused as I felt.

Lucia moaned. She had her head bent down, presumably in a great deal of pain. Luc moved toward her but stopped suddenly when she raised a hand to halt him. As we watched, two huge dark wings sprouted from behind her shoulders. She got to her feet and her wings opened up completely, their feathers iridescent and glowing in the moonlight. Before our eyes, she grew several inches taller, her face began to morph into a much older, very beautiful woman. She shook her head and the tiara fell off, her long dark hair tumbled over her bare shoulders, her figure became even more buxom and curvaceous, and the dress was stretched to its limits to contain her curves.

We were all struck motionless by what we had all witnessed.

"This is who I am. No longer a little girl. I am Lucia, daughter of Luc Nightingale, King of Hell. Powerful in my own right. I am ready to be trained as your successor. Believe me I will make one Hell of a Queen of the Underworld."

THE END

ABOUT THE AUTHOR

Savannah Blaize lives in Melbourne, Australia, after emigrating from Scotland many years ago. She enjoys writing fiction of all genres, in which the reader can visualise and step inside the world she creates. When she creates a story, the scenes run like a movie reel in her head, and the consistent feedback is that they create the same visual experience for her readers.

Savannah is proud member of the Melbourne Romance Writers Guild, The Romance writers of Australia and the Sisters In Crime. She is passionate about reading across genres, about writing her stories in which her imagination can run free, and about connecting with her readers.

Devil In The Details is the second book of the Heart Of The Devil Series. The first book, Deal With The Devil was published in September 2020.

Her first novel From Paris To Forever was published in 2017. Her second novel The Class Reunion was published in 2018. Her novellas If The Shoe Fits and A Tartan Christmas were published in 2020.